Bug-Eyed Monsters

Previous anthologies edited by
Bill Pronzini and Barry N. Malzberg

SHARED TOMORROWS: Science Fiction
  in Collaboration (1979)

THE END OF SUMMER: Science Fiction
  of the Fifties (1979)

DARK SKINS, DARK DREAMS: Crime in Science
  Fiction (1978)

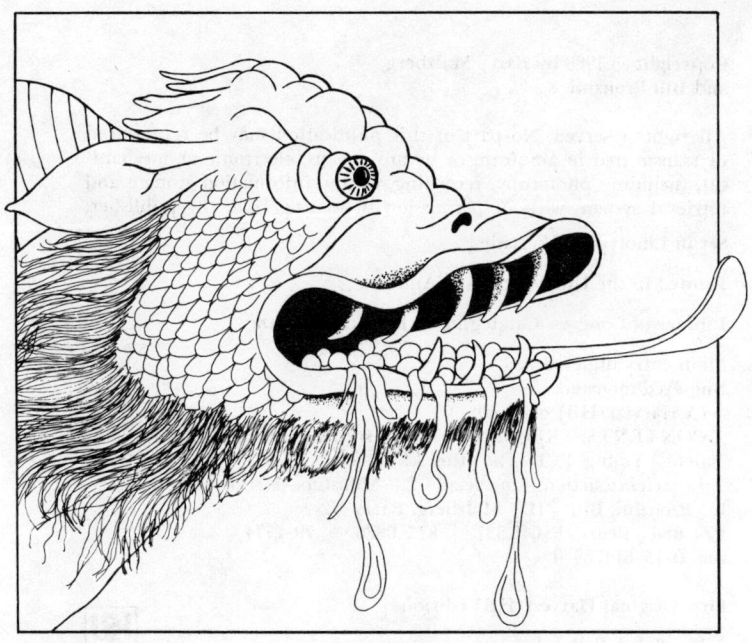

Bug-Eyed Monsters

Edited by Bill Pronzini and Barry N. Malzberg

A Harvest/HBJ Original
Harcourt Brace Jovanovich   New York and London

Copyright © 1980 by Barry Malzberg
and Bill Pronzini

All rights reserved. No part of this publication may be reproduced or transmitted in any form or by any means, electronic or mechanical, including photocopy, recording, or any information storage and retrieval system, without permission in writing from the publisher.

Set in Linotype Baskerville

Printed in the United States of America

Library of Congress Cataloging in Publication Data

Main entry under title:
Bug-eyed monsters.
 (A Harvest/HBJ original)
 CONTENTS: Knight, D. Stranger station.—Bloch, R. Talent.—Young, R. F. The other kids.—[etc.]
 1. Science fiction, American. 2. Monsters—Fiction
I. Pronzini, Bill. II. Malzberg, Barry N.
PZ1.B86 1980 [PS648.S3] 813'.0876 79-2771
ISBN 0-15-614789-0

First Original Harvest/HBJ edition

A B C D E F G H I J

STRANGER STATION, by Damon Knight. Copyright © 1956 by Fantasy House, Inc. First published in *The Magazine of Fantasy & Science Fiction*. Reprinted by permission of the author.

TALENT, by Robert Bloch. Copyright © 1960 by Digest Productions Corp. First published in *Worlds of If*. Reprinted by permission of the author and his agents, Scott Meredith Literary Agency, Inc., 845 Third Avenue, New York, NY 10022.

THE OTHER KIDS, by Robert F. Young. Copyright © 1956 by King-Size Publications, Inc. First published in *Fantastic Universe*. Reprinted by permission of the author.

THE MIRACLE OF THE LILY, by Clare Winger Harris. Copyright © 1927 by E. P. Co., Inc. First published in *Amazing Stories*. Reprinted by arrangement with the author's agent, Forrest J. Ackerman, who is holding a check for the author or her heir; please contact at 2495 Glendower Ave., Hollywood, CA 90027.

THE BUG-EYED MUSICIANS, by Laurence M. Janifer. Copyright © 1959 by Galaxy Publishing Co. First published in *Galaxy*. Reprinted by permission of the author.

PUPPET SHOW, by Fredric Brown. Copyright © 1962 by H. M. H. Publishing Co. First published in *Playboy*. Reprinted by permission of Scott Meredith Literary Agency, Inc., 845 Third Avenue, New York, NY 10022.

WHEREVER YOU ARE, by Poul Anderson. Copyright © 1959 by Street & Smith Publications, Inc. First published in *Astounding* as by Winston P. Sanders. Reprinted by permission of the author and his agents, Scott Meredith Literary Agency, Inc., 845 Third Avenue, New York, NY 10022.

MIMIC, by Donald A. Wollheim. Copyright © 1942 by Fictioneers, Inc.; copyright © 1969 by Donald A. Wollheim. First published in *Astonishing Stories*. Reprinted by permission of the author.

THE FACELESS THING, by Edward D. Hoch. Copyright © 1963 by Health Knowledge, Inc. First published in *The Magazine of Horror*. Reprinted by permission of the author.

THE RULL, by A. E. Van Vogt. Copyright © 1948 by Street & Smith Publications, Inc.; copyright renewed © 1976 by A. E. Van Vogt. First published in *Astounding*. Reprinted by permission of the author and his agent, Forrest J. Ackerman, 2495 Glendower Ave., Hollywood, CA 90027.

FRIEND TO MAN, by C. M. Kornbluth. Copyright © 1951 by Avon Publications, Inc. First published in *10-Story Fantasy*. Reprinted by permission of Robert P. Mills, Ltd., agents for the estate of C. M. Kornbluth.

THE LAST ONE LEFT, by Bill Pronzini and Barry N. Malzberg. Copyright © 1980 by Mercury Press, Inc. First published in *The Magazine of Fantasy & Science Fiction*. Reprinted by permission of the authors.

HOSTESS, by Isaac Asimov. Copyright © 1951 by World Editions, Inc. First published in *Galaxy Science Fiction*. Reprinted by permission of the author.

CONTENTS

Introduction	3
Stranger Station *Damon Knight*	7
Talent *Robert Bloch*	39
The Other Kids *Robert F. Young*	55
The Miracle of the Lily *Clare Winger Harris*	61
The Bug-Eyed Musicians *Laurence M. Janifer*	85

Puppet Show *Fredric Brown*	97
Portfolio (Cartoons) *Gahan Wilson*	111
Wherever You Are *Poul Anderson*	119
Mimic *Donald A. Wollheim*	153
The Faceless Thing *Edward D. Hoch*	163
The Rull *A. E. Van Vogt*	171
Friend to Man *C. M. Kornbluth*	203
The Last One Left *Bill Pronzini and Barry N. Malzberg*	215
Hostess *Isaac Asimov*	221

Those which we call monsters are not so with God.

—Montaigne, *Essays II*

Bug-Eyed Monsters

Introduction

The Bug-Eyed Monster has been an important, if not always approbated, subtextual figure of science fiction virtually from the field's inception as a distinct subgenre of American popular fiction.*

Established almost thirty years before then by H. G. Wells in his 1898 novel *The War of the Worlds* (a work

---

* In March 1926 with the appearance of the first issue of Hugo Gernsback's *Amazing Stories*.

made even more famous by Orson Welles's 1938 radio adaptation), the BEM* had his heyday in the 1920s and 1930s. Such writers as Raymond Z. Gallun, Edmond Hamilton, and H. P. Lovecraft built their careers on the seemingly endless confrontation between man and hideous beings from alien worlds (or, on occasion, from right here on Earth). And the monsters of that era *were* hideous, as evidenced by hundreds of pulp magazine covers: grotesque life forms sometimes dripping slime or ichor, often with great bulging eyes and clutching tentacles, often bent on wanton destruction of human life. (Earth-type females, scantily clad, seemed to be their favorite targets—an interesting if not biologically sound phenomenon. But then again, all BEMs appeared to be males, which may or may not be the result of either alien or human sexism; so their preference may not be such an unsound phenomenon after all.)

The reasons for this proliferation of monsters in the twenties and thirties? One, of course, is that science fiction was then still in puberty, suffering growth pangs and almost but not quite ready to throw off its onus as a juvenile art form. But the primary reason, perhaps, is this: if science fiction, as critic Brian Aldiss claims in *The Billion-Year Spree*, is the image of the unspeakable human heart given shape as the Grotesque Other, and if Mary Shelley's *Frankenstein* is truly our first science-fiction novel, then the Bug-Eyed Monster is the unassimilable vision of ourselves, safely distanced, invariably rejected (for BEMs almost always came to a bad end).

---

* Science fiction fans like acronyms as much as politicians or bureaucrats do. FIAWOL (Fandom Is A Way Of Life) did battle with FIJAGDH (Fandom Is Just A God-Damned Hobby) in the thirties; their older and wiser descendants settled in the fifties for the understanding of TINSTAAFL (There Is No Such Thing As A Free Lunch).

Introduction 5

Although A. E. Van Vogt, among others, continued to champion the cause of the extraterrestrial monster in the 1940s—and although the terrestrial or supernatural monster remained in favor in the pages of *Weird Tales* during that same period—most s-f writers had by then shied away to more serious subject matter, such as the Atomic Bomb and other wonders of modern technology. This general shunning of the BEM became even more pronounced in the fifties, perhaps science fiction's finest and most dazzlingly inventive decade; and by 1958, after the last of the old pulps and most of the low-quality digests born during the magazine boom of that decade had collapsed, the remaining art directors had cleaned up their act: covers on *Astounding, Galaxy, Fantasy & Science Fiction* et al. depicted sedate technological imaginings or astronomical wonders, and it was possible, sometimes even politic, to read a science-fiction magazine without covering it with plain brown wrapping paper or hiding it behind one's elementary chemistry textbook. The monsters were all but extinct.

Now and then during the past twenty years, a nostalgic editor or unreconstructed art director would feature a BEM for old times' sake, usually in a humorous vein. But in those two decades science fiction as a whole became a Sophisticated Literary Medium: interface between man and his technology in this terrifying post-technological era; chronicler of Doppler Shifts and Black Holes and maddened astronauts battling psychosis on the First Venus Sweep; keeper of the flame and guider of the way. Bug-Eyed Monsters, it has been said, are like the dreams of childhood: no one can take them seriously anymore; they can only be mocked or evoked in deprecation. Apocalypse is the ticket now—that, and the outposts of science.

It was more *fun*, however, in the old days.

And it is in the spirit of fun—a harkening back to those

more innocent days when BEMs menaced the girls in the brass brassieres—that we present this anthology. Which is not to imply that the stories here are old-fashioned or undistinguished; indeed, they are some of the best and most entertaining to be found in the field, offering a wide variety of approaches to and variations on the BEM theme.

There are evocative studies of human/alien relationships (Damon Knight's "Stranger Station," Fredric Brown's "Puppet Show," Isaac Asimov's "Hostess," A. E. Van Vogt's "The Rull"); satirical humor (Poul Anderson's "Wherever You Are," our own "The Last One Left"); horrific visions (C. M. Kornbluth's "Friend to Man," Donald Wollheim's "Mimic"); a pair of poignant short-shorts (Robert F. Young's "The Other Kids," Edward D. Hoch's "The Faceless Thing"); and just plain entertainment (Robert Bloch's "Talent," Laurence M. Janifer's "The Bug-Eyed Musicians"). In short, a little something for every science-fictional taste. *Plus*, as a bonus, six of Gahan Wilson's funny and mordant monster cartoons.

Part of understanding what we are and where we are going, someone wrote a long time ago, is understanding where we have been. The Bug-Eyed Monster is where science fiction has been—and in its own way it wasn't such a bad place to be, either.

The BEM is dead; long live the BEM.

—Bill Pronzini and
Barry N. Malzberg

June 1979

"Stranger Station" is a virtuoso performance—arguably, one of the two finest BEM stories ever written (the other being, of course, H. G. Wells's The War of the Worlds). *Once you've met Paul Wesson, the new Station watchman, and the alien that "reminded him of all the loathsome, crawling, creeping things the Earth was full of," you're not likely to forget them, or the fate that awaits them on Stranger Station.*

Damon Knight (b. 1922) achieved a reputation as one of the most polished craftsmen to publish consistently in the 1950s: short fiction for H. L. Gold's Galaxy, *Anthony Boucher's* Magazine of Fantasy & Science Fiction, *and other publications; and such excellent novels as* Hell's Pavement *and* A for Anything. *But because he does little fiction these days, he is best known to modern readers as a critic and anthologist (his brilliantly perceptive collection of science-fiction criticism,* In Search of Wonder, *is still in print today, twenty-five years after initial publication; the* Orbit *series of original s-f anthologies is widely regarded, as are numerous other collections.) Knight once stated that he felt "Stranger Station" was a basic and not very original 1950s metaphoric horror vision—which just shows that even the best of critics, particularly when examining their own work, have blind spots.*

Stranger Station

Damon Knight

The clang of metal echoed hollowly down through the Station's many vaulted corridors and rooms. Paul Wesson stood listening for a moment as the rolling echoes died away. The maintenance rocket was gone, heading back to Home; they had left him alone in Stranger Station.

Stranger Station! The name itself quickened his imagination. Wesson knew that both orbital stations had been named a century ago by the then British administration of the satellite service: "Home" because the larger, inner station handled the traffic of Earth and its colonies; "Stranger" because the outer station was designed specifically for dealings with foreigners . . . beings from outside the solar system. But even that could not diminish the wonder of Stranger Station, whirling out here alone in the dark—waiting for its once-in-two-decades visitor. . . .

One man, out of all Sol's billions, had the task and privilege of enduring the alien's presence when it came. The two races, according to Wesson's understanding of the subject, were so fundamentally different that it was painful for them to meet. Well, he had volunteered for the job, and he thought he could handle it—the rewards were big enough.

He had gone through all the tests, and against his own expectations he had been chosen. The maintenance crew had brought him up as dead weight, drugged in a survival hamper; they had kept him the same way while they did their work, and then had brought him back to consciousness. Now they were gone. He was alone.

. . . But not quite.

"Welcome to Stranger Station, Sergeant Wesson," said a pleasant voice. "This is your alpha network speaking. I'm here to protect and serve you in every way. If there's anything you want, just ask me."

Wesson had been warned, but he was still shocked at the human quality of it. The alpha networks were the last word in robot brains—computers, safety devices, personal servants, libraries, all wrapped up in one, with something so close to "personality" and "free will" that experts were still arguing the question. They were rare and fantastically expensive; Wesson had never met one before.

"Thanks," he said now, to the empty air. "Uh—what do I call you, by the way? I can't keep saying, 'Hey, alpha network.'"

"One of your recent predecessors called me Aunt Nettie."

Wesson grimaced. Alpha network—Aunt Nettie. He hated puns; that wouldn't do. "The Aunt part is all right," he said. "Suppose I call you Aunt Jane. That was my mother's sister; you sound like her, a little bit."

"I am honored," said the invisible mechanism politely. "Can I serve you any refreshments now? Sandwiches? A drink?"

"Not just yet," said Wesson.

He turned away. That seemed to end the conversation as far as the network was concerned. A good thing; it was all right to have it for company, speaking when spoken to, but if it got talkative ...

The human part of the Station was in four segments: bedroom, living room, dining room, bath. The living room was comfortably large and pleasantly furnished in greens and tans: the only mechanical note in it was the big instrument console in one corner. The other rooms, arranged in a ring around the living room, were tiny: just space enough for Wesson, a narrow encircling corridor, and the mechanisms that would serve him. The whole place was spotlessly clean, gleaming and efficient in spite of its twenty-year layoff.

This is the gravy part of the run, Wesson told himself. The month before the alien came—good food, no work, and an alpha network for conversation. "Aunt Jane, I'll have a small steak now," he said to the network. "Medium rare, with hash-brown potatoes, onions and mushrooms, and a glass of lager. Call me when it's ready."

"Right," said the voice pleasantly. Out in the dining room, the autochef began to hum and cluck self-importantly. Wesson wandered over and inspected the instrument console. Airlocks were sealed and tight, said the dials; the air was cycling. The Station was in orbit, and rotating on its axis with a force at the perimeter, where Wesson was, of one *g*. The internal temperature of this part of the Station was an even 73°.

The other side of the board told a different story; all the dials were dark and dead. Sector Two, occupying a volume some eighty-eight thousand times as great as this one, was not yet functioning.

Wesson had a vivid mental image of the Station, from photographs and diagrams—a 500-foot duralumin sphere, onto which the shallow 30-foot disk of the human section had been stuck apparently as an afterthought. The whole cavity of the sphere, very nearly—except for a honeycomb of supply and maintenance rooms, and the all-important, recently enlarged vats—was one cramped chamber for the alien. . . .

The steak was good, bubbling crisp outside the way he liked it, tender and pink inside. "Aunt Jane," he said with his mouth full, "this is pretty soft, isn't it?"

"The steak?" asked the voice, with a faintly anxious note.

Wesson grinned. "Never mind," he said. "Listen, Aunt Jane, you've been through this routine . . . how many times? Were you installed with the Station, or what?"

"I was not installed with the Station," said Aunt Jane primly. "I have assisted at three contacts."

"Um. Cigarette," said Wesson, slapping his pockets. The autochef hummed for a moment, and popped a pack of G.I.'s out of a vent. Wesson lit up. "All right," he said, "you've been through this three times. There are a lot of things you can tell me, right?"

"Oh, yes, certainly. What would you like to know?"

Wesson smoked, leaned back reflectively, green eyes narrowed. "First," he said, "read me the Pigeon report—you know, from the *Brief History*. I want to see if I remember it right."

"Chapter Two," said the voice promptly. "First contact with a non-Solar intelligence was made by Commander Ralph C. Pigeon on July 1, 1987, during an emergency landing on Titan. The following is an excerpt from his official report:

"*'While searching for a possible cause for our mental disturbance, we discovered what appeared to be a gigantic construction of metal on the far side of the ridge. Our distress grew stronger with the approach to this construction, which was polyhedral and approximately five times the length of the Cologne.*

"*'Some of those present expressed a wish to retire, but Lt. Acuff and myself had a strong sense of being called or summoned in some indefinable way. Although our uneasiness was not lessened, we therefore agreed to go forward and keep radio contact with the rest of the party while they returned to the ship.*

"*'We gained access to the alien construction by way of a large, irregular opening ... The internal temperature was minus seventy-five degrees Fahrenheit; the atmosphere appeared to consist of methane and ammonia ... Inside the second chamber, an alien creature was waiting for us. We felt the distress which I have tried to describe, to a much greater degree than before, and also the sense of summoning or pleading ... We observed that the creature was exuding a thick yellowish fluid from certain joints or pores in its surface. Though disgusted, I managed to collect a sample of this exudate, and it was later forwarded for analysis...'*

"The second contact was made ten years later by Commodore Crawford's famous Titan Expedition—"

"No, that's enough," said Wesson. "I just wanted the Pigeon quote." He smoked, brooding. "It seems kind of chopped off, doesn't it? Have you got a longer version in your memory banks anywhere?"

There was a pause. "No," said Aunt Jane.

"There was more to it when I was a kid," Wesson complained nervously. "I read that book when I was twelve, and I remember a long description of the alien . . . that is, I remember its being there." He swung around. "Listen, Aunt Jane—you're a sort of universal watchdog, that right? You've got cameras and mikes all over the Station?"

"Yes," said the network, sounding—was it Wesson's imagination?—faintly injured.

"Well, what about Sector Two—you must have cameras up there, too, isn't that so?"

"Yes."

"All right, then you can tell me. What do the aliens look like?"

There was a definite pause. "I'm sorry, I can't tell you that," said Aunt Jane.

"No," said Wesson, "I didn't think you could. You've got orders not to, I guess, for the same reason those history books have been cut since I was a kid. Now, what would the reason be? Have you got any idea, Aunt Jane?"

There was another pause. "Yes," the voice admitted.

"Well?"

"I'm sorry, I can't—"

"—tell you that," Wesson repeated along with it. "All right. At least we know where we stand."

"Yes, sergeant. Would you like some dessert?"

"No dessert. One other thing. *What happens to Station watchmen, like me, after their tour of duty?*"

"They are upgraded to Class Seven, students with unlimited leisure, and receive outright gifts of seven thousand stellors, plus free Class One housing—"

"Yeah, I know all that," said Wesson, licking his dry

lips. "But here's what I'm asking you. The ones you knew —what kind of shape were they in when they left here?"

"The usual human shape," said the voice brightly. "Why do you ask, sergeant?"

Wesson made a discontented gesture. "Something I remember from a bull session at the Academy. I can't get it out of my head; I know it had something to do with the Station. Just a part of a sentence—*'blind as a bat, and white bristles all over.'* Now, would that be a description of the alien . . . or the watchman when they came to take him away?"

Aunt Jane went into one of her heavy pauses. "All right, I'll save you the trouble," said Wesson. "You're sorry, you can't tell me that."

"I *am* sorry," said the robot, sincerely.

Aunt Jane was a model companion. She had a record library of thousands of hours of music; she had films to show him, and micro-printed books that he could read on the scanner in the living room; or if he preferred, she would read to him. She controlled the Station's three telescopes, and on request would give him a view of Earth, or the Moon, or Home. . . .

But there was no news. Aunt Jane would obligingly turn on the radio receiver if he asked her, but nothing except static came out. That was the thing that weighed most heavily on Wesson, as time passed: the knowledge that radio silence was being imposed on all ships in transit, on the orbital stations, and on the planet-to-space transmitters. It was an enormous, almost a crippling handicap. Some information could be transmitted over relatively short distances by photophone, but ordinarily the whole complex traffic of the spacelanes depended on radio.

But this coming alien contact was so delicate a thing that

even a radio voice, out here where the Earth was only a tiny disk twice the size of the Moon, might upset it. It was so precarious a thing, Wesson thought, that only one man could be allowed in the Station while the alien was there, and to give that man the company that would keep him sane, they had to install an alpha network....

"Aunt Jane?"

The voice answered promptly, "Yes, Paul."

"This distress that the books talk about—you wouldn't know what it is, would you?"

"No, Paul."

"Because robot brains don't feel it, right?"

"Right, Paul."

"So tell me this—why do they need a man here at all? Why can't they get along with just you?"

A pause. "I don't know, Paul." The voice sounded faintly wistful.

He got up from the living-room couch and paced restlessly back and forth. "Let's have a look at Earth," he said. Obediently, the viewing screen on the console glowed into life: there was the blue Earth, swimming deep below him, in its first quarter, jewel-bright. "Switch it off," Wesson said.

"A little music?" suggested the voice, and immediately began to play something soothing, full of woodwinds.

"*No,*" said Wesson. The music stopped.

Wesson's hands were trembling; he had a caged and frustrated feeling.

The fitted suit was in its locker beside the air lock. Wesson had been topside in it once or twice; there was nothing to see up there, just darkness and cold. But he had to get out of this squirrel-cage. He took the suit down.

"Paul," said Aunt Jane anxiously, "are you feeling nervous?"

"Yes," he snarled.

"Then don't go into Sector Two," said Aunt Jane.

"Don't tell me what to do, you hunk of tin!" said Wesson with sudden anger. He zipped up the front of his suit.

Aunt Jane was silent.

The air lock, an upright tube barely large enough for one man, was the only passage between Sector One and Sector Two. It was also the only exit from Sector One; to get here in the first place, Wesson had had to enter the big lock at the "south" pole of the sphere, and travel all the way down inside by drop-hole and catwalk. He had been drugged unconscious at the time, of course. When the time came, he would go out the same way; neither the maintenance rocket nor the tanker had any space, or time, to spare.

At the "north" pole opposite, there was a third air lock, this one so huge it could easily have held an interplanet freighter. But that was nobody's business—no human being's.

In the beam of Wesson's helmet lamp, the enormous central cavity of the Station was an inky gulf that sent back only remote, mocking glimmers of light. The near walls sparkled with hoarfrost. Sector Two was not yet pressurized; there was only a diffuse vapor that had leaked through the airseal, and had long since frozen into the powdery deposit that lined the walls. The metal rang cold under his shod feet; the vast emptiness of the chamber was the more depressing because it was airless, unwarmed and unlit. *Alone*, said his footsteps; *alone* ...

He was thirty yards up the catwalk when his anxiety suddenly grew stronger. Wesson stopped in spite of himself, and turned clumsily, putting his back to the wall. The support of the solid wall was not enough. The catwalk seemed threatening to tilt underfoot, dropping him into the gulf.

Wesson recognized this drained feeling, this metallic taste at the back of his tongue. It was fear.

The thought ticked through his head, *They want me to be afraid.* But why? Why now? Of what?

Equally suddenly, he knew. The nameless pressure tightened, like a great fist closing, and Wesson had the appalling sense of something so huge that it had no limits at all, descending, with a terrible endless swift slowness. . . .

His first month was up.

The alien was coming.

As Wesson turned, gasping, the whole huge structure of the Station around him seemed to dwindle to the size of an ordinary room . . . and Wesson with it, so that he seemed to himself like a tiny insect, frantically scuttling down the walls toward safety.

Behind him as he ran, the Station *boomed*.

In the silent rooms, all the lights were burning dimly. Wesson lay still, looking at the ceiling. Up there, his imagination formed a shifting, changing image of the alien—huge, shadowy, formlessly menacing.

Sweat had gathered in globules on his brow. He stared, unable to look away.

"That was why you didn't want me to go topside, huh, Aunt Jane?"

"Yes. The nervousness is the first sign. But you gave me a direct order, Paul."

"I know it," he said vaguely, still staring fixedly at the ceiling. "A funny thing . . . Aunt Jane?"

"Yes, Paul."

"You won't tell me what it looks like, right?"

"*No*, Paul."

"I don't want to know. Lord, I don't *want* to know... Funny thing, Aunt Jane, part of me is just pure funk—I'm so scared, I'm nothing but a jelly—"

"I know," said the voice gently.

"—and part is real cool and calm, as if it didn't matter. Crazy, the things you think about. You know?"

"What things, Paul?"

He tried to laugh. "I'm remembering a kids' party I went to twenty... twenty-five years ago. I was, let's see, I was nine. I remember, because that was the same year my father died.

"We were living in Dallas then, in a rented mobile-house, and there was a family in the next tract with a bunch of redheaded kids. They were always throwing parties; nobody liked them much, but everybody always went."

"Tell me about the party, Paul."

He shifted on the couch. "This one, this one was a Hallowe'en party. I remember the girls had on black and orange dresses, and the boys mostly wore spirit costumes. I was about the youngest kid there, and I felt kind of out of place. Then all of a sudden one of the redheads jumps up in a skull mask, hollering, 'C'mon, everybody get ready for hidenseek.' And he grabs *me*, and says, '*You* be it,' and before I can even move, he shoves me into a dark closet. And I hear that door lock behind me."

He moistened his lips. "And then—you know, in the darkness—I feel something hit my *face*. You know, cold and clammy, like, I don't know, something dead....

"I just hunched up on the floor of that closet, waiting for that thing to touch me again. You know? That thing, cold and kind of gritty, hanging up there. You know what it was? A cloth glove, full of ice and bran cereal. A joke. Boy, that was one joke I never forgot.... Aunt Jane?"

"Yes, Paul."

"Hey, I'll bet you alpha networks make great psychs, huh? I could lie here and tell you anything, because you're just a machine—right?"

"Right, Paul," said the network sorrowfully.

"Aunt Jane, Aunt Jane . . . It's no use kidding myself along, I can *feel* that thing up there, just a couple of yards away."

"I know you can, Paul."

"I can't stand it, Aunt Jane."

"You can if you think you can, Paul."

He writhed on the couch. "It's—it's dirty, it's clammy. My God, is it going to be like that for *five months*? I can't, it'll kill me, Aunt Jane."

There was another thunderous boom, echoing down through the structural members of the Station. "What's that?" Wesson gasped. "The other ship—casting off?"

"Yes. Now he's alone, just as you are."

"Not like me. He can't be feeling what I'm feeling. Aunt Jane, you don't know . . ."

Up there, separated from him only by a few yards of metal, the alien's enormous, monstrous body hung. It was that poised weight, as real as if he could touch it, that weighed down his chest.

Wesson had been a space-dweller for most of his adult life, and knew even in his bones that if an orbital station ever collapsed, the "under" part would not be crushed but would be hurled away by its own angular momentum. This was not the oppressiveness of planetside buildings, where the looming mass above you seemed always threatening to fall: this was something else, completely distinct, and impossible to argue away.

It was the scent of danger, hanging unseen up there in the dark, waiting, cold and heavy. It was the recurrent nightmare of Wesson's childhood—the bloated unreal shape, no-color, no-size, that kept on hideously falling toward his face. . . . It was the dead puppy he had pulled out of the creek, that summer in Dakota . . . wet fur, limp head, cold, cold, *cold*. . . .

With an effort, Wesson rolled over on the couch and lifted himself to one elbow. The pressure was an insistent chill weight on his skull; the room seemed to dip and swing around in slow circles.

Wesson felt his jaw muscles contorting with the strain as he knelt, then stood erect. His back and legs tightened; his mouth hung painfully open. He took one step, then another, timing them to hit the floor as it came upright.

The right side of the console, the one that had been dark, was lighted. Pressure in Sector Two, according to the indicator, was about one and a third atmospheres. The air lock indicator showed a slightly higher pressure of oxygen and argon; that was to keep any of the alien atmosphere from contaminating Sector One, but it also meant that the lock would no longer open from either side.

"Lemme see Earth," he gasped.

The screen lighted up as he stared into it. "It's a long way down," he said. A long, long way down to the bottom of that well. . . . He had spent ten featureless years as a servo tech in Home Station. Before that, he'd wanted to be a pilot, but had washed out the first year—couldn't take the math. But he had never once thought of going back to Earth.

"Aunt Jane, Aunt Jane, it's beautiful," he mumbled.

Down there, he knew, it was spring; and in certain places, where the edge of darkness retreated, it was morning: a watery blue morning like the sea light caught in an agate, a morning with smoke and mist in it; a morning of stillness and promise. Down there, lost years and miles away, some tiny dot of a woman was opening her microscopic door to listen to an atom's song. Lost, lost, and packed away in cotton wool, like a specimen slide: one spring morning on Earth.

Black miles above, so far that sixty Earths could have been piled one on another to make a pole for his perch, Wesson swung in his endless circle within a circle. Yet, vast as was the gulf beneath him, all this—earth, Moon, orbital stations, ships; yes, the Sun and all the rest of his planets, too—was the merest sniff of space, to be pinched up between thumb and finger.

Beyond—there was the true gulf. In that deep night, galaxies lay sprawled aglitter, piercing a distance that could only be named in a meaningless number, a cry of dismay: O,O,O....

Crawling and fighting, blasting with energies too big for them, men had come as far as Uranus. But if a man had been tall enough to lie with his boots toasting in the Sun and his head freezing at Pluto, still he would have been too small for that overwhelming emptiness. Here, not at Pluto, was the outermost limit of man's empire: here the Outside funneled down to meet it, like the pinched waist of an hourglass: here, and only here, the two worlds came near enough to touch. Ours—and Theirs.

Down at the bottom of the board, now, the golden dials were faintly alight, the needles trembling ever so little on their pins.

Deep in the vats, the vats, the golden liquid was trickling down: *"Though disgusted, I took a sample of the exudate and it was forwarded for analysis...."*

Space-cold fluid, trickling down the bitter walls of the tubes, forming little pools in the cups of darkness; goldenly agleam there, half-alive. The golden elixir. One drop of the concentrate would arrest aging for twenty years—

Stranger Station 21

keep your arteries soft, tonus good, eyes clear, hair pigmented, brain alert.

That was what the tests of Pigeon's sample had showed. That was the reason for the whole crazy history of the "alien trading post"—first a hut on Titan, then later, when people understood more about the problem, Stranger Station.

Once every twenty years, an alien would come down out of Somewhere, and sit in the tiny cage we had made for him, and make us rich beyond our dreams—rich with life . . . and still we did not know why.

Above him, Wesson imagined he could see that sensed body a-wallow in the glacial blackness, its bulk passively turning with the Station's spin, bleeding a chill gold into the lips of the tubes: drip, drop.

Wesson held his head. The pressure inside made it hard to think; it felt as if his skull were about to fly apart. "Aunt Jane," he said.

"Yes, Paul." The kindly, comforting voice: like a nurse. The nurse who stands beside your cot while you have painful, necessary things done to you.

"Aunt Jane," said Wesson, "do you know why they keep coming back?"

"No," said the voice precisely. "It is a mystery."

Wesson nodded. "I had," he said, "an interview with Gower before I left Home. You know Gower? Chief of the Outworld Bureau. Came up especially to see me."

"Yes?" said Aunt Jane encouragingly.

"Said to me, 'Wesson, you got to find out. Find out if we can count on them to keep up the supply. You know? There's fifty million more of us,' he says, 'than when you were born. We need more of the stuff, and we got to know if we can count on it. Because,' he says, 'you know what would happen if it stopped?' Do you know, Aunt Jane?"

"It would be," said the voice, "a catastrophe."

"That's right," Wesson said respectfully. "It would. Like, he says to me, 'What if the people in the Nefud area were cut off from the Jordan Valley Authority? Why, there'd be millions dying of thirst in a week.

" 'Or what if the freighters stopped coming to Moon Base. Why,' he says, 'there'd be thousands starving and smothering.'

"He says, 'Where the water is, where you can get food and air, people are going to settle, and get married, you know? and have kids.'

"He says, 'If the so-called longevity serum stopped coming . . .' Says, 'Every twentieth adult in the Sol family is due for his shot this year.' Says, 'Of those, almost twenty per cent are one hundred fifteen or older.' Says, 'The deaths in that group, in the first year, would be at least three times what the actuarian tables call for.' " Wesson raised a strained face. "I'm thirty-four, you know?" he said. "That Gower, he made me feel like a baby."

Aunt Jane made a sympathetic noise.

"Drip, drip," said Wesson hysterically. The needles of the tall golden indicators were infinitesimally higher. "Every twenty years, we need more of the stuff, so somebody like me has to come out and take it for five lousy months. And one of *them* has to come out and sit there, and *drip. Why*, Aunt Jane? What for? Why should it matter to them whether we live a long time or not? Why do they keep on coming back? What do they take *away* from here?"

But to these questions, Aunt Jane had no reply.

All day and every day, the lights burned cold and steady in the circular gray corridor around the rim of Sector One. The hard gray flooring had been deeply scuffed in that circular path before Wesson ever walked there: the corridor existed for that only, like a treadmill in a squirrel cage; it said "Walk," and Wesson walked. A man would go crazy if he sat still, with that squirming, indescribable pressure on his head; and so Wesson paced off the miles, all day and every day, until he dropped like a dead man in the bed at night.

He talked, too, sometimes to himself, sometimes to the listening alpha network; sometimes it was difficult to tell which. "Moss on a rock," he muttered, pacing. "Told him, wouldn't give twenty mills for any damn shell. . . . Little pebbles down there, all colors." He shuffled on in silence for a while. Abruptly: "I don't see *why* they couldn't have given me a cat."

Aunt Jane said nothing. After a moment Wesson went on, "Nearly everybody at Home has a cat, for God's sake, or a goldfish or something. You're all right, Aunt Jane, but I can't *see* you. My God, I mean if they couldn't send a man a woman for company, what I mean, my God, I never liked *cats*." He swung around the doorway into the bedroom, and absent-mindedly slammed his fist into the bloody place on the wall.

"But a cat would have been *something*," he said.

Aunt Jane was still silent.

"Don't pretend your damn feelings are hurt, I know you, you're only a damn machine," said Wesson. "Listen, Aunt Jane, I remember a cereal package one time that had a horse and a cowboy on the side. There wasn't much room, so about all you saw was their faces. It used to strike me funny how much they looked alike. Two ears on the top with hair in the middle. Two eyes. Nose. Mouth with teeth in it. I was thinking, we're kind of distant cousins, aren't we, us and the horses. But compared to that thing up there—we're *brothers*. You know?"

"Yes," said Aunt Jane, quietly.

"So I keep asking myself, why couldn't they have sent a horse, or a cat, *instead* of a man? But I guess the answer is, because only a man could take what I'm taking. God, only a man. Right?"

"Right," said Aunt Jane, with deep sorrow.

Wesson stopped at the bedroom doorway again and shuddered, holding onto the frame. "Aunt Jane," he said in a low, clear voice, "You take pictures of *him* up there, don't you?"

"Yes, Paul."

"And you take pictures of me. And then what happens? After it's all over, who looks at the pictures?"

"I don't know," said Aunt Jane humbly.

"You don't know. But whoever looks at 'em, it doesn't do any good. Right? We got to find out why, why, why . . . And we never do find out, do we?"

"No," said Aunt Jane.

"But don't they figure that if the man who's going through it could see him, he might be able to tell something? That other people couldn't? Doesn't that make sense?"

"That's out of my hands, Paul."

He sniggered. "That's funny. Oh, that's funny." He chortled in his throat, reeling around the circuit.

"Yes, that's funny," said Aunt Jane.

"Aunt Jane, tell me what happens to the watchmen."

". . . I can't tell you that, Paul."

He lurched into the living room, sat down before the console, beat on its smooth, cold metal with his fists. "What are you, some kind of monster? Isn't there any blood in your veins, damn it, or oil or *anything*?"

"Please, Paul—"

"Don't you see, all I want to know, can they talk? Can they tell anything after their tour is over?"

". . . No, Paul."

He stood upright, clutching the console for balance. "They can't? No, I figured. And you know why?"

"No."

"Up there," said Wesson obscurely. "Moss on the rock."

"Paul, what?"

"We get changed," said Wesson, stumbling out of the room again. "We get changed. Like a piece of iron next to a magnet. Can't help it. You—nonmagnetic, I guess. Goes right through you, huh, Aunt Jane? You don't get changed. You stay here, wait for the next one."

"Yes," said Aunt Jane.

"You know," said Wesson pacing, "I can tell how he's lying up there. Head *that* way, tail the other. Am I right?"

". . . Yes," said Aunt Jane.

Wesson stopped. "Yes," he said intently. "So you *can* tell me what you see up there, can't you, Aunt Jane?"

"No. Yes. It isn't allowed."

"Listen, Aunt Jane, *we'll die* unless we can find out what makes those aliens tick! Remember that." Wesson leaned against the corridor wall, gazing up. "He's turning now—around this way. Right?"

"Right."

"Well, what else is he doing? Come on, Aunt Jane!"

A pause. "He is twitching his . . ."

"What?"

"I don't know the words."

"My God, my God," said Wesson, clutching his head, "of course there aren't any words." He ran into the living room, clutched the console and stared at the blank screen. He pounded the metal with his fist. "You've got to show me, Aunt Jane, come on and show me, show me!"

"It isn't allowed," Aunt Jane protested.

"You've got to do it just the same, or we'll *die*, Aunt

Jane—millions of us, billions, and it'll be your fault, get it, *your fault*, Aunt Jane!"

"*Please*," said the voice. There was a pause. The screen flickered to life, for an instant only. Wesson had a glimpse of something massive and dark, but half transparent, like a magnified insect—a tangle of nameless limbs, whiplike filaments, claws, wings . . .

He clutched the edge of the console.

"Was that all right?" Aunt Jane asked.

"Of course! What do you think, it'll kill me to look at it? Put it back, Aunt Jane, put it back!"

Reluctantly, the screen lighted again. Wesson stared, and went on staring. He mumbled something.

"What?" said Aunt Jane.

"*Life of my love, I loathe thee*," said Wesson, staring. He roused himself after a moment and turned away. The image of the alien stayed with him as he went reeling into the corridor again; he was not surprised to find that it reminded him of all the loathsome, crawling, creeping things the Earth was full of. That explained why he was not supposed to see the alien, or even know what it looked like—because that fed his hate. And it was all right for him to be afraid of the alien, but he was not supposed to hate it . . . why not? Why not?

His fingers were shaking. He felt drained, steamed, dried up and withered. The one daily shower Aunt Jane allowed him was no longer enough. Twenty minutes after bathing, the acid sweat dripped again from his armpits, the cold sweat was beaded on his forehead, the hot sweat was in his palms. Wesson felt as if there were a furnace inside him, out of control, all the dampers drawn. He knew that under stress, something of the kind did happen to a man: the body's chemistry was altered—more adrenalin, more glycogen in the muscles; eyes brighter, digestion retarded.

That was the trouble—he was burning himself up, unable to fight the thing that tormented him, or to run from it.

After another circuit, Wesson's steps faltered. He hesitated, and went into the living room. He leaned over the console, staring. From the screen, the alien stared blindly up into space. Down in the dark side, the golden indicators had climbed: the vats were more than two-thirds filled.

... to *fight*, or *run* ...

Slowly Wesson sank down in front of the console. He sat hunched, head bent, hands squeezed tight between his knees, trying to hold onto the thought that had come to him.

If the alien felt a pain as great as Wesson's—or greater—

Stress might alter the alien's body chemistry, too.

Life of my love, I loathe thee.

Wesson pushed the irrelevant thought aside. He stared at the screen, trying to envisage the alien, up there, wincing in pain and distress—sweating a golden sweat of horror....

After a long time, he stood up and walked into the kitchen. He caught the table edge to keep his legs from carrying him on around the circuit. He sat down.

Humming fondly, the autochef slid out a tray of small glasses—water, orange juice, milk. Wesson put the water glass to his stiff lips; the water was cool, and hurt his throat. Then the juice, but he could drink only a little of it; then he sipped the milk. Aunt Jane hummed approvingly.

Dehydrated—how long had it been since he had eaten, or drunk? He looked at his hands. They were thin bundles of sticks, ropy-veined, with hard yellow claws. He could see the bones of his forearms under the skin, and his heart's beating stirred the cloth at his chest. The pale hairs on his arms and thighs—were they blond, or white?

The blurred reflections in the metal trim of the dining room gave him no answers—only pale faceless smears of gray. Wesson felt light-headed and very weak, as if he had just ended a bout of fever. He fumbled over his ribs and shoulder-bones. He was thin.

He sat in front of the autochef for a few minutes more, but no food came out. Evidently Aunt Jane did not think he was ready for it, and perhaps she was right. *Worse for them than for us,* he thought dizzily. *That's why the Station's so far out; why radio silence, and only one man aboard. They couldn't stand it at all, otherwise.* . . . Suddenly he could think of nothing but sleep—the bottomless pit, layer after layer of smothering velvet, numbing and soft. . . . His leg muscles quivered and twitched when he tried to walk, but he managed to get to the bedroom and fall on the mattress. The resilient block seemed to dissolve under him. His bones were melting.

He woke with a clear head, very weak, thinking cold and clear: *When two alien cultures meet, the stronger must transform the weaker with love or hate.* "Wesson's Law," he said aloud. He looked automatically for pencil and paper, but there was none, and he realized he would have to tell Aunt Jane, and let her remember it.

"I don't understand," she said.

"Never mind, remember it anyway. You're good at that, aren't you?"

"Yes, Paul."

"All right. . . . I want some breakfast."

He thought about Aunt Jane, so nearly human, sitting up here in her metal prison, leading one man after another through the torments of hell . . . nursemaid, protector, torturer. They must have known that something would have to give. . . . But the alphas were comparatively new;

nobody understood them very well. Perhaps they really thought that an absolute prohibition could never be broken.

... the stronger must transform the weaker ...

I'm *the stronger,* he thought. *And that's the way it's going to be.* He stopped at the console, and the screen was blank. He said angrily, "Aunt Jane!" And with a guilty start, the screen flickered into life.

Up there, the alien had rolled again in his pain. Now the great clustered eyes were staring directly into the camera; the coiled limbs threshed in pain: the eyes were staring, asking, pleading...

"*No,*" said Wesson, feeling his own pain like an iron cap, and he slammed his hand down on the manual control. The screen went dark. He looked up, sweating, and saw the floral picture over the console.

The thick stems were like antennae, the leaves thoraxes, the buds like blind insect-eyes. The whole picture moved slightly, endlessly, in a slow waiting rhythm.

Wesson clutched the hard metal of the console and stared at the picture, with sweat cold on his brow, until it turned into a calm, meaningless arrangement of lines again. Then he went into the dining room, shaking, and sat down. After a moment he said, "Aunt Jane, does it get worse?"

"No. From now on, it gets better."

"How long?" he asked vaguely.

"One month."

A month, getting "better" . . . that was the way it had always been, with the watchman swamped and drowned, his personality submerged. Wesson thought about the men who had gone before him—Class Seven citizenship, with unlimited leisure, and Class One housing, yes, sure ... in a sanatorium.

His lips peeled back from his teeth, and his fists clenched hard. *Not me!* he thought.

He spread his hands on the cool metal to steady them. He said, "How much longer do they usually stay able to talk?"

"You are already talking longer than any of them."

Then there was a blank. Wesson was vaguely aware, in snatches, of the corridor walls moving past, and the console glimpsed, and of a thunderous cloud of ideas that swirled around his head in a beating of wings. The aliens: what did they want? And what happened to the watchmen in Stranger Station?

The haze receded a little, and he was in the dining room again, staring vacantly at the table. Something was wrong.

He ate a few spoonfuls of the gruel that autochef served him, then pushed it away; the stuff tasted faintly unpleasant. The machine hummed anxiously and thrust a poached egg at him, but Wesson got up from the table.

The Station was all but silent. The resting rhythm of the household machines throbbed in the walls, unheard. The blue-lit living room was spread out before him like an empty stage-setting, and Wesson stared as if he had never seen it before.

He lurched to the console and stared down at the pictured alien on the screen: heavy, heavy, asprawl with pain in the darkness. The needles of the golden indicators were high, the enlarged vats almost full. *It's too much for him*, Wesson thought with grim satisfaction. The peace that followed the pain had not descended as it was supposed to; no, not this time!

He glanced up at the painting over the console: heavy crustacean limbs that swayed gracefully.

He shook his head violently. *I won't let it; I won't give in!* He held the back of one hand close to his eyes. He saw the dozens of tiny cuneiform wrinkles stamped into the skin over the knuckles, the pale hairs sprouting, the pink shiny flesh of recent scars. *I'm human*, he thought. But when he let his hand fall onto the console, the bony fingers seemed to crouch like crustaceans' legs, ready to scuttle.

Sweating, Wesson stared into the screen. Pictured there, the alien met his eyes, and it was as if they spoke to each other, mind to mind, an instantaneous communication that needed no words. There was a piercing sweetness in it, a melting, dissolving luxury of change into something that would no longer have any pain. . . . A pull, a calling.

Wesson straightened up slowly, carefully, as if he held some fragile thing in his mind that must not be handled roughly, or it would disintegrate. He said hoarsely, "Aunt Jane!"

She made some responsive noise.

He said, "Aunt Jane, I've got the answer! The whole thing! Listen, now, wait—listen!" He paused a moment to collect his thoughts. *"When two alien cultures meet, the stronger must transform the weaker with love or hate.* Remember? You said you didn't understand what that meant. I'll *tell* you what it means. When these—monsters—met Pigeon a hundred years ago on Titan, *they knew* we'd have to meet again. They're spreading out, colonizing, and so are we. We haven't got interstellar flight yet, but give us another hundred years, we'll *get* it. *We'll wind up out there, where they are.* And they can't stop us. Because they're not killers, Aunt Jane, it isn't in them. They're *nicer* than us. See, they're like the missionaries, and we're the South Sea Islanders. *They* don't kill their enemies, oh no—perish the thought!"

She was trying to say something, to interrupt him, but he rushed on. "Listen! The longevity serum—that was a lucky accident. But they played it for all it's worth. Slick and smooth—they come and give us the stuff free—they don't ask for a thing in return. Why not? Listen.

"They come here, and the shock of that first contact makes them sweat out that golden gook we need. Then, the last month or so, the pain always eases off. Why? Because the two minds, the human and alien, they stop fighting each other. Something gives way, it goes soft and there's a mixing together. And that's where you get the human casualties of this operation—the bleary men that come out of here not even able to talk human language any more. Oh, I suppose they're happy—happier than I am!—because they've got something big and wonderful inside 'em. Something that you and I can't even understand. But if you took them and put them together again with the aliens who spent time here, *they could all live together —they're adapted.*

"That's what they're aiming for!" He struck the console with his fist. "Not now—but a hundred, two hundred years from now! When we start expanding out to the stars— when we go a-conquering—we'll have already been conquered! Not by weapons, Aunt Jane, not by hate—by love! Yes, love! *Dirty, stinking, low-down, sneaking love!*"

Aunt Jane said something, a long sentence, in a high, anxious voice.

"What?" said Wesson irritably. He couldn't understand a word.

Aunt Jane was silent. "What, what?" Wesson demanded, pounding the console. "Have you got it through your tin head, or not? *What?*"

Aunt Jane said something else, tonelessly. Once more, Wesson could not make out a single word.

He stood frozen. Warm tears started suddenly out of his eyes. "Aunt Jane—" he said. He remembered, *You are already talking longer than any of them.* Too late? Too late?

He tensed, then whirled and sprang to the closet where the paper books were kept. He opened the first one his hand struck.

The black letters were alien squiggles on the page, little humped shapes, without meaning.

The tears were coming faster, he couldn't stop them: tears of weariness, tears of frustration, tears of hate. "*Aunt Jane!*" he roared.

But it was no good. The curtain of silence had come down over his head. He was one of the vanguard—the conquered men, the ones who would get along with their stranger brothers, out among the alien stars.

The console was not working any more; nothing worked when he wanted it. Wesson squatted in the shower stall, naked, with a soup bowl in his hands. Water droplets glistened on his hands and forearms; the pale short hairs were just springing up, drying.

The silvery skin of reflection in the bowl gave him back nothing but a silhouette, a shadow man's outline. He could not see his face.

He dropped the bowl and went across the living room, shuffling the pale drifts of paper underfoot. The black lines on the paper, when his eyes happened to light on them, were worm-shapes, crawling things, conveying nothing. He rolled slightly in his walk; his eyes were glazed. His head twitched, every now and then, sketching a useless motion to avoid pain.

Once the bureau chief, Gower, came to stand in his way. "You fool," he said, his face contorted in anger, "you were supposed to go on to the end, like the rest. Now look what you've done!"

"I found out, didn't I?" Wesson mumbled, and as he brushed the man aside like a cobweb, the pain suddenly grew more intense. Wesson clasped his head in his hands with a grunt, and rocked to and fro a moment, uselessly, before he straightened and went on. The pain was coming in waves now, so tall that at their peak his vision dimmed out, violet, then gray.

It couldn't go on much longer. Something had to burst.

He paused at the bloody place and slapped the metal with his palm, making the sound ring dully up into the frame of the Station: *rroom, rroom.*

Faintly an echo came back: *boooom.*

Wesson kept going, smiling a faint and meaningless smile. He was only marking time now, waiting. Something was about to happen.

The dining-room doorway sprouted a sudden sill and tripped him. He fell heavily, sliding on the floor, and lay without moving beneath the slick gleam of the autochef.

The pressure was too great: the autochef's clucking was swallowed up in the ringing pressure, and the tall gray walls buckled slowly in. . . .

The Station lurched.

Wesson felt it through his chest, palms, knees and elbows: the floor was plucked away for an instant and then swung back.

The pain in his skull relaxed its grip a little. Wesson tried to get to his feet.

There was an electric silence in the Station. On the second try, he got up and leaned his back against a wall. *Cluck*, said the autochef suddenly, hysterically, and the vent popped open, but nothing came out.

He listened, straining to hear. What?

The station bounced beneath him, making his feet jump like a puppet's; the wall slapped his back hard, shuddered and was still; but far off through the metal cage came a long angry groan of metal, echoing, diminishing, dying. Then silence again.

The Station held its breath. All the myriad clickings and pulses in the walls were suspended; in the empty rooms the lights burned with a yellow glare, and the air hung stagnant and still. The console lights in the living room glowed like witchfires. Water in the dropped bowl, at the bottom of the shower stall, shone like quicksilver, waiting.

The third shock came. Wesson found himself on his hands and knees, the jolt still tingling in the bones of his body, staring at the floor. The sound that filled the room ebbed away slowly and ran down into the silences: a resonant metallic hollow sound, shuddering away now along the girders and hull plates, rattling tinnily into bolts and fittings, diminishing, noiseless, gone. The silence pressed down again.

The floor leaped painfully under his body: one great resonant blow that shook him from head to foot.

A muted echo of that blow came a few seconds later, as if the shock had traveled across the Station and back.

The bed, Wesson thought, and scrambled on hands and knees through the doorway, along a floor curiously tilted, until he reached the rubbery block.

The room burst visibly upward around him, squeezing the block flat. It dropped back as violently, leaving Wesson bouncing helpless on the mattress, his limbs flying. It came to rest, in a long reluctant groan of metal.

Wesson rolled up on one elbow, thinking incoherently, *Air, the air lock.* Another blow slammed him down into the mattress, pinched his lungs shut, while the room danced grotesquely over his head. Gasping for breath in the ringing silence, Wesson felt a slow icy chill rolling toward him across the room . . . and there was a pungent smell in the air. *Ammonia!* he thought; and the odorless, smothering methane with it.

His cell was breached. The burst membrane was fatal: the alien's atmosphere would kill him.

Wesson surged to his feet. The next shock caught him off balance, dashed him to the floor. He arose again, dazed and limping; he was still thinking confusedly, *The air lock, get out.*

When he was halfway to the door, all the ceiling lights went out at once. The darkness was like a blanket around his head. It was bitter cold now in the room, and the pungent smell was sharper. Coughing, Wesson hurried forward. The floor lurched under his feet.

Only the golden indicators burned now: full to the top, the deep vats brimming, golden-lipped, gravid, a month before the time. Wesson shuddered.

Water spurted in the bathroom, hissing steadily on the tiles, rattling in the plastic bowl at the bottom of the shower stall. The lights winked on and off again. In the dining room, he heard the autochef clucking and sighing. The freezing wind blew harder: he was numb with cold to the hips. It seemed to Wesson abruptly that he was not at the top of the sky at all, but down, *down* at the bottom of the sea . . . trapped in this steel bubble, while the dark poured in.

The pain in his head was gone, as if it had never been there, and he understood what that meant: Up there, the great body was hanging like butcher's carrion in the darkness. Its death struggles were over, the damage done.

Wesson gathered a desperate breath, shouted, "Help me! The alien's dead! He kicked the Station apart—the methane's coming! Get help, do you hear me? *Do you hear me?*"

Silence. In the smothering blackness, he remembered: *She can't understand me any more. Even if she's alive.*

He turned, making an animal noise in his throat. He groped his way on around the room, past the second doorway. Behind the walls, something was dripping with a slow cold tinkle and splash, a forlorn night sound. Small, hard floating things rapped against his legs. Then he touched a smooth curve of metal: the air lock.

Eagerly he pushed his feeble weight against the door. It didn't move. And it didn't move. Cold air was rushing out around the door frame, a thin knife-cold stream, but the door itself was jammed tight.

The suit! He should have thought of that before. If he just had some pure air to breathe, and a little warmth in his fingers . . . But the door of the suit locker would not move, either. The ceiling must have buckled.

And that was the end, he thought, bewildered. There were no more ways out. But there *had* to be— He pounded on the door until his arms would not lift any more; it did not move. Leaning against the chill metal, he saw a single light blink on overhead.

The room was a wild place of black shadows and swimming shapes—the book leaves, fluttering and darting in the air stream. Schools of them beat wildly at the walls, curling over, baffled, trying again; others were swooping around the outer corridor, around and around: he could see them whirling past the doorways, dreamlike, a white drift of silent paper in the darkness.

The acrid smell was harsher in his nostrils. Wesson choked, groping his way to the console again. He pounded it with his open hand: he wanted to see Earth.

But when the little square of brightness leaped up, it was the dead body of the alien that Wesson saw.

It hung motionless in the cavity of the Station, limbs dangling stiff and still, eyes dull. The last turn of the screw had been too much for it: but Wesson had survived . . .

For a few minutes.

The dead alien face mocked him; a whisper of memory floated into his mind: *We might have been brothers.* ... All at once, Wesson passionately wanted to believe it—wanted to give in, turn back. That passed. Wearily he let himself sag into the bitter *now*, thinking with thin defiance, *It's done—hate wins. You'll have to stop this big giveaway—can't risk this happening again. And we'll hate you for that—and when we get out to the stars—*

The world was swimming numbly away out of reach. He felt the last fit of coughing take his body, as if it were happening to someone else beside him.

The last fluttering leaves of paper came to rest. There was a long silence in the drowned room.

Then:

"Paul," said the voice of the mechanical woman brokenly; "Paul," it said again, with the hopelessness of lost, unknown, impossible love.

The "Talent" possessed by young Andrew Benson, as those who knew him testify, is a most unusual one indeed—for a human or an extraterrestrial (and there is some question as to which Andrew might be). In fact, one could say that this talent of his is decidedly monstrous.

Robert Bloch (b. 1917) published his first short story in Weird Tales *nearly a half-century ago, at the tender age of seventeen, and has followed it with several hundred more to date. Plus a dozen or so collections and a score of science-fiction, fantasy/horror, and mystery novels. Plus large numbers of radio, television, and film scripts. Plus innumerable nonfiction pieces of different types. Although he is best known to the general reader as the author of Psycho, it is such sometimes grim, sometimes pun-filled and comic—and usually horrific—visions as "Talent," "Enoch," "Yours Truly, Jack the Ripper,"* Night-World, *and the recently published* Strange Eons *which are most highly lauded by aficionados of science fiction and the macabre. BEMs in one form or another, human or alien, are one of his specialties, as you'll shortly discover in the pages that follow.*

Talent

Robert Bloch

It is perhaps a pity that nothing is known of Andrew Benson's parents.

The same reasons which prompted them to leave him as a foundling on the steps of the St. Andrews Orphanage also caused them to maintain a discreet anonymity. The event occurred on the morning of March 3rd, 1943—the war era, as you probably recall—so in a way the child may be regarded as a wartime casualty. Similar occurrences were by no means rare during those days, even in Pasadena, where the Orphanage was located.

After the usual tentative and fruitless inquiries, the good Sisters took him in. It was there that he acquired his first name, from the patron and patronymic saint of the establishment. The "Benson" was added some years later, by the couple who eventually adopted him.

It is difficult, at this late date, to determine what sort of a child Andrew was; orphanage records are sketchy, at best, and Sister Rosemarie, who acted as supervisor of the boys' dormitory, is long since dead. Sister Albertine, the primary grades teacher of the Orphanage School, is now—to put it as delicately as possible—in her senility, and her testimony is necessarily colored by knowledge of subsequent events.

That Andrew never learned to talk until he was nearly seven years old seems almost incredible; the forced gregarity and the conspicuous lack of individual attention characteristic of orphanage upbringing would make it appear as though the ability to speak is necessary for actual survival in such an environment from infancy onward. Scarcely more credible is Sister Albertine's theory that Andrew knew how to talk but merely refused to do so until he was well into his seventh year.

For what it is worth, she now remembers him as an unusually precocious youngster, who appeared to possess an intelligence and understanding far beyond his years. Instead of employing speech, however, he relied on pantomime, an art at which he was so brilliantly adept (if Sister Albertine is to be believed) that his continuing silence seemed scarcely noticeable.

"He could imitate anybody," she declares. "The other children, the Sisters, even the Mother Superior. Of course I had to punish him for that. But it was remarkable, the way he was able to pick up all the little mannerisms and facial expressions of another person, just at a glance. And that's all it took for Andrew—just a mere glance.

"Visitors' Day was Sunday. Naturally, Andrew never had any visitors, but he liked to hang around the corridor and watch them come in. And afterwards, in the dormitory at night, he'd put in a regular performance for the other boys. He could impersonate every single man, woman or child who'd come to the Orphanage that day—the way they walked, the way they moved, every action and gesture. Even though he never said a word, nobody made the mistake of thinking Andrew was mentally deficient. For a while, Dr. Clement had the idea he might be a mute."

Dr. Roger Clement is one of the few persons who might be able to furnish more objective data concerning Andrew Benson's early years. Unfortunately, he passed away in 1954, a victim of a fire which also destroyed his home and his office files.

It was Dr. Clement who attended Andrew on the night that he saw his first motion picture.

The date was 1949, some Saturday evening in the late fall of the year. The Orphanage received and showed one film a week, and only children of school age were permitted to attend. Andrew's inability—or unwillingness—to speak had caused some difficulty when he entered primary grades that September, and several months went by before he was allowed to join his classmates in the auditorium for the Saturday night screenings. But it is known that he eventually did so.

The picture was the last (and probably the least) of the Marx Brothers movies. Its title was *Love Happy*, and if it is remembered by the general public at all today, that is due to the fact that the film contained a brief walk-on appearance by a then-unknown blonde bit player named Marilyn Monroe.

But the Orphanage audience had other reasons for regarding it as memorable. Because *Love Happy* was the picture that sent Andrew Benson into his trance.

Long after the lights came up again in the auditorium the child sat there, immobile, his eyes staring glassily at the blank screen. When his companions noticed and sought to arouse him he did not respond; one of the Sisters (possibly Sister Rosemarie) shook him, and he promptly collapsed in a dead faint. Dr. Clement was summoned, and he administered to the patient. Andrew Benson did not recover consciousness until the following morning.

And it was then that he talked.

He talked immediately, he talked perfectly, he talked fluently—but not in the manner of a six-year-old child. The voice that issued from his lips was that of a middle-aged man. It was a nasal, rasping voice, and even without the accompanying grimaces and facial expressions it was instantaneously and unmistakably recognizable as the voice of Groucho Marx.

Andrew Benson mimicked Groucho in his Sam Grunion role to perfection, word for word. Then he "did" Chico Marx. After that he relapsed into silence again, and for a moment it was thought he had reverted to his mute phase. But it was an eloquent silence, and soon it became evident that he was imitating Harpo. In rapid succession, Andrew created recognizable vocal and visual portraits of Raymond Burr, Melville Cooper, Eric Blore and the other actors who played small roles in the picture. His impersonations seemed uncanny to his companions, and the Sisters were not unimpressed.

"Why, he even *looked* like Groucho," Sister Albertine insists.

Ignoring the question of how a towheaded moppet of six can achieve a physical resemblance to Groucho Marx without benefit (or detriment) of make-up, it is nevertheless an established fact that Andrew Benson gained immediate celebrity as a mimic within the small confines of the Orphanage.

And from that moment on, he talked regularly, if not freely. That is to say, he replied to direct questions, he recited his lessons in the classroom, and responded with the outward forms of politeness required by Orphanage discipline. But he was never loquacious, or even communicative, in the ordinary sense. The only time he became spontaneously articulate was immediately following the showing of a weekly movie.

There was no recurrence of his initial seizure, but each Saturday night screening brought in its wake a complete dramatic recapitulation by the gifted youngster. During the fall of '49 and the winter of '50, Andrew Benson saw many movies. There was *Sorrowful Jones*, with Bob Hope; *Tarzan's Magic Fountain*; *The Fighting O'Flynn*; *The Life of Riley*; *Little Women*, and a number of other films, current and older. Naturally, these pictures were subject to approval by the Sisters before being shown, and as a result movies depicting or emphasizing violence were not included. Still, several Westerns reached the Orphanage screen, and it is significant that Andrew Benson reacted in what was to become a characteristic fashion.

"Funny thing," declares Albert Dominguez, who attended the Orphanage during the same period as Andrew Benson and is one of the few persons located who is willing to admit, let alone discuss, the fact. "At first Andy imitated everybody—all the men, that is. He never imitated none of the women. But after he started to see Westerns, it got so he was choosey, like. He just imitated the villains. I don't mean like when us guys was playing cowboys—you know, when one guy is the Sheriff and one is a gunslinger. I mean he imitated villains all the time. He could talk like 'em, he could even look like 'em. We used to razz hell out of him, you know?"

It is probably as a result of the "razzing" that Andrew Benson, on the evening of May 17th, 1950, attempted to slit the throat of Frank Phillips with a table-knife. Probably—although Albert Dominguez claims that the older boy offered no provocation, and that Andrew Benson was exactly duplicating the screen role of a western desperado in an old Charles Starrett movie.

The incident was hushed up, apparently, and no action taken; we have little information on Andrew Benson's growth and development between the summer of 1950 and the autumn of 1955. Dominguez left the orphanage, nobody else appears willing to testify, and Sister Albertine had retired to a rest-home. As a result, there is nothing available concerning what may well have been Andrew's crucial, formative years. The meager records of his classwork seem satisfactory enough, and there is nothing to indicate that he was a disciplinary problem to his instructors. In June of 1955 he was photographed with the rest of his classmates upon the occasion of graduation from eighth grade. His face is a mere blur, an almost blank smudge in a sea of preadolescent countenances. What he actually looked like at that age is hard to tell.

The Bensons thought that he resembled their son, David.

Little David Benson had died of polio in 1953, and two years later his parents came to St. Andrews Orphanage seeking to adopt a boy. They had David's picture with them, and they were frank to state that they sought a physical resemblance as a guide to making their choice.

Did Andrew Benson see that photograph? Did—as has been subsequently theorized by certain irresponsible alarmists—he see certain *home movies* which the Bensons had taken of their child?

We must confine ourselves to the known facts, which are, simply, that Mr. and Mrs. Louis Benson, of Pasadena, California, legally adopted Andrew Benson, aged 12, on December 9th, 1955.

And Andrew Benson went to live in their home, as their son. He entered the public high school. He became the owner of a bicycle. He received an allowance of one dollar a week. And he went to the movies.

Andrew Benson went to the movies, and there were no restrictions. No restrictions at all. For several months, that is. During this period he saw comedies, dramas, Westerns, musicals, melodramas. He must have seen melodramas. Was there a film, released early in 1956, in which an actor played the role of a gangster who pushed a victim out of a second-story window?

Knowing what we do today, we must suspect that there must have been. But at the time, when the actual incident occurred, Andrew Benson was virtually exonerated. He and the other boy had been "scuffling" in a classroom after school, and the boy had "accidentally fallen." At least, this is the official version of the affair. The boy—now Pvt. Raymond Schuyler, USMC—maintains to this day that Benson deliberately tried to kill him.

"He was spooky, that kid," Schuyler insists. "None of us ever really got close to him. It was like there was nothing to get close to, you know? I mean, he kept changing off so. From one day to the next you could never figure out what he was going to be like. Of course we all knew he imitated these movie actors—he was only a freshman but already he was a big shot in the dramatic club—but it was as though he imitated all the time. One minute he'd be real quiet, and the next, wham! You know that story, the one about Jekyll and Hyde? Well, that was Andrew Benson. Afternoon he grabbed me, we weren't even talking to each other. He just came up to me at the window and I swear to

God he changed right before my eyes. It was as if he all of a sudden got about a foot taller and fifty pounds heavier, and his face was real wild. He pushed me out of the window, without one word. Of course I was scared spitless, and maybe I just thought he changed. I mean, nobody can actually do a thing like that, can they?"

This question, if it arose at all at the time, remained unanswered. We do know that Andrew Benson was brought to the attention of Dr. Max Fahringer, child psychiatrist and part-time guidance counselor at the school, and that his initial examination disclosed no apparent abnormalities of personality or behavior patterns. Dr. Fahringer did, however, have several long talks with the Bensons, and as a result Andrew was forbidden to attend motion pictures. The following year, Dr. Fahringer voluntarily offered to examine young Andrew—undoubtedly his interest had been aroused by the amazing dramatic abilities the boy was showing in his extracurricular activities at the school.

Only one such interview ever took place, and it is to be regretted that Dr. Fahringer neither committed his findings to paper nor communicated them to the Bensons before his sudden, shocking death at the hands of an unknown assailant. It is believed (or was believed by the police, at the time) that one of his former patients, committed to an institution as a psychotic, may have been guilty of the crime.

All that we know is that it occurred some short while following a local re-run of the film, *Man in the Attic*, in which Jack Palance essayed the role of Jack the Ripper.

It is interesting, today, to examine some of the so-called "horror movies" of those years, including the re-runs of earlier vehicles starring Boris Karloff, Bela Lugosi, Peter Lorre and a number of other actors.

Talent 47

We cannot say with any certainty, of course, that Andrew Benson was violating the wishes of his foster parents and secretly attending motion pictures. But if he did, it was quite likely that he would frequent the smaller neighborhood houses, many of which specialized in re-runs. And we do know, from the remarks of fellow classmates during these high school years, that "Andy" was familiar—almost omnisciently so—with the mannerisms of these performers.

The evidence is oftentimes conflicting. Joan Charters, for example, is willing to "swear on a stack of Bibles" that Andrew Benson, at the age of fifteen, was "a dead ringer for Peter Lorre—the same bug eyes and everything." Whereas Nick Dossinger, who attended classes with Benson a year later, insists that he "looked just like Boris Karloff."

Granted that adolescence may bring about a considerable increase in height during the period of a year, it is nevertheless difficult to imagine how a "dead ringer for Peter Lorre" could metamorphose into an asthenic Karloff type.

A mass of testimony is available concerning Andrew Benson during those years, but almost all of it deals with his phenomenal histrionic talent and his startling skill at "ad lib" impersonations of motion picture actors. Apparently he had given up mimicking his associates and contemporaries almost entirely.

"He said he liked to do actors better, because they were bigger," says Don Brady, who appeared with him in the senior play. "I asked him what he meant by 'bigger' and he said it was just that—actors were bigger on the screen, sometimes twenty feet tall. He said, 'Why bother with little people when you can be big?' Oh, he was a real offbeat character, that one."

The phrases recur. "Oddball," and "screwball," and

"real gone" are picturesque, but hardly enlightening. And there seems to be little recollection of Andrew Benson as a friend or classmate, in the ordinary role of adolescence. It's the imitator who is remembered, with admiration and, frequently, with distaste bordering on actual apprehension.

"He was so good he scared you. But that's when he was doing those impersonations, of course. The rest of the time, you scarcely knew he was around."

"Classes? I guess he did all right. I didn't notice him much."

"Andrew was a fair student. He could recite when called upon, but he never volunteered. His marks were average. I got the impression he was rather withdrawn."

"No, he never dated much. Come to think of it, I don't think he went out with girls at all. I never paid much attention to him, except when he was on stage, of course."

"I wasn't really what you call close to Andy. I don't know anybody who seemed to be friends with him. He was so quiet, outside of the dramatics. And when he got up there, it was like he was a different person—he was real great, you know? We all figured he'd end up at the Pasadena Playhouse."

The reminiscences of his contemporaries are frequently apt to touch upon matters which did not directly involve Andrew Benson. The years 1956 and 1957 are still remembered, by high school students of the area in particular, as the years of the curfew. It was a voluntary curfew, of course, but it was nevertheless strictly observed by most of the female students during the period of the "werewolf murders"—that series of savage, still-unsolved crimes which terrorized the community for well over a year. Certain cannibalistic aspects of the slaying of the five young women led to the "werewolf" appellation on the part of the sensation-mongering press. The *Wolf Man* series made by Universal had been revived, and perhaps this had something to do with the association.

But to return to Andrew Benson; he grew up, went to school, and lived the normal life of a dutiful stepson. If his foster parents were a bit strict, he made no complaints. If they punished him because they suspected he sometimes slipped out of his room at night, he made no complaint or denials. If they seemed apprehensive lest he be disobeying their set injunctions not to attend the movies, he offered no overt defiance.

The only known clash between Andrew Benson and his family came about as a result of their flat refusal to allow a television set in their home. Whether or not they were concerned about the possible encouragement of Andrew's mimicry or whether they had merely developed an allergy to Lawrence Welk and his ilk is difficult to determine. Nevertheless, they balked at the acquisition of a TV set. Andrew begged and pleaded, pointed out that he "needed" television as an aid to a future dramatic career. His argument had some justification, for in his senior year, Andrew had indeed been "scouted" by the famous Pasadena Playhouse, and there was even some talk of a future professional career without the necessity of formal training.

But the Bensons were adamant on the television question; as far as we can determine, they remained adamant right up to the day of their death.

The unfortunate circumstances occurred at Balboa, where the Bensons owned a small cottage and maintained a little cabin cruiser. The elder Bensons and Andrew were heading for Catalina Channel when the cruiser overturned in choppy waters. Andrew managed to cling to the craft until rescued, but his foster parents were gone. It was a common enough accident; you've probably seen something just like it in the movies a dozen times.

Andrew, just turned eighteen, was left an orphan once more—but an orphan in full possession of a lovely home, and with the expectation of coming into a sizeable inheritance when he reached twenty-one. The Benson estate was administered by the family attorney, Justin L. Fowler, and he placed young Andrew on an allowance of forty dollars a week—an amount sufficient for a recent graduate of high school to survive on, but hardly enough to maintain him in luxury.

It is to be feared that violent scenes were precipitated between the young man and his attorney. There is no point in recapitulating them here, or in condemning Fowler for what may seem—on the surface of it—to be the development of a fixation.

But up until the night that he was struck down by a hit-and-run driver in the street before his house, Attorney Fowler seemed almost obsessed with the desire to prove that the Benson lad was legally incompetent, or worse. Indeed, it was his investigation which led to the uncovering of what few facts are presently available concerning the life of Andrew Benson.

Certain other hypotheses—one hesitates to dignify them with the term "conclusions"—he apparently extrapolated from these meager findings, or fabricated them out of thin air. Unless, of course, he did manage to discover details which he never actually disclosed. Without the support of such details there is no way of authenticating what seem to be a series of fantastic conjectures.

A random sampling, as remembered from various conversations Fowler had with the authorities, will suffice.

"I don't think the kid is even human, for that matter. Just because he showed up on those orphanage steps, you call him a foundling. Changeling might be a better word for it. Yes, I know they don't believe in such things any more. And if you talk about life-forms from other planets, they laugh at you and tell you to join the Fortean Society. So happens, I'm a member.

"Changeling? It's probably a more accurate term than the narrow meaning implies. I'm talking about the way he changes when he sees these movies. No, don't take my word for it—ask anyone who's ever seen him act. Better still, ask those who never saw him on a stage, but just watched him imitate movie performers in private. You'll find out he did a lot more than just imitate. He *becomes* the actor. Yes, I mean he undergoes an actual physical transformation. Chameleon. Or some other form of life. Who can say?

"No, I don't pretend to understand it. I know it's not 'scientific' according to the way you define science. But that doesn't mean it's impossible. There are a lot of life-forms in the universe, and we can only guess at some of them. Why shouldn't there be one that's abnormally sensitive to mimicry?

"You know what effect the movies can have on so-called 'normal' human beings, under certain conditions. It's a hypnotic state, for this movie-viewing, and you can ask the psychologists for confirmation. Darkness, concentration, suggestion—all the elements are present. And there's post-hypnotic suggestion, too. Again, psychiatrists will back me up on that. Most people tend to identify with various characters on the screen. That's where our hero worship comes in, that's why we have western-movie fans, and detective fans, and all the rest. Supposedly ordinary people come out of the theater and fantasy themselves as the heroes and heroines they saw up there on the screen; imitate them, too.

"That's what Andrew Benson did of course. Only suppose he could carry it one step further? Suppose he was capable of *being* what he saw portrayed? And he chose to *be* the villains? I tell you, it's time to investigate those killings of a few years back, all of them. Not just the murder of those girls, but the murder of the two doctors who examined Benson when he was a child, and the death of his foster parents, too. I don't think any of these things were accidents. I think some people got too close to the secret, and Benson put them out of the way.

"Why? How should I know why? Any more than I know what he's looking for when he watches the movies. But he's looking for something, I can guarantee that. Who knows what purpose such a life-form can have, or what he intends to do with his power? All I can do is warn you."

It is easy to dismiss Attorney Fowler as a paranoid type, though perhaps unfair, in that we cannot evaluate the reasons for his outburst. That he knew (or believed he knew) something is self-evident. As a matter of fact, on the very evening of his death he was apparently about to put his findings on paper.

Deplorably, all that he ever set down was a preamble, in the form of a quotation from Eric Voegelin, concerning rigid pragmatic attitudes of "scientism," so-called:

"(1) the assumption that the mathematized science of natural phenomena is a model science to which all other sciences ought to conform; (2) that all realms of being are accessible to the methods of the sciences of phenomena; and (3) that all reality which is not accessible to sciences of phenomena is either irrelevant or, in the more radical form of the dogma, illusionary."

But Attorney Fowler is dead, and we deal with the living; with Max Schick, for example, the motion-picture and television agent who visited Andrew Benson at his home shortly after the death of the elder Bensons, and offered him an immediate contract.

"You're a natural," Schick declared. "Never mind with the Pasadena Playhouse bit. I can spot you right now, believe me! With what you got, we'll back Brando right off the map! Of course, we gotta start small, but I know just the gimmick. Main thing is to establish you in a starring slot right away. None of this stock-contract jazz, get me? The studios aren't handing 'em out any more in the first place, and even if you landed one, you'd end up on Cloud Nowhere. No, the deal is to get you a lead and billing right off the bat. And like I said, I got the angle.

"We go to a small independent producer, get it? Must be a dozen of 'em operating right now, and all of 'em making the same thing. Only one kind of picture that combines low budgets with big grosses, and that's a science fiction movie.

"Yeah, you heard me, a science fiction movie. Whaddya mean, you never saw one? Are you kidding? How about that? You mean you never saw any science fiction pictures at all?

"Oh, your folks, eh? Had to sneak out? And they only show that kind of stuff at the downtown houses?

"Well look, kid, it's about time, that's all I can say. It's about time! Hey, just so's you know what we're talking about, you better get on the ball and take in one right away. Sure, I'm positive, there must be one playing a downtown first run now. Why don't you go this afternoon? I got some work to finish up here at the office—run you down in my car and you can go on to the show, meet me back there when you get out.

"Sure, you can take the car after you drop me off. Be my guest."

So Andrew Benson saw his first science fiction movie. He drove there and back in Max Schick's car (coincidentally enough, it was the late afternoon of the day when Attorney Fowler became a hit-and-run victim) and Schick has good reason to remember Andrew Benson's reappearance at his office just after dusk.

"He had a look on his face that was out of this world," Schick says.

" 'How'd you like the picture?' I ask him.

" 'It was wonderful,' he tells me. 'Just what I've been looking for all these years. And to think I didn't know.'

" 'Didn't know what?' I ask. But he isn't talking to me any more. You can see that. He's talking to himself.

" 'I thought there must be something like that,' he says. 'Something better than Dracula, or Frankenstein's Monsters, or all the rest. Something bigger, more powerful. Something I could really be. And now I know. And now I'm going to.' "

Max Schick is unable to maintain coherency from this point on. But his direct account is not necessary. We are, unfortunately, all too well aware of what happened next.

Max Schick sat there in his chair and watched Andrew Benson *change*.

He watched him *grow*. He watched him put forth the eyes, the stalks, the writhing tentacles. He watched him twist and tower, filling the room and then *overflowing* until the flimsy stucco walls collapsed and there was nothing but the green, gigantic horror, the sixty-foot-high monstrosity that may have been born in a screenwriter's brain or may have been spawned beyond the stars, but certainly existed and drew nourishment from realms far from a three-dimensional world or three-dimensional concepts of sanity.

Max Schick will never forget that night and neither, of course, will anybody else.

That was the night the monster destroyed Los Angeles....

It has often been said that the short-short is the most difficult of all literary forms to master; this seems particularly true in science fiction, which for the most part deals with complex ideas rather than simple incidences. But "The Other Kids" is an example of what can *be done in the s-f short-short by a talented writer—a combination of idea and incidence that results in a powerful cautionary statement about men and about those we call monsters.*

Robert F. Young (b. 1917) has been a popular and prolific writer of science fiction for three decades. His stories regularly appear in The Magazine of Fantasy & Science Fiction, *among other publications in the field, and several have been honored in best-of-the-year anthologies edited over the past quarter-century by such diverse critical tastes as Everett Bleiler and T. E. Dikty, Judith Merrill, Harry Harrison and Brian W. Aldiss, and Terry Carr. These and some of his other fine stories appear in two collections,* The Worlds of Robert F. Young *(1965) and* A Glass of Stars *(1968).*

The Other Kids

Robert F. Young

By the time the two army officers came up in the jeep half the population of the little town was standing along the edge of the meadow. It wasn't a particularly large crowd, but it was a nasty one. There were shotguns in it, and rifles and knives and lead pipes and baseball bats.

Captain Blair waited till the two truckloads of soldiers arrived, then he pushed his way through the crowd to the meadow. Lieutenant Simms followed.

The sheriff was standing in front of the crowd, a brand-new .270 balanced in the crook of his arm. He nodded to the captain. "Thought I'd better let the army in on this," he said in a thin rasping voice. "It's a little out of my line."

The captain squinted at the saucer. It sat in the middle of the meadow, gleaming in the October sunlight. It looked like a king-size Aladdin's lamp; an Aladdin's lamp without chimney or base, and totally lacking in ornamentation. The captain had read most of the accounts about saucers and he had always been impressed by their dimensions, though he had never admitted it to anyone.

This one was disappointing. It was a distinct letdown. It was so small it couldn't possibly contain more than a crew of one, unless you postulated pint-size Martians. The captain was disgusted. He was sacrificing his Sunday morning sack time for nothing.

Still, he reconsidered, it *was* the first authentic saucer, and if it contained any kind of life at all, pint-size or otherwise, he would be the first human to contact it. There would be generals on the scene before long of course, and probably even chiefs of staff. But until they got there the responsibility was his. A tiny gold leaf fluttered before his eyes.

He turned to the lieutenant, who was quite young and who, in the captain's private opinion, had no business in this man's army. "Deploy the men," the captain said. Then he turned to the sheriff. "Get those people the hell out of here where they won't get hurt!"

The meadow came to life. The crowd shuffled back just far enough to give the impression of compliance, muttered just loud enough to imply resentment, and parted just wide enough to let the soldiers through. The soldiers came running, rifles at port, and deployed around the saucer at

The Other Kids 57

the lieutenant's direction, each man dropping to prone position.

The lieutenant rejoined the captain and the two officers stood looking at the little saucer. The lieutenant was having trouble with a memory. It concerned something that had happened to him when he was a small boy, but the trouble was he couldn't recall exactly what it was that had happened. All he could remember was the part that led up to the part he *wanted* to remember.

He could recall the circumstances clearly enough: the house in the new neighborhood, the morning after the first snow—the snow had been white and wonderful when he had looked at it from his strange bedroom window, and all he could think of while he was getting dressed was running outside and finding out was it good for packing and building a snowman and maybe a fort, and playing games...

He heard the shouts and laughter of the other neighborhood kids while he was eating breakfast and he was so excited he couldn't finish his cereal. He gulped down his milk, choking a little, and ran into the hall for his coat and leggings. His mother made him wear the wool scarf that always prickled his neck, and she buttoned the flaps of his toboggan hat in under his chin.

He ran out into the bright morning—

And there the memory stopped. Try as he would, the lieutenant couldn't recall the rest of it. Finally he gave up and devoted his attention to the saucer. The memory had no business in his mind at such a time anyway, and he couldn't understand what had evoked it.

"Do you think we'll have trouble, sir?" he asked the captain.

"We didn't come out here on a picnic, Lieutenant. Of course there'll be trouble. This may even be an act of war."

"Or of peace."

The captain's seamed face grew red. "Do you consider sneaking down during the night, eluding our radar, and landing way out here in the sticks an act of peace, Lieutenant?"

"But it's such an insignificant little ship—if it is a ship. It's almost like a toy. Why, I'll bet if you rubbed it a genie would appear."

"Lieutenant, I consider your attitude unmilitary. You're talking like a child."

"Sorry, sir."

The morning had grown quiet. The sound of the crowd had diminished to an occasional shuffling of restless feet and an occasional mutter of voices. The soldiers lay silently in the dun meadow grass. High in the cloudless sky a V of geese soared sedately south.

Suddenly the village church bell began to peal. The sound washed over the fields in sonorous, shocking waves. Even the captain jumped a little. But he recovered himself so quickly that no one noticed. He lit a cigarette slowly and deliberately.

"I hope all you men remembered to bring your hymn books," he said in a loud voice.

Nervous laughter rippled round the circle of waiting soldiers. "Hallelujah!" someone shouted. The old man was a good Joe after all.

The last peal of the bell lingered for a long time, then gradually trailed away. The crowd whispered to itself, but remained intact. The sheriff pulled out a red bandanna handkerchief and began polishing the barrel of his .270. He stood just behind the two officers.

The saucer gleamed enigmatically in the sunlight. The captain's eyes were starting to ache and he looked away for a moment to rest them. When he looked back the top half of the saucer was rising like the top section of a clam shell.

It rose slowly, up and back, flashing in the sunlight. Presently it stopped and something climbed out of its interior and slipped to the ground. Something with big bright eyes and too many limbs.

The captain drew his .45. Rifle bolts snickered around the circle of soldiers.

"It looks like it's been injured," the lieutenant said. "See, one of its arms—"

"Draw your weapon, Lieutenant!"

The lieutenant drew his .45.

The genie stood in the shadow of the ship, its luminous eyes glowing palely. A morning wind crept down from the hills and riffled the meadow grass. The sun shone brightly.

Presently the genie moved out of the shadow. It started forward, in the direction of the two officers. It was a livid green in color and it definitely had too many limbs, most of them legs. It was impossible to tell whether the creature was running or walking.

The captain's voice was tight. "Give the order to fire, Lieutenant!"

"But sir, I'm sure it's harmless."

"You blind? It's attacking us!"

The sheriff's rasping voice had thickened. "Sure it's attacking us," he said, his breath hot on the lieutenant's neck.

The lieutenant said nothing. The rest of the memory was emerging from his subconscious where it had been hiding for fifteen years.

He was running out of the house again, and into the bright morning. He started across the street to where the other kids were playing in the snow. He didn't see the snowball. It had been packed tight and it had been thrown hard. It struck him squarely in the face, exploding in blind numbing pain.

He stopped in the middle of the street. At first he

couldn't see, but after a while his eyes cleared. But only for a moment. Then they were blind again, blind with tears, and he was running back to the house, back to the warm comfort of his mother's arms—

The captain's voice was taut. "I'll give you one more chance, Lieutenant. Give the order to fire!"

The lieutenant stood silently, his face contorted with the remembered pain.

"Fire!" the captain screamed.

The morning detonated.

The captain and the soldiers and the sheriff shot the genie. The genie's eyes went out like shattered electric light bulbs and it collapsed into a tangle of arms and legs.

The lieutenant shot the captain. The captain's face looked silly as he slipped slowly to the ground. His officer's cap had come off and so had the top of his head.

After that the lieutenant was running. He looked wildly around for the house but it wasn't there any longer. And that was odd, he thought. It had been there a moment ago.

One of the other kids was shouting something in a thin rasping voice but he did not stop. He kept on running. He had to find the house, the security of the house, the warmth of his mother's arms—

The second snowball struck him squarely in the back of the head. It wasn't half as bad as the first one had been. The first one had hurt all the way through him. The first one had never stopped hurting. This one didn't hurt at all. There was just a sudden flash of brightness, and then nothing—

Nothing at all.

"The Miracle of the Lily" offers a strong extrapolative view of man's eternal battle with the insect, plus an ironic surprise twist on the theme. And, of course, it also offers some dandy BEMs. Although the story may show its age a bit compared to modern science fiction (it was originally published in the April 1928 issue of Amazing Stories), *it is nonetheless a first-rate and unusual example of early s-f.*

Clare Winger Harris was a pioneer woman "scientifiction" writer of the Gernsback era. Her first story, "A Runaway World," was published in the July 1926 issue of Weird Tales. *Ten subsequent stories appeared between 1927 and 1930 in* WT, Amazing, Wonder Stories Quarterly, *and other magazines; one, "Fate of the Poseidonia," won a prize in a 1927* Amazing Stories *contest. All eleven stories were gathered into a hardcover collection entitled* Away from the Here and Now *in 1947, at about the time she surfaced in Los Angeles science-fiction circles (only to disappear again in the early fifties, this time without resurfacing). Along with a collaboration with Miles J. Breuer, "A Baby on Neptune" (a.k.a. "Child of Neptune"), "The Miracle of the Lily" is considered to be her finest work.*

The Miracle of the Lily

Clare Winger Harris

CHAPTER I
The Passing of a Kingdom

Since the comparatively recent résumé of the ancient order of agriculture I, Nathano, have been asked to set down the extraordinary events of the past two thousand years, at the beginning of which time the supremacy of man, chief of the mammals, threatened to come to an untimely end.

Ever since the dawn of life upon this globe, life, which it seemed had crept from the slime of the sea, only two great types had been the rulers: the reptiles and the mammals. The former held undisputed sway for eons, but gave way eventually before the smaller but intellectually superior mammals. Man himself, the supreme example of the ability of life to govern and control inanimate matter, was master of the world with apparently none to dispute his right. Yet, so blinded was he with pride over the continued exercise of his power on Earth over other lower types of mammals and the nearly extinct reptiles, that he failed to notice the slow but steady rise of another branch of life, different from his own; smaller, it is true, but no smaller than he had been in comparison with the mighty reptilian monsters that roamed the swamps in Mesozoic times.

These new enemies of man, though seldom attacking him personally, threatened his downfall by destroying his chief means of sustenance, so that by the close of the twentieth century, strange and daring projects were laid before the various governments of the world with an idea of fighting man's insect enemies to the finish. These pests were growing in size, multiplying so rapidly and destroying so much vegetation, that eventually no plants would be left to sustain human life. Humanity suddenly woke to the realization that it might suffer the fate of the nearly extinct reptiles. Would mankind be able to prevent the encroachment of the insects? And at last man *knew* that unless drastic measures were taken *at once*, a third great class of life was on the brink of terrestrial sovereignty.

Of course no great changes in development come suddenly. Slow evolutionary progress had brought us up to the point where, with the application of outside pressure, we were ready to handle a situation that, a century before, would have overwhelmed us.

I reproduce here in part a lecture delivered by a great

The Miracle of the Lily

American scientist, a talk which, sent by radio throughout the world, changed the destiny of mankind: but whether for good or for evil I will leave you to judge at the conclusion of this story.

"Only in comparatively recent times has man succeeded in conquering natural enemies: flood, storm, inclemency of climate, distance. And now we face an encroaching menace to the whole of humanity. Have we learned more and more of truth and of the laws that control matter only to succumb to the first real danger that threatens us with extermination? Surely, no matter what the cost, you will rally to the solution of our problem, and I believe, friends, that I have discovered the answer to the enigma.

"I know that many of you, like my friend Professor Fair, will believe my ideas too extreme, but I am convinced that unless you are willing to put behind you those notions which are old and not utilitarian, you cannot hope to cope with the present situation.

"Already, in the past few decades, you have realized the utter futility of encumbering yourselves with superfluous possessions that had no useful virtue, but which, for various sentimental reasons, you continued to hoard, thus lessening the degree of your life's efficiency by using for it time and attention that should have been applied to the practical work of life's accomplishments. You have given these things up slowly, but I am now going to ask you to relinquish the rest of them *quickly*; everything that interferes in any way with the immediate disposal of our enemies, the insects."

At this point, it seems that my worthy ancestor, Professor Fair, objected to the scientist's words, asserting that efficiency at the expense of some of the sentimental virtues was undesirable and not conducive to happiness, the real goal of man. The scientist, in his turn, argued that happiness was available only through a perfect adaptability to one's environment, and that efficiency *sans* love, mercy and the softer sentiments was the short cut to human bliss.

It took a number of years for the scientist to put over his scheme of salvation, but in the end he succeeded, not so much from the persuasiveness of his words as because prompt action of some sort was necessary. There was not enough food to feed the people of the earth. Fruit and vegetables were becoming a thing of the past. Too much protein food in the form of meat and fish was injuring the race, and at last the people realized that for fruits and vegetables, or their nutritive equivalent, they must turn from the field to the laboratory: from the farmer to the chemist. Synthetic food was the solution to the problem. There was no longer any use in planting and caring for foodstuffs destined to become the nourishment of man's most deadly enemy.

The last planting took place in 2900, but there was no harvest. The voracious insects took every green shoot as soon as it appeared, and even trees, which had previously withstood the attacks of the huge insects, were by this time stripped of every vestige of greenery.

The vegetable world suddenly ceased to exist. Over the barren plains, which had been gradually filling with vast cities, man-made fires brought devastation to every living bit of greenery, so that in all the world there was no food for the insect pests.

CHAPTER II
Man or Insect?

Extract from the diary of Delfair, a descendant of Professor Fair, who had opposed the daring scientist.

From the borders of the great state-city of Iowa, I was witness to the passing of one of the great kingdoms of earth—the vegetable, and I can not find words to express the grief that overwhelms me as I write of its demise, for I loved all growing things. Many of us realized that Earth was no longer beautiful; but if beauty meant death, better life in the sterility of the metropolis.

The viciousness of the thwarted insects was a menace that we had foreseen and yet failed to take into adequate account. On the city-state borderland, life is constantly imperiled by the attacks of well-organized bodies of our dreaded foe.

(*Note*: The organization that now exists among the ants, bees and other insects, testifies to the possibility of the development of military tactics among them in the centuries to come.)

Robbed of their source of food, they have become emboldened to such an extent that they will take any risks to carry human beings away for food, and after one of their well-organized raids, the toll of human life is appalling.

But the great chemical laboratories where our synthetic food is made, and our oxygen plants, we thought were impregnable to their attacks. In that we were mistaken.

Let me say briefly that since the destruction of all vegetation, which furnished a part of the oxygen essential to human life, it became necessary to manufacture this gas artificially for general diffusion through the atmosphere.

I was flying to my work, which is in Oxygen Plant No. 21, when I noticed a peculiar thing on the upper speedway near Food Plant No. 3,439. Although it was night, the various levels of the state-city were illuminated as brightly as by day. A pleasure vehicle was going with prodigious speed westward. I looked after it in amazement. It was unquestionably the car of Eric, my co-worker at Oxygen Plant No. 21. I recognized the gay color of its body, but to verify my suspicions beyond the question of a doubt, I turned my volplane in pursuit and made out the familiar license number. What was Eric doing away from the plant before I had arrived to relieve him from duty?

In hot pursuit, I sped above the car to the very border of the state-city, wondering what unheard-of errand took him to the land of the enemy, for the car came to a sudden stop at the edge of what had once been an agricultural area. Miles ahead of me stretched an enormous expanse of black sterility; at my back was the teeming metropolis, five levels high—if one counted the hangar-level, which did not cover the residence sections.

I had not long to wait, for almost immediately my friend appeared. What a sight he presented to my incredulous gaze! He was literally covered from head to foot with the two-inch ants that, next to the beetles, had proved the greatest menace in their attacks upon humanity. With wild incoherent cries he fled over the rock and stubble-burned earth.

As soon as my stunned senses permitted, I swooped down toward him to effect a rescue, but even as my plane touched the barren earth, I saw that I was too late, for he fell, borne down by the vicious attacks of his myriad foes. I knew it was useless for me to set foot upon the ground, for my fate would be that of Eric. I rose ten feet and seizing my poison-gas weapon, let its contents out upon the tiny black evil things that swarmed below. I did not bother with my mask, for I planned to rise immediately, and it was not a moment too soon. From across the waste-land, a dark cloud eclipsed the stars and I saw coming toward me a horde of flying ants interspersed with larger flying insects, all bent upon my annihilation. I now took my mask and prepared to turn more gas upon my pursuers, but alas, I had used every atom of it in my attack upon the non-flying ants! I had no recourse but flight, and to this I immediately resorted, knowing that I could outdistance my pursuers.

When I could no longer see them, I removed my gas mask. A suffocating sensation seized me. I could not breathe! How high had I flown in my endeavor to escape the flying ants? I leaned over the side of my plane, expecting to see the city far, far below me. What was my utter amazement when I discovered that I was scarcely a thousand feet high! It was not altitude that was depriving me of the life-giving oxygen.

A drop of three hundred feet showed me inert specks of humanity lying about the streets. Then I knew; *the oxygen plant was not in operation!* In another minute I had on my oxygen mask, which was attached to a small portable tank for emergency use, and I rushed for the vicinity of the plant. There I witnessed the first signs of life. Men equipped with oxygen masks were trying to force entrance into the locked building. Being an employee, I possessed knowledge of the combination of the great lock, and I opened the door, only to be greeted by a swarm of ants that commenced a concerted attack upon us.

The floor seemed to be covered with a moving black rug, the corner nearest the door appearing to unravel as we entered, and it was but a few seconds before we were covered with the clinging, biting creatures, who fought with a supernatural energy born of despair. Two very active ants succeeded in getting under my helmet. The bite of their sharp mandibles and the effect of their poisonous formic acid became intolerable. Did I dare remove my mask while the air about me was foul with the gas discharged from the weapons of my allies? While I felt the attacks elsewhere upon my body gradually diminishing as the insects succumbed to the deadly fumes, the two upon my face waxed more vicious under the protection of my mask. One at each eye, they were trying to blind me. The pain was unbearable. Better the suffocating death-gas than the torture of lacerated eyes! Frantically I removed the headgear and tore at the shiny black fiends. Strange to tell, I discovered that I could breathe near the vicinity of the great oxygen tanks, where enough oxygen lingered to support life at least temporarily. The two vicious insects, no longer protected by my gas mask, scurried from me like rats from a sinking ship and disappeared behind the oxygen tanks.

This attack of our enemies, though unsuccessful on their part, was dire in its significance, for it had shown more cunning and ingenuity than anything that had ever preceded it. Heretofore, their onslaughts had been confined to direct attacks upon us personally or upon the synthetic-food laboratories, but in this last raid they had shown an amazing cleverness that portended future disaster, unless they were checked at once. It was obvious they had ingeniously planned to smother us by the suspension of work at the oxygen plant; knowing that they themselves could exist in an atmosphere containing a greater percentage of carbon dioxide. Their scheme, then, was to raid our laboratories for food.

CHAPTER III
Lucanus the Last

A Continuation of Delfair's Account

Although it was evident that the cessation of all plant life spelled inevitable doom for the insect inhabitants of Earth, their extermination did not follow as rapidly as one might have supposed. There were years of internecine warfare. The insects continued to thrive, though in decreasing numbers, upon stolen laboratory foods, bodies of human beings, and finally upon each other, at first capturing enemy species and at last even resorting to a cannibalistic procedure. Their rapacity grew in inverse proportion to their waning numbers, until the meeting of even an isolated insect might mean death, unless one were equipped with poison gas and prepared to use it upon a second's notice.

I am an old man now, though I have not yet lived quite two centuries, but I am happy in the knowledge that I have lived to see the last living insect which was held in captivity. It was an excellent specimen of the stag-beetle (*Lucanus*) and the years have testified that it was the sole survivor of a form of life that might have succeeded man upon this planet. This beetle was caught weeks after we had previously seen what was supposed to be the last living thing upon the globe, barring man and the sea life. Untiring search for years has failed to reveal any more insects, so that at last man rests secure in the knowledge that he is monarch of all he surveys.

I have heard that long, long ago man used to gaze with a fearful fascination upon the reptilian creatures which he displaced, and just so did he view this lone specimen of a type of life that might have covered the face of the earth, but for man's ingenuity.

It was this unholy lure that drew me one day to view the captive beetle in his cage in district 404 at Universapolis. I was amazed at the size of the creature, for it looked larger than when I had seen it by television, but I reasoned that upon that occasion there had been no object near with which to compare its size. True, the broadcaster had announced its dimensions, but the statistics concretely given had failed to register a perfect realization of its prodigious proportions.

As I approached the cage, the creature was lying with its dorsal covering toward me and I judged it measured fourteen inches from one extremity to the other. Its smooth horny sheath gleamed in the bright artificial light. (It was confined on the third level.) As I stood there, mentally conjuring a picture of a world overrun with billions of such creatures as the one before me, the keeper approached the cage with a meal-portion of synthetic food. Although the food has no odor, the beetle sensed the man's approach, for it rose on its jointed legs and came toward us, its horn-like prongs moving threateningly; then apparently remembering its confinement, and the impotency of an attack, it subsided and quickly ate the food which had been placed within its prison.

The food consumed, it lifted itself to its hind legs, partially supported by a box, and turned its great eyes upon me. I had never been regarded with such utter malevolence before. The detestation was almost tangible and I shuddered involuntarily. As plainly as if he spoke, I knew that Lucanus was perfectly cognizant of the situation and in his gaze I read the concentrated hate of an entire defeated race.

I had no desire to gloat over his misfortune; rather a great pity toward him welled up within me. I pictured myself alone, the last of my kind, held up for ridicule before the swarming hordes of insects who had conquered my people, and I knew that life would no longer be worth the living.

Whether he sensed my pity or not I do not know, but he continued to survey me with unmitigated rage, as if he would convey to me the information that his was an implacable hatred that would outlast eternity.

Not long after this he died, and a world long since intolerant of ceremony surprised itself by interring the beetle's remains in a golden casket, accompanied by much pomp and splendor.

I have lived many long years since that memorable event, and undoubtedly my days here are numbered, but I can pass on happily, convinced that in this sphere man's conquest of his environment is supreme.

CHAPTER IV
Efficiency Maximum

In a direct line of descent from Professor Fair and Delfair, the author of the preceding chapter, comes Thanor, whose journal is given in this chapter.

Am I a true product of the year 2928? Some times I am convinced that I am hopelessly old-fashioned, an anachronism, that should have existed a thousand years ago. In no other way can I account for the dissatisfaction I feel in a world where efficiency has at last reached a maximum.

I am told that I spring from a line of ancestors who were not readily acclimated to changing conditions. I love beauty, yet I see none of it here. There are many who think our lofty buildings that tower two and three thousand feet into the air are beautiful, but while they are architectural splendors, they do not represent the kind of loveliness I crave. Only when I visit the sea do I feel any satisfaction for a certain yearning in my soul. The ocean alone shows the handiwork of God. The land bears evidence only of man.

As I read back through the diaries of my sentimental ancestors I find occasional glowing descriptions of the world that was; the world before the insects menaced human existence. Trees, plants and flowers brought delight into the lives of people as they wandered among them in vast open spaces, I am told, where the earth was soft beneath the feet, and flying creatures, called birds, sang among the greenery. True, I learn that many people had not enough to eat, and that uncontrollable passions governed them, but I do believe it must have been more interesting than this methodical, unemotional existence. I cannot understand why many people were poor, for I am told that Nature as manifested in the vegetable kingdom was very prolific; so much so that year after year quantities of food rotted on the ground. The fault, I find by my reading, was not with Nature but with man's economic system which is now perfect, though this perfection really brings few of us happiness, I think.

Now there is no waste; all is converted into food. Long ago man learned how to reduce all matter to its constituent elements, of which there are nearly a hundred in number, and from them to rebuild compounds for food. The old axiom that nothing is created or destroyed, but merely changed from one form to another, has stood the test of ages. Man, as the agent of God, has simply performed the miracle of transmutation himself instead of waiting for natural forces to accomplish it as in the old days.

At first humanity was horrified when it was decreed that it must relinquish its dead to the laboratory. For too many eons had man closely associated the soul and body, failing to comprehend the body as merely a material agent, through which the spirit functioned. When man knew at last of the eternal qualities of spirit, he ceased to regard the discarded body with reverential awe, and saw in it only the same molecular constituents which comprised all matter about him. He recognized only material basically the same as that of stone or metal: material to be reduced to its atomic elements and rebuilt into matter that would render service to living humanity, that portion of matter wherein spirit functions.

The drab monotony of life is appalling. Is it possible that man had reached his height a thousand years ago and should have been willing to resign Earth's sovereignty to a coming order of creatures destined to be man's worthy successor in the eons to come? It seems that life is interesting only when there is a struggle, a goal to be reached through an evolutionary process. Once the goal is attained, all progress ceases. The huge reptiles of preglacial ages rose to supremacy by virtue of their great size, and yet was it not the excessive bulk of those creatures that finally wiped them out of existence? Nature, it seems, avoids extremes. She allows the fantastic to develop for awhile and then wipes the slate clean for a new order of development. Is it not conceivable that man could destroy himself through excessive development of his nervous system, and give place for the future evolution of a comparatively simple form of life, such as the insects were at man's height of development? This, it seems to me, was the great plan; a scheme with which man dared to interfere and for which he is now paying by the boredom of existence.

The earth's population is decreasing so rapidly, that I fear another thousand years will see a lifeless planet hurtling through space. It seems to me that only a miracle will save us now.

CHAPTER V
The Year 3928

The Original Writer, Nathano, Resumes the Narrative

My ancestor, Thanor, of ten centuries ago, according to the records he gave to my great-grandfather, seems to voice the general despair of humanity which, bad enough in his times, has reached the *nth* power in my day. A soulless world is gradually dying from self-inflicted boredom.

As I have ascertained from the perusal of the journals of my forebears, even antedating the extermination of the insects, I come of a stock that clings with sentimental tenacity to the things that made life worth while in the old days. If the world at large knew of my emotional musings concerning past ages, it would scarcely tolerate me, but surrounded by my thought-insulator, I often indulge in what fancies I will, and such meditation, coupled with a love for a few ancient relics from the past, have led me to a most amazing discovery.

Several months ago I found among my family relics a golden receptacle two feet long, one and a half in width and one in depth, which I found upon opening, to contain many tiny square compartments, each filled with minute objects of slightly varying size, texture and color.

"Not sand!" I exclaimed as I closely examined the little particles of matter.

Food? After eating some, I was convinced that their nutritive value was small in comparison with a similar quantity of the products of our laboratories. What were the mysterious objects?

Just as I was about to close the lid again, convinced that I had one over-sentimental ancestor whose gift to posterity was absolutely useless, my pocket-radio buzzed and the voice of my friend, Stentor, the interplanetary broadcaster, issued from the tiny instrument.

"If you're going to be home this afternoon," said Stentor, "I'll skate over. I have some interesting news."

I consented, for I thought I would share my "find" with this friend whom I loved above all others, but before he arrived I had again hidden my golden chest, for I had

The Miracle of the Lily

decided to await the development of events before sharing its mysterious secret with another. It was well that I did this for Stentor was so filled with the importance of his own news that he could have given me little attention at first.

"Well, what is your interesting news?" I asked after he was comfortably seated in my adjustable chair.

"You'd never guess," he replied with irritating leisureliness.

"Does it pertain to Mars or Venus?" I queried. "What news of our neighbor planets?"

"You may know it has nothing to do with the self-satisfied Martians," answered the broadcaster, "but the Venusians have a very serious problem confronting them. It is in connection with the same old difficulty they have had ever since interplanetary radio was developed forty years ago. You remember that, in their second communication with us, they told us of their continual warfare on insect pests that were destroying all vegetable food? Well, last night after general broadcasting had ceased, I was surprised to hear the voice of the Venusian broadcaster. He is suggesting that we get up a scientific expedition to Venus to help the natives of his unfortunate planet solve their insect problem as we did ours. He says the Martians turn a deaf ear to their plea for help, but he expects sympathy and assistance from Earth, who has so recently solved these problems for herself."

I was dumbfounded at Stentor's news.

"But the Venusians are farther advanced mechanically than we," I objected, "though they are behind us in the natural sciences. They could much more easily solve the difficulties of space-flying than we could."

"That is true," agreed Stentor, "but if we are to render them material aid in freeing their world from devastating insects, we must get to Venus. The past four decades have proved that we cannot help them merely by verbal instructions."

"Now, last night," Stentor continued, with warming enthusiasm, "Wanyana, the Venusian broadcaster, informed me that scientists on Venus are developing interplanetary television. This, if successful, will prove highly beneficial in facilitating communication, and it may even do away with the necessity of interplanetary travel, which I think is centuries ahead of us yet."

"Television, though so common here on Earth and on Venus, has seemed an impossibility across the ethereal void," I said, "but if it becomes a reality, I believe it will be the Venusians who will take the initiative, though of course they will be helpless without our friendly cooperation. In return for the mechanical instructions they have given us from time to time, I think it no more than right that we should try to give them all the help possible in freeing their world, as ours has been freed, of the insects that threaten their very existence. Personally, therefore, I hope it can be done through radio and television rather than by personal excursions."

"I believe you are right," he admitted, "but I hope we can be of service to them soon. Ever since I have served in the capacity of official interplanetary broadcaster, I have liked the spirit of goodfellowship shown by the Venusians through their spokesman, Wanyana. The impression is favorable in contrast to the superciliousness of the inhabitants of Mars."

We conversed for some time, but at length he rose to take his leave. It was then I ventured to broach the subject that was uppermost in my thoughts.

"I want to show you something, Stentor," I said, going into an adjoining room for my precious box and returning shortly with it. "A relic from the days of an ancestor named Delfair, who lived at the time the last insect, a beetle, was kept in captivity. Judging from his personal account, Delfair was fully aware of the significance of the changing times in which he lived, and contrary to the majority of his contemporaries, possessed a sentimentality of soul that has proved an historical asset to future generations. Look, my friend, these he left to posterity!"

I deposited the heavy casket on a table between us and lifted the lid, revealing to Stentor the mystifying particles.

The face of Stentor was eloquent of astonishment. Not unnaturally his mind took somewhat the same route as mine had followed previously, though he added atomic-power units to the list of possibilities. He shook his head in perplexity.

"Whatever they are, there must have been a real purpose behind their preservation," he said at last. "You say this old Delfair witnessed the passing of the insects? What sort of a fellow was he? Likely to be up to any tricks?"

"Not at all," I asserted rather indignantly, "he seemed a very serious-minded chap; worked in an oxygen plant and took an active part in the last warfare between men and insects."

Suddenly Stentor stooped over and scooped up some of the minute particles into the palm of his hand—and then he uttered a maniacal shriek and flung them into the air.

"Great God, man, do you know what they are?" he screamed, shaking violently.

"No, I do not," I replied quietly, with an attempt at dignity I did not feel.

"Insect eggs!" he cried, and shuddering with terror, he made for the door.

I caught him on the threshold and pulled him forcibly back into the room.

"Now see here," I said sternly, "not a word of this to anyone. Do you understand? I will test out your theory in every possible way but I want no public interference."

At first he was obstinate, but finally yielded to threats when supplications were impotent.

"I will test them," I said, "and will endeavor to keep hatchings under absolute control, should they prove to be what you suspect."

It was time for the evening broadcasting, so he left, promising to keep our secret and leaving me regretting that I had taken another into my confidence.

CHAPTER VI
The Miracle

For days following my unfortunate experience with Stentor, I experimented upon the tiny objects that had so terrified him. I subjected them to various tests for the purpose of ascertaining whether or not they bore evidence of life, whether in egg, pupa or larva stages of development. And to all my experiments, there was but one answer. No life was manifest. Yet I was not satisfied, for chemical tests showed that they were composed of organic matter. Here was an inexplicable enigma! Many times I was on the verge of consigning the entire contents of the chest to the flames. I seemed to see in my mind's eye the world again over-ridden with insects, and that calamity due to the indiscretions of one man! My next impulse was to turn over my problem to scientists, when a suspicion of the truth dawned upon me. These were seeds, the germs of plant life, and they might grow. But alas, where? Over all the earth man has spread his artificial dominion. The state-city has been succeeded by what could be termed the nation-

The Miracle of the Lily

city, for one great floor of concrete or rock covers the country.

I resolved to try an experiment, the far-reaching influence of which I did not at that time suspect. Beneath the lowest level of the community edifice in which I dwell, I removed, by means of a small atomic excavator, a slab of concrete large enough to admit my body. I let myself down into the hole and felt my feet resting on a soft dark substance that I knew to be dirt. I hastily filled a box of this, and after replacing the concrete slab, returned to my room, where I proceeded to plant a variety of the seeds.

Being a product of an age when practically to wish for a thing in a material sense is to have it, I experienced the greatest impatience, while waiting for any evidences of plant life to become manifest. Daily, yes hourly, I watched the soil for signs of a type of life long since departed from the earth, and was about convinced that the germ of life could not have survived the centuries, when a tiny blade of green proved to me that a miracle, more wonderful to me than the works of man through the ages, was taking place before my eyes. This was an enigma so complex and yet so simple, that one recognized in it a direct revelation of Nature.

Daily and weekly I watched in secret the botanical miracle. It was my one obsession. I was amazed at the fascination it held for me—a man who viewed the marvels of the fortieth century with unemotional complacency. It showed me that Nature is manifest in the simple things which mankind has chosen to ignore.

Then one morning, when I awoke, a white blossom displayed its immaculate beauty and sent forth its delicate fragrance into the air. The lily, a symbol of new life, resurrection! I felt within me the stirring of strange emotions I had long believed dead in the bosom of man. But the message must not be for me alone. As of old, the lily would be the symbol of life for all!

With trembling hands, I carried my precious burden to a front window where it might be witnessed by all who passed by. The first day there were few who saw it, for only rarely do men and women walk; they usually ride in speeding vehicles of one kind or another, or employ electric skates, a delightful means of locomotion, which gives the body some exercise. The fourth city level, which is reserved for skaters and pedestrians, is kept in a smooth glasslike condition. And so it was only the occasional pedestrian, walking on the outer border of the fourth level, upon which my window faced, who first carried the news of the growing plant to the world, and it was not long before it was necessary for civic authorities to disperse the crowds that thronged to my window for a glimpse of a miracle in green and white.

When I showed my beautiful plant to Stentor, he was most profuse in his apology and came to my rooms every day to watch it unfold and develop, but the majority of people, long used to businesslike efficiency, were intolerant of the sentimental emotions that swayed a small minority, and I was commanded to dispose of the lily. But a figurative seed had been planted in the human heart, a seed that could not be disposed of so readily, and this seed ripened and grew until it finally bore fruit.

CHAPTER VII
Ex Terreno

It is a very different picture of humanity that I paint ten years after the last entry in my diary. My new vocation is farming, but it is farming on a far more intensive scale

The Miracle of the Lily

than had been done two thousand years ago. Our crops never fail, for temperature and rainfall are regulated artificially. But we attribute our success principally to the total absence of insect pests. Our small agricultural areas dot the country like the parks of ancient days and supply us with a type of food, no more nourishing but more appetizing than that produced in the laboratories. Truly we are living in a marvelous age! If the earth is ours completely, why may we not turn our thoughts toward the other planets in our solar-system? For the past ten or eleven years the Venusians have repeatedly urged us to come and assist them in their battle for life. I believe it is our duty to help them.

Tomorrow will be a great day for us and especially for Stentor, as the new interplanetary television is to be tested, and it is possible that for the first time in history, we shall see our neighbors in the infinity of space. Although the people of Venus were about a thousand years behind us in many respects, they have made wonderful progress with radio and television. We have been in radio communication with them for the last half century and they shared with us the joy of the establishment of our Eden. They have always been greatly interested in hearing Stentor tell the story of our subjugation of the insects that threatened to wipe us out of existence, for they have exactly that problem to solve now; judging from their reports, we fear that theirs is a losing battle. Tomorrow we shall converse face to face with the Venusians! It will be an event second in importance only to the first radio communications interchanged fifty years ago. Stentor's excitement exceeds that displayed at the time of the discovery of the seeds.

Well, it is over and the experiment was a success, but alas for the revelation!

The great assembly halls all over the continent were packed with humanity eager to catch a first glimpse of the Venusians. Prior to the test, we sent our message of friendship and good will by radio, and received a reciprocal one from our interplanetary neighbors. Alas, we were ignorant at that time! Then the television receiving apparatus was put into operation, and we sat with breathless interest, our eyes intent upon the crystal screen before us. I sat near Stentor and noted the feverish ardor with which he watched for the first glimpse of Wanyana.

At first hazy mist-like spectres seemed to glide across the screen. We knew these figures were not in correct perspective. Finally, one object gradually became more opaque, its outlines could be seen clearly. Then across that vast assemblage, as well as thousands of others throughout the world, there swept a wave of speechless horror, as its full significance burst upon mankind.

The figure that stood facing us was a huge six-legged beetle, not identical in every detail with our earthly enemies of past years, but unmistakably an insect of gigantic proportions! Of course it could not see us, for our broadcaster was not to appear until afterward, but it spoke, and we had to close our eyes to convince ourselves that it was the familiar voice of Wanyana, the leading Venusian radio broadcaster. Stentor grabbed my arm, uttered an inarticulate cry and would have fallen but for my timely support.

"Friends of Earth, as you call your world," began the object of horror, "this is a momentous occasion in the annals of the twin planets, and we are looking forward to seeing one of you, and preferably Stentor, for the first time, as you are now viewing one of us. We have listened many times, with interest, to your story of the insect pests which threatened to follow you as lords of your planet. As you have often heard us tell, we are likewise molested with

The Miracle of the Lily

insects. Our fight is a losing one, unless we can soon exterminate them."

Suddenly, the Venusian was joined by another being, a colossal ant, who bore in his forelegs a tiny light-colored object which he handed to the beetle-announcer, who took it and held it forward for our closer inspection. It seemed to be a tiny ape, but was so small we could not ascertain for a certainty. We were convinced, however, that it was a mammalian creature, an "insect" pest of Venus. Yet in it we recognized rudimentary man as we know him on earth!

There was no question as to the direction in which sympathies instinctively turned, yet reason told us that our pity should be given to the intelligent reigning race who had risen to its present mental attainment through eons of time. By some quirk or freak of nature, way back in the beginning, life had developed in the form of insects instead of mammals. Or (the thought was repellent) had insects in the past succeeded in displacing mammals, as they might have done here on earth?

There was no more television that night. Stentor would not appear, so disturbed was he by the sight of the Venusians, but in the morning, he talked to them by radio and explained the very natural antipathy we experienced in seeing them or in having them see us.

Now they no longer urge us to construct ether-ships and go to help them dispose of their "insects." I think they are afraid of us, and their very fear has aroused in mankind an unholy desire to conquer them.

I am against it. Have we not had enough of war in the past? We have subdued our own world and should be content with that, instead of seeking new worlds to conquer. But life is too easy here. I can plainly see that. Much as he may seem to dislike it, man is not happy unless he has some enemy to overcome, some difficulty to surmount.

Alas, my greatest fears for man were groundless!

A short time ago, when I went out into my field to see how my crops were faring, I found a six-pronged beetle voraciously eating. No—man will not need to go to Venus to fight "insects."

Nowhere is it written that BEMs cannot be cultured and therefore make important contributions to the arts. Quite the contrary. For it is written (in "The Galactic Almanack," a splendidly funny series which ran intermittently in Galaxy *for almost twenty years) that artistic contributions, among a host of others, were made by a large number of alien life forms. "The Bug-Eyed Musicians" tells of some of the more profound BEM accomplishments in the field of music.*

Laurence M. Janifer (b. 1933) has been a full-time free-lance writer for almost a quarter of a century. He has published over thirty novels and 300 magazine pieces in a variety of fields; in science fiction he is best known for his three collaborative "Mark Phillips" novels with Randall Garrett, Supermind, Brain Twister, *and* The Impossibles, *and for his 1964* You Sane Men. *Recently he has begun a series of novels and stories featuring a "professional survivor" named Gerald Knave. He has testified in print that he was forced by H. L. Gold, a tough and exacting editor, to rewrite "The Bug-Eyed Musicians" eight times before it was accepted—which may be one reason it was his only contribution to "The Galactic Almanack" (the major contributors were Edward Wellen and John Brunner), and in fact constituted his only appearance in* Galaxy *itself.*

The Bug-Eyed Musicians

Laurence M. Janifer

This first selection deals entirely with the Music Section of the Almanack. Passed over in this anthology, which is intended for general readership, are all references to the four-dimensional doubly extensive polyphony of Green III (interested parties are referred to "Time in Reverse, or the Musical Granny Knot," by Alfid Carp, *Papers of the Rigel Musicological Society*) or, for reasons of local censorship, the notices regarding Shem VI, VII and IX and the racial-sex "music" which is common on those planets.

All dates have been made conformable with the Terran Calendar (as in the standard Terran edition of the Almanack) by application of Winstock Benjamin's Least Square Variable Time Scale.

FEBRUARY 17: Today marks the birth date of Freem Freem, of Dubhe IV, perhaps the most celebrated child prodigy in musical history. Though it is, of course, true that he appeared in no concerts after the age of twelve, none who have seen the solidographs of his early performances can ever forget the intent face, the tense, accurate motions of the hands, the utter perfection of Freem's entire performance.

His first concert, given at the age of four, was an amazing spectacle. Respected critics refused to believe that Freem was as young as his manager (an octopoid from Fomalhaut) claimed, and were satisfied only by the sworn affidavit of Glerk, the well-known Sirian, who was present at the preliminary interviews.

Being a Sirian, Glerk was naturally incapable of dissimulation, and his earnest supersonics soon persuaded the critics of the truth. Freem was, in actuality, only four years old.

In the next eight years, Freem concertized throughout the Galaxy. His triumph on Deneb at the age of six, the stellar reception given him by a deputation of composers and critics from the Lesser Magellanic Cloud when he appeared in that sector, and the introduction (as an encore) of his single composition, the beloved *Memories of Old Age*, are still recalled.

And then, at the age of eleven, Freem's concerts ceased. Music-lovers throughout the Galaxy were stunned by the news that their famed prodigy would appear no longer. At the age of twelve, Freem Freem was dead.

Terrans have never felt this loss as deeply as other Galactic races, and it is not difficult to see why. The standard "year" of Dubhe IV equals 300 Earth years; to the short-lived Terrans, Freem Freem had given his first concert at the age of 1200, and had died at the ripe old age of 3600 years.

"Calling a 1200-year-old being a child prodigy," states the Terran Dictionary of Music and Musicians, rather tartly, "is the kind of misstatement up with which we shall not put."

Particularly noteworthy is the parallel attitude expressed by the inhabitants of Terk I, whose "year" is approximately three Terran days, to the alleged "short" life of Wolfgang Amadeus Mozart.

MAY 12: Wilrik Rotha Rotha Delk Shkulma Tik was born on this date in 8080. Although he/she is renowned both as the creator of symphonic music on Wolf XVI and as the progenitor of the sole Galactic Censorship Law which remains in effect in this enlightened age, very little is actually known about the history of that law.

The full story is, very roughly, as follows:

In 8257, a composition was published by the firm of Scholer and Dichs (Sirius), the Concerto for Wood-Block and Orchestra by Tik. Since this was not only the first appearance of any composition by Tik, but was in fact the first composition of any kind to see publication from his planet of Wolf XVI, the musical world was astonished at the power, control and mastery the piece showed.

A review which is still extant stated: "It is not possible that a composition of such a high level of organization should be the first to proceed from a composer—or from an entire planet. Yet we must recognize the merit and worth of Tik's Concerto, and applaud the force of the composer, in a higher degree than usual."

Even more amazing than the foregoing was the speed with which Tik's compositions followed one another. The Concerto was followed by a sonata, Tik's *Tosk*, his/her Free-Fall Ballet for Centipedals, *Lights! Action! Comrades!*, a symphony, an Imbroglio for Unstrung Violin, and fourteen Wolfish Rhapsodies—*all within the year*!

Scholars visited Wolf XVI, and reported once again that there was no musical history on the planet.

Success, fame and money were Tik's. Succeeding compositions were received with an amount of enthusiasm that would have done credit to any musician.

And Wolf XVI seemed to awaken at his/her touch. Within ten years, there was a school of composition established there, and works of astounding complexity and beauty came pouring forth. The "great flowering," as it was called, seemed to inspire other planets as well—to name only a few, Dog XII, Goldstone IX and Trent II (whose inhabitants, dwelling underwater for the most part, had never had anything like a musical history).

Tik's own income began to go down as the process continued. Then the astonishing truth was discovered.

Tik was not a composer at all—merely an electronics technician! He/she had recorded the sounds of the planet's main downtown business center and slowed the recording to half-speed. Since the inhabitants of Wolf XVI converse in batlike squeals, this slowing resulted in a series of patterns which fell within sonic range, and which had all of the scope and the complexity of music itself.

The other planets had copied the trick and soon the Galaxy was glutted with this electronic "music." The climax came when a judge on Paolo III aided in the recording of a court trial over which he presided. During the two weeks of subsonic testimony, speech and bustle, he supervised recording apparatus and, in fact, announced that he had performed the actual "arrangement" involved: speeding up the recordings so that the two-week subsonic trial became a half-hour fantasia.

The judge lost the subsequent election and irrationally placed the blame on the recording (which had not been well-received by the critics). Single-handed, he restored the state of pure music by pushing through the Galactic Assembly a censorship rule requiring that all recording companies, musicians, technicians and composers be limited to the normal sonic range of the planet on which they were working.

Tik himself, after the passage of this law, eked out a bare living as a translator from the supersonic. He died, alone and friendless, in 9501.

JUNE 4: The composition, on this date, in 8236, of Wladislaw Wladislaw's Concertino for Enclosed Harp stirs reflections in musical minds of the inventor and first virtuoso on this instrument, the ingenious Barsak Gh. Therwent of Canopus XII. Nowadays, with compositions for that instrument as common as the *chadlas* of Gh. Therwent's home planet, we are likely to pass over the startling and almost accidental circumstance that led to his marvelous discovery.

As a small boy, Gh. Therwent was enamored of music and musicians; he played the *gleep*-flute before the age of eight and, using his hair-thin minor arms, was an accomplished performer on the Irish (or small open) harp in his fifteenth year. A tendency to confuse the strings of the harp with his own digital extremities, however, seemed serious enough to rule out a concert career for the young *flalk,* and when an Earth-made piano was delivered to the home of a neighbor who fancied himself a collector of baroque instruments, young Gh. was among the first to attempt playing on it.

Unfortunately, he could not muster pressure sufficient in his secondary arms and digits to depress the keys; more, he kept slipping between them. It was one such slip that led to his discovery of the enclosed strings at the back of the piano (a spinet).

The subtle sonorities of plucked strings at the back of a closed chamber excited him, and he continued research into the instrument in a somewhat more organized manner. Soon he was able to give a concert of music which he himself had arranged—and when Wladislaw Wladislaw dedicated his composition to Gh., the performer's future was assured.

The rest of his triumphant story is too well known to repeat here. The single observation on Gh. Therwent's playing, however, by the composer Ratling, is perhaps worthy of note.

"He don't play on the white keys, and he don't play on the black keys," said Ratling, with that cultivated lack of grammar which made him famous as an eccentric. "He plays in the cracks!"

JULY 23: On this date, the Hrrshtk Notes were discovered in a *welf*-shop cellar on Deneb III.

These notes are, quite certainly, alone in their originality, and in the force which they have had on the growth of subsequent musicians.

To begin at the beginning: it is well established that Ludwig Hrrshtk, perhaps the most widely known Denebian composer, died of overwork in his prime. His compositions, until the famous T85 discoveries of G'g Rash, were almost alone in their universal appeal. Races the Galaxy over have thrilled to Hrrshtk's Second Symphony, his Concerto for Old Men, and the inspiring Classic Mambo Suite. It is, as a matter of fact, said that G'g Rash himself was led to his discovery by considering the question:

"How can many different races, experiencing totally different emotions in totally different ways, agree on the importance of a single musical composition by Hrrshtk? How can all share a single emotional experience?"

His researches delved deeply into the Hrrshtk compositions, and a tentative theory based on the Most Common Harmonic, now shown to have been totally mistaken, led to the T85 discoveries.

The Hrrshtk notes, however, found long afterward, provide the real answer.

Among a pile of sketches and musical fragments was found a long list—or, rather, a series of lists. In the form of a Galactic Dictionary, the paper is divided into many columns, each headed with the name of a different planet.

Rather than describe this document, we are printing an excerpt from it herewith:

DENEB III	TERRA	MARS
Love	Anger	Hunger
Hate	Joy	F'rit
Prayer	Madness	Sadness
Vilb	NPE	Non-F'rit
FOMALHAUT II	**SIRIUS VII**	
Sadness	Madness	
Prayer	Love	
Full	Joy	
Golk	NPE	

In completed form, the document contains over one hundred and fifty separate listings for race, and over six hundred separate emotional or subject headings. In some places (like the Terra and Sirius listing for Vilb, above), the text is marked NPE, and this has been taken to mean No Precise Equivalent. For instance, such a marking appears after the Denebian *shhr* for both Terra and Mars, although Sirius has the listing *grk* and Fomalhaut *plarat in the desert*.

Hrrshtk may be hailed, therefore, as the discoverer of the Doctrine of Emotional Equivalency, later promulgated in a different form by Space Patrol Psychiatrist Rodney Garman. Further, the document alluded to above explains a phrase in Hrrshtk's noted letter to Dibble Young, which has puzzled commentators since its first appearance.

Hrrshtk is here alluding to the composition of his Revolutionary Ode, which all Terra knows as the most perfect expression of true love to be found in music:

"It's a Revolutionary Ode to me, my friend—but not to you. As we say here, one man's mood is another man's passion."

SEPTEMBER 1: On this date in the year 9909, Treth Schmaltar died on his home planet of Wellington V. All the Galaxy knows his famous Symphonic Storm Suite; less known, but equally interesting, is the history and development of its solo instrument.

The natives of Wellington V feed on airborne plankton, which is carried by the vibrations of sound or speech. This was a little-known fact for many years, but did account for the joy with which the first explorers on Wellington V were greeted. Their speech created waves that fed the natives.

When eating, the natives emit a strange humming noise, due to the action of the peculiar glottis. These facts drove the first settlers, like Treth Schmaltar, to the invention of a new instrument.

This was a large drumlike construction with a small hole

The Bug-Eyed Musicians 93

in its side through which airborne plankton could enter. Inside the drum, a Wellingtonian crouched. When the drum was beaten, the air vibrations drove plankton into the native's mouth, and he ate and hummed.

(A mechanical device has since replaced the native. This is, of course, due to the terrific expense of importing both natives and plankton to other planets than Wellington V for concerts.)

Thus, a peculiarity of native life led not only to the Symphonic Storm Suite, but to such lovely compositions as Schmaltar's Hum-Drum Sonata.

SEPTEMBER 30: The victimization of the swanlike inhabitants of Harsh XII, perhaps the most pitiful musical scandal of the ages, was begun by Ferd Pill, born on this date in 8181. Pill, who died penitent in a neuterary of the Benedictine Order, is said to have conceived his idea after perusing some early Terran legends about the swan.

He never represented himself as the composer, but always as the agent or representative of a Harsh XII inhabitant. In the short space of three years, he sold over two hundred songs, none of great length but all, as musicians agree to this day, of a startling and almost un-Hnau-like beauty.

When a clerk in the records department of Pill's publishers discovered that Pill, having listed himself as the heir of each of the Harsh XII composers, was in fact collecting their money, an investigation began.

That the composers were in fact dead was easily discovered. That Pill was their murderer was the next matter that came to light.

In an agony of self-abasement, Pill confessed his crime. "The Harshians don't sing at all," he said. "They don't make a sound. But—like the legendary swan of old Terra—

they do deliver themselves of one song in dying. I murdered them in order to record these songs, and then sold the recordings."

Pill's subsequent escape from the prison in which he was confined, and his trip to the sanctuary of the neuetary, were said to have been arranged by the grateful widow of one of the murdered Harshians, who had been enabled by her mate's death to remarry with a younger and handsomer Harshian.

DECEMBER 5: Today marks the birthday of Timmis Calk, a science teacher of Lavoris II.

Calk is almost forgotten today, but his magnificent Student Orchestra created a storm both of approval and protest when it was first seen in 9734. Critics on both sides of what rapidly became a Galaxywide controversy were forced, however, to acknowledge the magnificent playing of the Student Orchestra and its great technical attainments.

Its story begins with Calk himself and his sweetheart, a lovely being named Silla.

Though Calk's love for Silla was true and profound, Silla did not return his affectionate feelings. She was an antiscientist, a musician. The sects were split on Lavoris II to such an extent that marriage between Calk and his beloved would have meant crossing the class lines—something which Silla, a music-lover, was unwilling to contemplate.

Calk therefore determined to prove to her that a scientist could be just as artistic as any musician. Months of hard work followed, until finally he was ready.

He engaged the great Drick Hall for his first concert—and the program consisted entirely of classical works of great difficulty. Beethoven's Ninth Symphony opened the program, and Fenk's Reversed Ode closed it. Calk had no time for the plaudits of critics and audience; he went searching for Silla.

But he was too late. She had heard his concert—and had immediately accepted the marriage proposal of a childhood sweetheart.

Calk nearly committed suicide. But at the last moment, he tossed the spraying-bottle away and went back to Silla.

"Why?" he said. "Why did you reject me, after hearing the marvelous music which I created?"

"You are not a musician, but a scientist," Silla said. "Any musician would have refrained from *growing* his orchestra from seeds."

Unable to understand her esthetic revulsion, Calk determined there and then to continue his work with the Student Orchestra (it made a great deal more money than science-teaching). Wrapping his rootlets around his branches, he rolled away from her with crackling dignity.

There are BEMs, as every reader and writer of science fiction knows, and then there are BEMs. And in no other story is that conundrum better demonstrated than in "Puppet Show"—a powerful and beautifully deceptive tale of extraterrestrials and humans meeting for the first time in the Arizona desert.

Fredric Brown (1906–1972) wrote mysteries and science fiction with equal distinction throughout his long career. He was one of the first and most prolific contributors of science fiction to Playboy *(where "Puppet Show" first appeared) and other magazines outside the genre; and he was universally conceded to be the best writer of the mordant short-short—most of the finest of which can be found in his 1961 (and recently reissued) collection* Nightmares and Geezenstacks *—in either field. His* What Mad Universe *(1949) and* Martians Go Home *(1955), both of which have also been reprinted in recent days, are splendid examples of his gifts as a novelist. And "Puppet Show" is likewise a splendid example of his gifts as a writer of short stories, ranking with "Arena," "The Weapon," and "Come and Go Mad" as his finest contribution to the short literature of science fiction.*

Puppet Show

Fredric Brown

Horror came to Cherrybell at a little after noon on a blistering hot day in August.

Perhaps that is redundant; *any* August day in Cherrybell, Arizona, is blistering hot. It is on Highway 89 about forty miles south of Tucson and about thirty miles north of the Mexican border. It consists of two filling stations, one on each side of the road to catch travelers going in both directions, a general store, a beer-and-wine-license-only tavern, a tourist-trap type trading post for tourists who can't wait until they reach the border to start buying serapes and huaraches, a deserted hamburger stand, and a few 'dobe houses inhabited by Mexican-Americans who work in Nogales, the border town to the south, and who, for God knows what reason, prefer to live in Cherrybell and commute, some of them in Model T Fords. The sign on the highway says, "Cherrybell, Pop. 42," but the sign exaggerates; Pop died last year—Pop Anders, who ran the now-deserted hamburger stand—and the correct figure is 41.

Horror came to Cherrybell mounted on a burro led by an ancient, dirty and gray-bearded desert rat of a prospector who later—nobody got around to asking his name for a while—gave the name of Dade Grant. Horror's name was Garth. He was approximately nine feet tall but so thin, almost a stick-man, that he could not have weighed over a hundred pounds. Old Dade's burro carried him easily, despite the fact that his feet dragged in the sand on either side. Being dragged through the sand for, as it later turned out, well over five miles hadn't caused the slightest wear on the shoes—more like buskins, they were—which constituted all that he wore except for a pair of what could have been swimming trunks, in robin's-egg blue. But it wasn't his dimensions that made him horrible to look upon; it was his *skin*. It looked red, raw. It looked as though he had been skinned alive, and the skin replaced upside down, raw side out. His skull, his face, were equally narrow or elongated; otherwise in every visible way he appeared human—or at least humanoid. Unless you counted such little things as the fact that his hair was a robin's-egg blue to match his trunks, as were his eyes and his boots. Blood red and light blue.

Casey, owner of the tavern, was the first one to see them

coming across the plain, from the direction of the mountain range to the east. He'd stepped out of the back door of his tavern for a breath of fresh, if hot, air. They were about a hundred yards away at that time, and already he could see the utter alienness of the figure on the lead burro. Just alienness at that distance, the horror came only at closer range. Casey's jaw dropped and stayed down until the strange trio was about fifty yards away, then he started slowly toward them. There are people who run at the sight of the unknown, others who advance to meet it. Casey advanced, however slowly, to meet it.

Still in the wide open, twenty yards from the back of the little tavern, he met them. Dade Grant stopped and dropped the rope by which he was leading the burro. The burro stood still and dropped its head. The stick-man stood up simply by planting his feet solidly and standing, astride the burro. He stepped one leg across it and stood a moment, leaning his weight against his hands on the burro's back, and then sat down in the sand. "High-gravity planet," he said. "Can't stand long."

"Kin I get water for my burro?" the prospector asked Casey. "Must be purty thirsty by now. Hadda leave water bags, some other things, so it could carry—" He jerked a thumb toward the red-and-blue horror.

Casey was just realizing that it *was* a horror. At a distance the color combination seemed a bit *outré*, but close— The skin was rough and seemed to have veins on the outside and looked moist (although it wasn't) and *damn* if it didn't look just like he had his skin peeled off and put back upside down. Or just peeled off, period. Casey had never seen anything like it and hoped he wouldn't ever see anything like it again.

Casey felt something behind him and looked over his shoulder. Others had seen now and were coming, but the nearest of them, a pair of boys, were ten yards behind him. "*Muchachos,*" he called out, "*Agua por el burro. Un pazal. Pronto.*"

He looked back and said, "What—? Who—?"

"Name's Dade Grant," said the prospector, putting out a hand, which Casey took absently. When he let go of it it jerked back over the desert rat's shoulder, thumb indicating the thing that sat on the sand. "*His* name's Garth, he tells me. He's an extra something or other, and he's some kind of minister."

Casey nodded at the stick-man and was glad to get a nod in return instead of an extended hand. "I'm Manuel Casey," he said. "What does he mean, an extra something?"

The stick-man's voice was unexpectedly deep and vibrant. "I am an extraterrestrial. And a minister plenipotentiary."

Surprisingly, Casey was a moderately well-educated man and knew both of those phrases; he was probably the only person in Cherrybell who would have known the second one. Less surprisingly, considering the speaker's appearance, he believed both of them. "What can I do for you, sir?" he asked. "But first, why not come in out of the sun?"

"No, thank you. It's a bit cooler here than they told me it would be, but I'm quite comfortable. This is equivalent to a cool spring evening on my planet. And as to what you can do for me, you can notify your authorities of my presence. I believe they will be interested."

Well, Casey thought, by blind luck he's hit the best man for his purpose within at least twenty miles. Manuel Casey was half-Irish, half-Mexican. He had a half brother who was half-Irish and half assorted-American, and the half brother was a bird colonel at Davis-Monthan Air Force Base in Tucson. He said, "Just a minute, Mr. Garth, I'll telephone. You, Mr. Grant, would you want to come inside?"

"Naw, I don't mind sun. Out in it all day every day. An' Garth here, he ast me if I'd stick with him till he was finished with what he's gotta do here. Said he'd gimme somethin' purty vallable if I did. Somethin'—a 'lectrononic—"

"An electronic battery-operated portable ore indicator," Garth said. "A simple little device, indicates presence of a concentration of ore up to two miles, indicates kind, grade, quantity and depth."

Casey gulped, excused himself, and pushed through the gathering crowd into his tavern. He had Colonel Casey on the phone in one minute, but it took him another four minutes to convince the colonel that he was neither drunk nor joking.

Twenty-five minutes after that there was a noise in the sky, a noise that swelled and then died as a four-man helicopter sat down and shut off its rotors a dozen yards from an extraterrestrial, two men and a burro. Casey alone had had the courage to rejoin the trio from the desert; there were other spectators, but they still held well back.

Colonel Casey, a major, a captain, and a lieutenant who was the helicopter's pilot all came out and ran over. The stick-man stood up, all nine feet of him; from the effort it cost him to stand you could tell that he was used to a much lighter gravity than Earth's. He bowed, repeated his name and identification of himself as an extraterrestrial and a minister plenipotentiary. Then he apologized for sitting down again, explained why it was necessary, and sat down.

The colonel introduced himself and the three who had come with him. "And now, sir, what can we do for you?"

The stick-man made a grimace that was probably intended as a smile. His teeth were the same light blue as his hair and eyes. "You have a cliché, 'take me to your leader.' I do not ask that. In fact, I *must* remain here. Nor do I ask that any of your leaders be brought here to me. That would be impolite. I am perfectly willing for you to represent them, to talk to you and let you question me. But I do ask one thing.

"You have tape recorders. I ask that, before I talk or answer questions, you have one brought. I want to be sure that the message your leaders eventually receive is full and accurate."

"Fine," the colonel said. He turned to the pilot. "Lieutenant, get on the radio in the whirlybird and tell them to get us a tape recorder faster than possible. It can be dropped by para— No, that'd take longer, rigging it for a drop. Have them send it by another helicopter." The lieutenant turned to go. "Hey," the colonel said. "Also fifty yards of extension cord. We'll have to plug it in inside Manny's tavern."

The lieutenant sprinted for the helicopter.

The others sat and sweated a moment and then Manuel Casey stood up. "That's a half an hour wait," he said, "and if we're going to sit here in the sun, who's for a bottle of cold beer? You, Mr. Garth?"

"It is a cold beverage, is it not? I am a bit chilly. If you have something hot—?"

"Coffee, coming up. Can I bring you a blanket?"

"No, thank you. It will not be necessary."

Casey left and shortly returned with a tray with half a dozen bottles of cold beer and a cup of steaming coffee. The lieutenant was back by then. Casey put down the tray and first served the stick-man, who sipped the coffee and said, "It is delicious."

Colonel Casey cleared his throat. "Serve our prospector friend next, Manny. As for us—well, drinking is forbidden on duty, but it was a hundred and twelve in the shade in Tucson, and this is hotter and also is *not* in the shade. Gentlemen, consider yourselves on official leave for as long as it takes you to drink one bottle of beer, or until the tape recorder arrives, whichever comes first."

The beer was finished first, but by the time the last of it had vanished, the second helicopter was within sight and sound. Casey asked the stick-man if he wanted more coffee. The offer was politely declined. Casey looked at Dade Grant and winked back, so Casey went in for two more bottles, one apiece for the civilian terrestrials. Coming back he met the lieutenant coming with the extension cord and returned as far as the doorway to show him where to plug it in.

When he came back, he saw that the second helicopter had brought its full complement of four, besides the tape recorder. There were, besides the pilot who had flown it, a technical sergeant who was skilled in the operation of the tape recorder and who was now making adjustments on it, and a lieutenant-colonel and a warrant officer who had come along for the ride or because they had been made curious by the request for a tape recorder to be rushed to Cherrybell, Arizona, by air. They were standing gaping at the stick-man and whispered conversations were going on.

The colonel said "Attention" quietly, but it brought complete silence. "Please sit down, gentlemen. In a rough circle. Sergeant, if you rig your mike in the center of the circle, will it pick up clearly what any one of us may say?"

"Yes, sir. I'm almost ready."

Ten men and one extraterrestrial humanoid sat in a rough circle, with the microphone hanging from a small tripod in the approximate center. The humans were sweating profusely; the humanoid shivered slightly. Just outside the circle, the burro stood dejectedly, its head low. Edging closer, but still about five yards away, spread out now in a semicircle, was the entire population of Cherrybell who had been at home at the time; the stores and the filling stations were deserted.

The technical sergeant pushed a button and the tape recorder's reel started to turn. "Testing . . . testing," he said. He held down the rewind button for a second and then pushed the playback button. "Testing . . . testing," said the recorder's speaker. Loud and clear. The sergeant pushed the rewind button, then the erase one to clear the tape. Then the stop button. "When I push the next button, sir," he said to the colonel, "we'll be recording."

The colonel looked at the tall extraterrestrial, who nodded, and then the colonel nodded at the sergeant. The sergeant pushed the recording button.

"My name is Garth," said the stick-man, slowly and clearly. "I am from a planet of a star which is not listed in your star catalogs, although the globular cluster in which it is one of ninety thousand stars, is known to you. It is, from here, in the direction of the center of the galaxy at a distance of a little over four thousand light-years.

"However, I am not here as a representative of my planet or my people, but as minister plenipotentiary of the Galactic Union, a federation of the enlightened civilizations of the galaxy, for the good of all. It is my assignment to visit you and decide, here and now, whether or not you are to be welcomed to join our federation.

"You may now ask questions freely. However, I reserve the right to postpone answering some of them until my decision has been made. If the decision is favorable, I will then answer all questions, including the ones I have postponed answering meanwhile. Is that satisfactory?"

"Yes," said the colonel. "How did you come here? A spaceship?"

"Correct. It is overhead right now, in orbit twenty-two thousand miles out, so it revolves with the earth and stays over this one spot. I am under observation from it, which is one reason I prefer to remain here in the open. I am to signal it when I want it to come down to pick me up."

"How do you know our language so fluently? Are you telepathic?"

"No, I am not. And nowhere in the galaxy is any race telepathic except among its own members. I was taught your language, for this purpose. We have had observers among you for many centuries—by *we*, I mean the Galactic Union, of course. Quite obviously I could not pass as an Earthman, but there are other races who can. Incidentally, they are not spies, or agents; they have in no way tried to affect you; they are observers and that is all."

"What benefits do we get from joining your union, if we are asked and if we accept?" the colonel asked.

"First, a quick course in the fundamental social sciences which will end your tendency to fight among yourselves and end or at least control your aggressions. After we are satisfied that you have accomplished that and it is safe for you to do so, you will be given space travel, and many other things, as rapidly as you are able to assimilate them."

"And if we are not asked, or refuse?"

"Nothing. You will be left alone; even our observers will be withdrawn. You will work out your own fate—either you will render your planet uninhabited and uninhabitable within the next century, or you will master social science yourselves and again be candidates for membership and again be offered membership. We will check from time to time and if and when it appears certain that you are not going to destroy yourselves, you will again be approached."

"Why the hurry, now that you're here? Why can't you stay long enough for our leaders, as you call them, to talk to you in person?"

"Postponed. The reason is not important but it is complicated, and I simply do not wish to waste time explaining."

"Assuming your decision is favorable, how will we get in touch with you to let you know *our* decision? You know enough about us, obviously, to know that *I* can't make it."

"We will know your decision through our observers. One condition of acceptance is full and uncensored publication in your newspapers of this interview, verbatim from the tape we are now using to record it. Also of all deliberations and decisions of your government."

"And other governments? We can't decide unilaterally for the world."

"Your government has been chosen for a start. If you accept we shall furnish the techniques that will cause the others to fall in line quickly—and those techniques do not involve force or the threat of force."

"They must be *some* techniques," said the colonel wryly, "if they'll make one certain country I don't have to name fall into line quickly, without even a threat."

"Sometimes the offer of reward is more significant than the use of threat. Do you think the country you do not wish to name would like your country colonizing planets of far stars before they even reach Mars? But that is a minor point, relatively. You may trust the techniques."

"It sounds almost too good to be true. But you said that you are to decide, here and now, whether or not we are to be invited to join. May I ask on what factors you will base your decision?"

"One is that I am—was, since I already have—to check your degree of xenophobia. In the loose sense in which you use it, that means fear of strangers. We have a word that has no counterpart in your vocabulary: it means fear of and revulsion toward *aliens*. I—or at least a member of my race—was chosen to make the first overt contact with you. Because I am what you call roughly humanoid—as you are what I would call roughly humanoid—I am probably more horrible, more repulsive to you than many completely different species would be. Because to you, I am a caricature of a human being, I am more horrible to you than a being who bears no remote resemblance to you.

"You may think you *do* feel horror at me, and revulsion, but believe me, you have passed that test. There *are* races in the galaxy who can never be members of the federation, no matter how they advance otherwise, because they are violently and incurably xenophobic; they could never face or talk to any alien of any species. They would either run screaming from him or try to kill him instantly. From watching you and these people"—he waved a long arm at the civilian population of Cherrybell not far outside the circle of the conference—"I know you feel revulsion at the sight of me, but believe me it is relatively slight and certainly curable. You have passed that test satisfactorily."

"And are there other tests?"

"One other. But I think it is time that I—" Instead of finishing the sentence, the stick-man lay back flat on the sand and closed his eyes.

The colonel started to his feet. "What in *hell?*" he said. He walked quickly around the mike's tripod and bent over the recumbent extraterrestrial, put an ear to the bloody-appearing chest.

As he raised his head, Dade Grant, the grizzled prospector, chuckled. "No heartbeat, Colonel, because no heart. But I may leave him as a souvenir for you and you'll find much more interesting things inside him than heart and guts. Yes, he is a puppet whom I have been operating—as your Edgar Bergen operates his—what's his name?—oh yes,

Charlie McCarthy. Now that he has served his purpose, he is deactivated. You can go back to your place, Colonel."

Colonel Casey moved back slowly. "Why?" he asked.

Dade Grant was peeling off his beard and wig. He rubbed a cloth across his face to remove make-up and was revealed as a handsome young man. He said, "What he told you, or what you were told through him, was true as far as it went. He is only a simulacrum, yes, but he is an exact duplicate of a member of one of the intelligent races of the galaxy, the one toward whom you would be disposed —if you were violently and incurably xenophobic—to be most horrified by, according to our psychologists. But we did not bring a real member of his species to make first contact because they have a phobia of their own, agoraphobia—fear of space. They are highly civilized and members in good standing of the federation, but they never leave their own planet.

"Our observers assure us you don't have *that* phobia. But they were unable to judge in advance the degree of your xenophobia and the only way to test it was to bring along something in lieu of someone to test it against, and presumably to let him make the initial contact."

The colonel sighed audibly. "I can't say this doesn't relieve me in one way. We could get along with humanoids, yes, and will when we have to. But I'll admit it's a relief to learn that the master race of the galaxy is, after all, human instead of only humanoid. What is the second test?"

"You are undergoing it now. Call me—" He snapped his fingers. "What's the name of Bergen's second-string puppet, after Charlie McCarthy?"

The colonel hesitated, but the tech sergeant supplied the answer. "Mortimer Snerd."

"Right. So call me Mortimer Snerd, and now I think it

is time that I—" He lay back flat on the sand and closed his eyes just as the stick-man had done a few minutes before.

The burro raised its head and put it into the circle over the shoulder of the tech sergeant. "That takes care of the puppets, Colonel," it said. "And now what's this bit about it being important that the master race be human or at least humanoid? What is a master race?"

The cartoons of Gahan Wilson are justifiably famous for their biting satirical humor and for the range of "things"—BEMS, ghouls, witches, demons, strange animals, stranger humans—which inhabit them. The six offered in evidence here are among his most mordant, and feature half a dozen monsters of the type you'll hope never to meet in a dark alley. Or, for that matter, in broad daylight.

In addition to supplying cartoons for newspaper syndication and such popular magazines as Playboy, *Wilson has for the past fifteen years contributed one each month to* The Magazine of Fantasy & Science Fiction *(the selections here are all from F&SF). And he also finds time to do occasional book review columns, introductions to fantasy/macabre anthologies and collections, and short stories every bit as caustically humorous as his cartoons. One of the latter is "M-1," something of a minor classic about a mysterious statue of Mickey Mouse several thousand feet high....*

Portfolio (Cartoons)

Gahan Wilson

"We've no idea what it is, but it makes a darling planter!"

"That's alright, boy! Here, boy! Forget it, boy! C'mon, boy . . ."

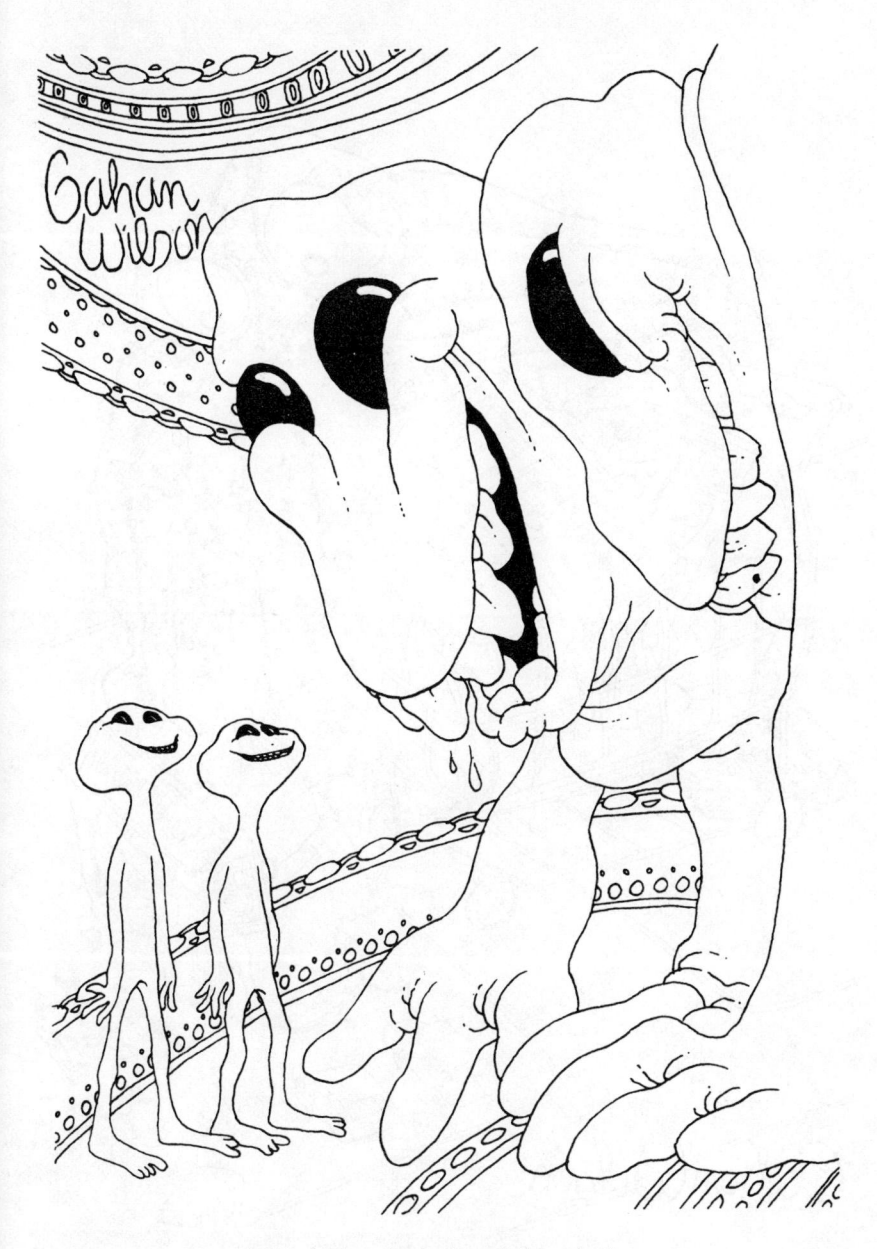

"OK, kids, ask the Earthlings in!"

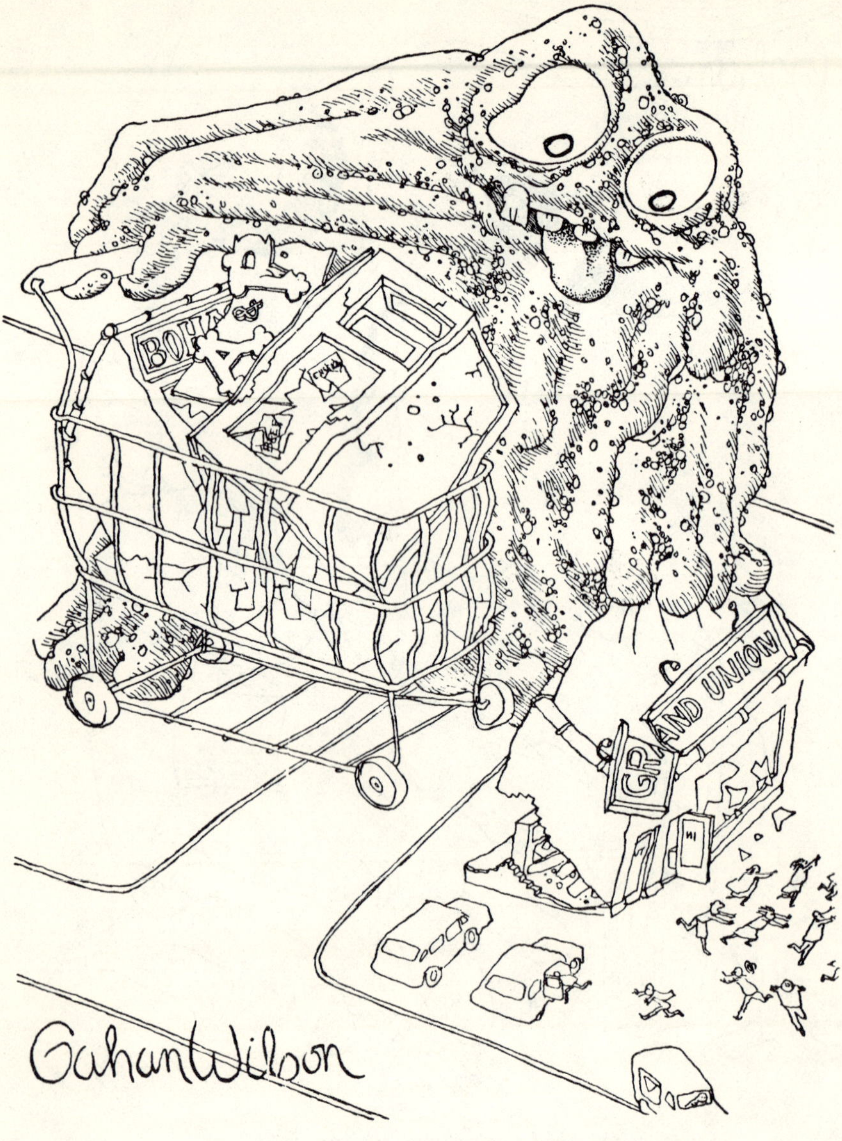
GRAND UNION
Gahan Wilson

"There's that funny noise again!"

"You know, Larry, with a smart lawyer you could make a lot of money!"

When "Wherever You Are" appeared in Astounding *in 1959, editor John W. Campbell wrote: "This one . . . is a bit confused. The bug-eyed reptilian monster is afraid of the girl, you see, and the hero doesn't know where he is, much less where the heroine is. . . ." The adventures of Ulrica Ormstad and Didymus Mudge on Epstein's Planet are every bit as tongue-in-cheek as Campbell's blurb, and involve some of the more fetching BEMs in the history of the species.*

Poul Anderson (b. 1926) is among the most loftily regarded of contemporary science-fiction writers; since his first published story in 1947, he has written almost fifty s-f novels and more than 400 short stories. (He has also authored a number of popular scientific works and mysteries of all lengths.) Several of his stories have won Hugo and Nebula awards. His 1968 novel Tau Zero *has been accorded considerable acclaim, but his first novel,* Brain Wave *(1954), is thought by many to be his best. The appearance of "Wherever You Are" in* Astounding *(under Anderson's pseudonym of Winston P. Sanders) inspired one of Kelly Freas's most inventive covers: an evocatively cowering Epsteinian BEM. The story has never before been anthologized.*

Wherever You Are

Poul Anderson

The monster laid a taloned hand on the girl's shoulder. She jumped, startled, and whirled about to face bulging red eyes. The monster opened jaws full of teeth that glowed.

The girl wrenched free. "What the devil do you want?" she yelled.

"Eek," said the monster, stepping back a pace. "*Urgu aki, Zivar.*"

The girl advanced threateningly. "The next time you forget your manners," she snapped, "the next time you forget who I am, you peasant, may heaven protect you!"

The monster wailed and scuttled down the path, as if hoping the man would come along and save him from the girl.

Ulrica Ormstad added a few soldierly oaths and followed. She knew they were wasted; nobody understood any Terrestrial language for several thousand kilometers. (Unless, she thought scornfully, you counted Didymus Mudge. But a corpulent help he was!) Nevertheless, her emotions needed a safety valve, and she could barely speak Harakunye, let alone swear in it.

Far down underneath, she admitted her anger stemmed from loneliness. And even, it might be, fear. She was trained to face battle, or storm, or the sudden failure of human engineering under conditions never foreseen by man. The situation here, on this island, held some of those elements. But basically it was another sort of dilemma, involving a worse way to die.

Therefore Ulrica Ormstad fell back on pride. She was a major in the militechnic service of New Scythia, free-born to full rights in Clan Swenson. Let the universe beware!

Long strides carried her quickly through the jungle. Its leaves were stiff and reddish blue: vegetation on Epstein's Planet photosynthesized, but the compound used was not chlorophyl. At first the pervasive smell had sickened her a little, but she soon grew used to it. Now, when she returned to her home world, or visited Mother Earth—if she ever did—their familiar biochemistry would stink for a while.

The native glowbugs, spectacularly clustered where thickets made a twilight, or the beautiful crystal flowers, or the delicate chiming of bellfruit, had ceased to interest her. She would swap it all for a chance to leave this hell-hole.

The game trail ended and Ulrica stepped out onto a broad white beach. The ship *Geyvadigur* lay anchored inside a sheltered lagoon: for the hidden sun was close enough to raise considerable tides, even in the absence of a satellite. Boats were drawn up on the sand, where the crew had pitched conical pink tents. The sailor whom she had frightened waited timidly. Doubtless Captain Zalakun wished to question her.

Ulrica sighed. She had gone walking in the jungle just to get away from the endless struggle with Harakunye grammar. For one honest human conversation, in any human language, she would trade her soul. Make it Swedish, and she'd throw in her sidearm.

Didymus Mudge emerged from one of the tents. He had been playing with a silly-looking affair inside, wooden frameworks and inclined planes, as indeed he had done for a week now. The ship's carpenter, who had been helping, squeaked at sight of Ulrica and tried to hide behind the man. Since Mudge stood only one hundred eighty centimeters tall, and even the smallest Epsteinian was three meters long including the tail, this was not very successful.

"Oh. Hello." Mudge tried to smile. "What were you doing, Miss Ormstad?"

Ulrica put hands on hips and glared downward. Mudge was slender as well as short, with sandy hair, cowlick, an undistinguished freckled face, and large blue eyes near-sighted behind contact lenses. His tattered gray zipsuit did not make him more impressive.

"I will give you three guesses," snorted the girl. "I have been making an atomic-powered aircraft with my bare hands? No. Then I have been weaving vines into a radio circuit, to call base and have them come get us? No. I have been practicing to swim all the way to Lonesome Landing? Still no. *Kors i Herrans namn!* And you are supposed to be bright enough to teach children!"

"I ... er ... yes," said the Earthman meekly.

Ulrica looked him up and down. She herself had the big bones and powerful muscles of a human breed which had spent generations under the gee-and-a-half of New Scythia. It did not make her less graceful, in a full-hipped full-breasted way; on her, a salt-stained tunic and clan kilt looked good. Thick brown braids lay tightly around a face of high cheekbones, straight nose, broad firm mouth, and wide-set green eyes. Even beneath the perpetually leaden sky of this planet, her skin glowed tawny.

"And still Earth manages to be the leader of the League," she murmured. "I do not understand it. I just plain do not." Louder: "Well, what have you been tinkering with? Are you making an abstraction ladder in there, to teach semantics? Better you learn to talk with these lizards first!"

"That isn't my forte," said Mudge in a defensive tone. "You were trained from childhood to pick up languages fast, tone discrimination, mnemonics— You might as well expect me, at my time of life, to take up ballet, as learn Harakunye from scratch in a week!"

Ulrica laughed.

"What is it?" asked Mudge.

"The thought of you in tights," she chortled, "doing a *pas de deux* with an Epsteinian."

"Some people have a strange sense of humor," grumbled Mudge. He rubbed his peeling nose. Enough ultraviolet had penetrated the clouds to give his untanned hide a bad sunburn.

"I have been so busy studying," said Ulrica. Mirth had

eased her, and she wanted to offer friendliness to this fellow castaway whom she had scarcely seen so far. "It was necessary I be able to talk with them. As soon as one sailor got restless, I let him go and started with another. I only stopped to eat and sleep. But you, what have you been working on?"

Mudge pointed to his wrist watch. "This was damaged," he said. "It kept running, and I know the precise time when it was deranged. But now it's either fast or slow, I'm not sure which. Checking it against my pulse suggests it is slow, but I have always had an irregular pulse. I—"

"*What?*" yelped Ulrica. "At this time you worry about your little tin watch?"

"It isn't either," said Mudge. "It's a very good seventeen-jewel Swiss chrono. My mother gave it to me at graduation. My graduation, that is, not hers. Though she does have a degree herself, from the same place, Boston Uni—"

"On a desert island," said Ulrica to heaven, "*x* thousand kilometers from the one human outpost on this entire planet, surrounded by natives of absolutely unknown culture and intentions, he worries about his graduation present. *Du store Gud!* Also *lieber Gott, nom du Dieu,* and *Bozhe moi!*"

"But wait," bleated Mudge. "It's important! Let me explain!"

Ulrica stalked down to the shore, trailing a string of remarks which ionized the air behind her.

The sailor stood patiently at a beached rowboat. He was a typical Epsteinian, which is to say he looked rather like a small slim tyrannosaur with a bulldog face and round coxcombed head. His scales were dark-blue on top, pale below, and zebra striped; his eyes were red and bulging, his teeth phosphorescent yellow. He wore merely crossed belts, one of which held a knife and one a pouch. The data book—thank a lifetime's Amazonian training for the quick-wittedness which had made Ulrica pocket that, along with a bottle of vitamin pills, when the spaceboat exploded—said the autochthones were not actually reptiles, being warm-blooded and placental. Neither were they mammals, lacking the appropriate glands as well as hair. They looked ferocious enough, but most of the *Geyvadigur* crew had shown Yes, Master personalities.

The officers, though, appeared to be something else again.

Ulrica entered the boat. The sailor launched it, jumped in, and rowed her out to the ship. Tension gathered within her. After the captain understood she was working on his language, he had turned the dull job of helping over to his crew. A few hours ago, one of the mates—Ulrica assumed that was their status—had interviewed her briefly and gone off wagging his tail. He must have reported she was now proficient enough to talk intelligently.

The ship loomed over her. Except for the ornate figurehead, it might at first glance have been an early Terrestrial steamer, with high stacks, monstrous sidewheels, and two schooner-rigged masts in case of emergency. Then you began to notice things. There probably wasn't a door on all Epstein's Planet, except at Lonesome Landing, likely to pinch a tail. Since the natives sat on those same organs, they had never invented chairs. The treads of all ladders, and the ratlines, were a meter apart. Ulrica had inspected the engines and been surprised to find them oil-burning steam turbines; why the craft then used paddles instead of screws could only be explained by the whimsical gods who, on Earth, had once put engines in the front of rear-wheel drive automobiles.

The *Geyvadigur* had both magnetic and spring-powered gyro compasses, but otherwise no hint of electromagnetic technology—which scuttled all hope of radioing for help. Quite likely the eternal damp atmosphere accounted for the Harakuni failure to study such phenomena, even though the nearby sun lit every night with fabulous auroras. Poverty of resources, or sheer historical accident, might explain the fact that there were no firearms aboard. The craft did, however, sport catapults, oil bombs, and flame throwers.

Ulrica would have felt better had her own pistol been of any use. But she had exhausted its charge against hungry sea snakes, as she and Mudge paddled their fragment of spaceboat toward this island; and when the vessel went, there hadn't been time to grab extra clips.

The sailor helped her up a Jacob's ladder. The decks were littered with his fellows, polishing, holystoning, splicing, the usual nautical chores. A mate stalked about with a barbed-wire whip, touching up an occasional back to encourage progress. Ulrica stamped as haughtily as possible to the captain's cabin. (Another foreign detail. It was a thatch hut, its walls lined with a tasteful collection of weapons and Epsteinian skulls.)

Captain Zalakun bared his fangs politely as the girl entered. Beside him squatted a gaunt male with an eyeglass and a sash whereon a dozen medals tinkled together. A sawtoothed scimitar lay drawn on the table. Combats between Epsteinians, whose scales bounced back a mere slash, must be awesome.

"Ssss," greeted the captain. "Coil your tail, *Zivar*."

At least he used the aristocratic title. The only alternative Ulrica had found in Harakunye was *Yaldazir*, which seemed a contraction of a phrase meaning "Offal of an unspeakable worm." If you weren't addressed by one title, you necessarily had the other.

She hunkered and waited.

Zalakun turned toward the eyeglass. *"Zivar,"* he said, "this is the monster called Orumastat, which we took from the sea with its slave four days ago." He meant Epsteinian days, of course, forty-six hours long. Turning to Ulrica: "Orumastat, this is the most glorious Feridur of Beradura, who heads our expedition. You have not seen him before because he was belowdecks playing *karosi*. Now that you can talk, Feridur of Beradura will let you know his magnanimous will."

Ulrica struggled to follow the speech. She was by no means fluent in Harakunye. In this conversation, she often had to ask what a word meant; or sometimes the natives were baffled by her accent. But, in effect, she answered: "That would be very pleasant to know."

The language barrier strained out sarcasm. Feridur lifted his monocle. "I say, captain," he asked, "are you sure it is a bona fide warrior? It didn't even sneer at me."

"It claims to be, *Zivar*," said Zalakun uncertainly. "And after all, if I may extrude a suggestion, your magnificent memory will recall tribes we have already encountered, prepared to fight bravely but given to soft female-type words on all other occasions."

"True. Yes. True." Feridur wiggled his tail tip. "And this creature is still more alien, eh, what? Great Kastakun, how hideous it is!"

"Hey!" bristled Ulrica. Then she sat back. Perhaps this was a compliment. She didn't know.

According to the data book, all Epsteinians encountered so far by humans had been amiable fishers and farmers. In the archipelagoes fringing the Northeast Ocean they were neolithic; further west, they had begun to use iron; and cursory flights above one of the small continents beyond had shown areas where there were cities and square-rigged ships.

The *Geyvadigur* was from Harakun, still further west—perhaps at the antipodes—and, apparently, still more advanced in technology. The vessel must have been chugging eastward for months, exploring, refueling often from the planet's many natural oil wells. Now it poised somewhere near the edge of the Northeast Ocean, with little but water ahead for half the world's circumference.

In short, this region was as strange to Zalakun and Feridur as it was to Ulrica and Mudge. By the same token, you could no more conclude what the Harakuni were like from reports on local primitives than an eighteenth-century Martian visiting Hawaii could have predicted the character of Europeans.

It behooved her to gang warily. But gang she must.

"Well, don't just sit there," said Feridur. "Speak. Or do tricks, or something." He yawned. "Great Kastakun! And to think I left my estates because I thought this wretched expedition would be an adventure! Why, I haven't collected ten decent skulls since we weighed anchor!"

"Ah, but *Zivar*," soothed Zalakun, "what an interesting skull Orumastat has."

"True," said Feridur, perking up. "Sensational. A collector's item. That is, if Orumastat gives me enough of a fight."

"Oh, but it is a guest," objected Zalakun. "I didn't mean Orumastat personally, but warriors of its tribe, after we contact them—"

"Quiet, you low creature," said Feridur.

The captain looked distressed. He tried another approach: "Orumastat may be too soft to be worthwhile. No scales."

"The *erkuma* of Akhvadin lacks scales," pointed out Feridur, "and yet if you meet one hand-to-hand and survive, its skull is jolly well worth fifty like yours."

"True," said Zalakun, banging his brow on the table. "I abase myself."

Ulrica stood up. The conversation seemed to be getting out of hand. "Just a moment, just a moment!" she exclaimed. "I did not come here to fight."

"No?" Feridur gaped idiotically and twiddled his eyeglass. "Not to fight? Whatever for, then?"

"It was shipwrecked, puissant one," said Zalakun.

"Eh, what? Shipwrecked? Nonsense. We haven't had any storms lately. Couldn't be shipwrecked. I mean to say, that's nonsense. Come, come, now, monster, out with it. Why are you here?"

"Shut up, you knock-kneed son of a frog!" snarled Ulrica. She kept her fraying temper just enough to say it in English.

"Eh? What say? Don't understand it. Terrible accent. If it's going to learn Harakunye, why can't it learn right? Answer me that." Feridur leaned back sulkily and toyed with his scimitar.

Zalakun gave him a glance of frustrated exasperation, then said to the girl: "Suppose you explain yourself from the beginning."

Ulrica had dreaded that request. The upper atmosphere of this planet was so thickly clouded that you never even saw its own sun, let alone the stars. She had learned without surprise that the Harakuni thought their world was flat. Even their boldest sailors never ventured more than a few hundred kilometers from land, and that only in familiar seas where compass and log made crude dead reckoning possible.

Briefly, she was tempted to say: "Mudge and I were coming down in a small ferry from the regular supply spaceship. We were letting the autopilot bring us in on a radio beam, and know only that we were several thousand kilometers west of Lonesome Landing. I have no idea what number that word 'several' really stands for. Some freakish backblast caused the engine to explode, the jet stream seized us and flung us far off course, we came down in a torn-off section on a dying grav-unit with capricious winds blowing us about, and hit the sea near this island. Every scrap of our equipment is lost or ruined. Doubtless aircraft are hunting for us, but what chance have we of being found on an entire, virtually unmapped planet, before our vitamin pills give out and we die? For we can eat the native life, but unless it is supplemented with Terrestrial vitamins we will soon get scurvy, beriberi, pellagra, and every other deficiency disease you can name."

But she didn't have Harakunye words to say it.

Instead, she ventured: "We are of a race different from yours. All our tribe are mighty warriors. We two went far from the island where we live, exploring in a boat that flew. But it suffered harm in the air and we fell here, where you soon found us."

"We spied your ruin descending and made haste to investigate," said Captain Zalakun. "I have been looking at the wreckage. That material like unbreakable glass is interesting, but why do you use such soft light metal instead of wood or iron?"

Ulrica sighed. "That is a long story," she answered. "There are many wonderful things we can show you, if you will only take us to our home." She was quite confident the *Geyvadigur* could reach Lonesome Landing in time. The ship must be capable of averaging at least five knots, which meant some fifteen hundred kilometers an Earth-week. The station was certainly less than five thousand kilometers away. There were pills left for three weeks; and, if necessary, several days more without vitamins would do no serious harm.

"We are anxious to know all the nations in your . . . er,

in the world," continued Ulrica persuasively. "We wish trade with them, and friendship." No need to elaborate on the civilizing program of the League. They might not appreciate that idea without advance propaganda.

"Trade?" Feridur brightened. "Skulls?"

"Well—" temporized Ulrica.

"See here," said Feridur in a reasonable tone, "either you want to fight and give a chap a chance to collect skulls, or else you're not worth contacting. Eh, what? Isn't that fair?"

"My splendid master," said Zalakun with strained politeness, "we have already discovered that few foreign peoples share the interest of us and our neighbors in craniology. There *are* other things in life, you know."

Feridur laid talons about the scimitar. His monocle glittered red. "Ssso," he murmured, "you think that, eh?"

Zalakun wriggled backward on his tail. "Oh, no, your awesomeness," he said hastily. "Not at all. Of course not!"

"Oh, so you do want to expand your own collection," purred Feridur. He tested saw edges with a thumb. "Well, well! I say! Maybe you would like to add the skull of your liege lord to the museum, eh, what?"

"Oh, no, no, *Zivar*," said Zalakun, sweating. "Wouldn't dream of it."

"So my skull isn't good enough for you. Is that it?"

"No, *Zivar*! Your skull is a thing of beauty."

"I'll oblige you any time, you know," said Feridur. "We can go ashore right this moment and have a whack at each other, eh?"

Zalakun licked rubbery lips. "Uh," he said. "Well, the fact is—"

"Ah, I know, I know. Not a drop of sporting blood in the whole dashed ship. Great Kastakun! Well, go on, then,

Yaldazir, talk to the monster. Two of a kind." Feridur yawned elaborately.

Ulrica felt embarrassed for the captain. After breathing hard for a while he resumed the conversation with her. "Where is this home of yours, Orumastat?"

"Somewhere . . . er . . . that way." Ulrica pointed out the window, past reefs and surf to a steel-gray eastward stretch of sea.

"Can you not be more precise? What archipelago?"

"No archipelago," said the girl. "It is a single island in the middle of an ocean. My people have seen from the air that the part of the world you must come from has many islands and two small continents, so that one is never far from land. But beyond the region where I think we are now, there is almost no land for . . . I don't know your measures. You could sail steadily for more than fifty of your days before seeing shore again."

"I say!" Feridur straightened. "You're sure, monster?"

"Not in detail," Ulrica admitted. "But I do know there is that much water somewhere to the east, ahead of you."

"But then . . . Great Kastakun, captain! I'm glad we found that out! We're heading straight homeward again!"

"To be sure," declared Zalakun, appalled. "Why, after so long a time at sea, one could not even guess at northward or southward drift. One might miss the shore you speak of completely. Even if the wind didn't fail in so long a voyage. For we could only steam twenty days at most before our oil bunkers were dry."

"It would not be that far to my island," said Ulrica.

"Hm-m-m . . . how far?"

"I am not certain. But no more than, uh, fifteen days."

"Fifteen days in open ocean!" gasped Zalakun.

He sat back, tongue hanging out, speechless with horror.

Feridur quizzed Ulrica through his monocle. "But I say," he objected, "what's the jolly old purpose in living so far away? Eh? It's unheard of. I mean to say, nobody lives in mid-ocean."

"Since we can fly at great speeds, we are not inconvenienced by distance," replied Ulrica. And colonizing an isolated speck would offend no natives: they didn't even realize it existed. No sense, though, in giving so pacifistic a reason to this warrior culture.

"But how do you find your way? Eh? Answer me that. Ha, ha, I've bally well got you there!" Feridur wagged a triumphant finger.

Ulrica decided that there was also no point in describing a radio net involving three small artificial satellites. "We have our methods," she said in a mysterious tone.

"By the Iron Reefs," murmured Zalakun. His tone held awe. "Of course you do! You must, or you couldn't have found that island in the first place. But to know exactly where you are, even when there's no land in sight, no current or cloud formations or— Why, that's a secret sought for as long as there have been ships!"

"We will gladly provide you with similar means," said Ulrica. "If, of course, you take us home."

"Naturally!" babbled Zalakun. He sprang to his feet, wagging his tail till the air whistled. "Jumping gods, master, what're a thousand bug-bitten skulls next to a prize like that? Just give us a line, *Zivar* Orumastat, give us a compass bearing and we'll hold true on it till you're home, though the sky fall down!"

"*Ah, nej!*" whispered Ulrica. She felt the blood sink from her face.

"What is it?" asked the captain. He came around the table and offered an arm. She leaned on it, badly in need of support.

"I just realized . . . I was so busy before that it only occurs to me now . . . I know where the island is," she said faintly. "But I can't give you a course. I don't know where *we* are!"

When Ulrica had gone aboard ship, Ardabadur, the carpenter, followed. There he directed a gang of sailors as they unloaded the completed Foucault bob, got it into a boat and ashore. While they carried it onward, he went to the tent where Didymus Mudge was at work.

He hesitated outside. The Earthling's operations had been fascinating, but enigmatic and delicate. Ardabadur didn't want to interrupt. Finally he stuck his head through the flap.

Mudge stood hunched over his apparatus. In the days since arriving here, he had gotten it to function rather well. Or, more accurately, Ardabadur had. They shared no words, but through gestures, drawings, and crude models Mudge had explained what he needed. Then the ship's excellent carpenter shop had prepared it for him—after which he tinkered, groaned, and sent it back for revision.

A ball of cast bronze rolled thunderously down an inclined plane. Mudge watched it while counting the swings of a small pendulum, carefully made from a leather cord and a lead weight in a leveled glass-sided box. When the ball reached ground, Mudge made a note. The Harakuni had paper and pencils. "Which is a mercy," he said aloud. "But *why* couldn't you have brought a clock along?"

Ardabadur hopped inside and squatted respectfully. Mudge ran a hand through rumpled hair and mopped sweat off his face. "I'm sure you have some chronometry," he said. "You have probably even measured the length of the day, and its seasonal variation. I know the long twilight confuses things, clouds always hiding the sun . . . but if you averaged enough observations for enough centuries, you could do it. So why didn't you bring a clock? Knowing this planet's rotation period, I could have corrected my watch according to your timepiece by simple arithmetic."

He tapped the chrono on his wrist. "I think a momentary surge of magnetism must have affected it," he went on. "It's antimagnetic, to be sure, but a disintegrating nuclear field can produce overwhelming forces. I suppose I'm lucky to be alive at all. Well, I know from the data book how long from sunrise to sunrise, so theoretically I could use that fact to tell me how fast or slow my watch is. But in practice, the clouds complicate observation too much for anything like accuracy; and *I* haven't got a hundred years in which to accumulate enough data for analysis."

Ardabadur wagged his tail knowingly, as if he understood English.

"Of course, time is of no obvious importance to you on shipboard," said Mudge. "Since you can't make astronomical sightings, and you don't even know astronomical phenomena exist, you cannot have invented navigation. You possess an inaccurate little hourglass to tell you when to change watch, and that's all."

He smiled, a weary lopsided grimace. "Well, I've gotten around the handicap," he said. "This makes my one-thousandth observation of time to roll down the plane. After calculation, I should be able to work out a very good correction factor for my watch." He patted the bulge in one hip pocket. "Do you know, my friend, I owe my life to whoever invented waterproof paper. Without it, the data book would be unreadable. It was a wet journey to this island. And this book compiles—not only the physical and mathematical constants needed anywhere in the universe—but all the information so far gathered about Epstein's Planet. Its mass, dimensions, orbital elements, rotational period, axial inclination, surface gravity, atmospheric composition, everything—or almost everything. Unfortunately, such quantities as magnetic deviation have hardly been mapped at all: otherwise I might try using that to locate us. The book does include tide tables, though, not only for Lonesome Landing but for several other selected spots, at which temperature, pelagic salinity, and whatever else occurred to the expeditions, have been measured."

He turned toward the exit. "But I am sure you came to show me something," he said. "Forgive me. I talk too much. However, it has been a very trying week on this island. I am used to talking, the feast of reason and the flow of soul and so on. My mother has always moved in intellectual circles. And then, I am a teacher by profession: basic science in the elementary grades."

Ardabadur led the way over the beach. Didymus Mudge continued to chatter. Perhaps he wanted to drown out the surf. Now, with the incoming solar tide, it had grown loud, an undergroundish sinister noise to his landlubber ears. Overhead scudded smoky rainclouds, and lightning flickered, high up in the permanent gray layers. The jungle talked in the wind with a million blue tongues.

"My mother was very dubious about my coming to Epstein's Planet," he said. "I had never been farther than Luna before, and then I had letters of recommendation to people she knows. On the other hand, it was an undeniable opportunity. The scientific and cultural staff here is already of respectable size, and is due for great expansion in the near future, when intensive work begins. The tendency is for married couples to be employed, and they have children, and the children need education. On a four-year contract, I could not only save a very good salary, but make valuable friendships among highly intellectual people. If only my mother could have come too, I would never have hesitated. But no opening was available for her. She finally agreed that I had a duty to my career."

Mudge looked around. He saw nothing but drifting sand, tents that snapped in the wind, waves and the alien ship. He leaned close to Ardabadur and hissed: "Frankly, and don't tell anyone, I thought it was high time I went somewhere by myself. I am thirty years old. After all!"

Then, blushing and stammering, he hurried on: "Miss . . . er . . . Major Orumastat isn't an instructor. Not of children, I mean. She was to organize defensive squads for the exploration teams, in case they meet hostility. Not that we would dream of provoking any such demonstration, I assure you. But—"

But by that time they had reached the Foucault bob, where a dozen sailors waited for orders. Ardabadur beamed like a picket fence and waved a hand at his creation.

Mudge examined it with care. It was as he had drawn, a hollow copper ball some one hundred and fifty centimeters across. When filled with sand, its mass would be enormous. A small loop and a very light stiff wire were affixed to the bottom. On top was a larger loop, riveted to ten meters of wire rope. As far as Mudge could see, it had been made with perfect symmetry and should give no trouble.

He said aloud: "We shall have to wait for calm weather. The wind would cause the pendulum to describe an ellipse today. But according to the data book, this region at this time of year is usually calm, so we can doubtless perform the experiment tomorrow. Let us set it all up now."

Ardabadur got his drift and barked orders. His assistants sprang to work. The sphere lay under a tall tree on the beach's edge which had been stripped of branches. A stout gallowslike crosspiece had been erected on the trunk, thirteen meters above ground. Now a pair of sailors swarmed up and affixed the loose end of the cable, so that the copper ball hung suspended. It swayed and toned in the wind. Mudge was gratified to note that it had little tendency to move in arcs; Ardabadur's suspension was well designed.

"Why are you helping me?" he mused aloud. "You have certainly spared no pains on my behalf, though you can have no idea why I want all this work done. Is it curiosity? Or boredom? For this has been a long dull time for you to lie anchored—I suppose on our account, until your captain knows more about us. I prefer to think you feel a genuine friendship and wish to assist a being in distress. Your officers seem to be perfect brutes, but all you common crewpeople are very quiet and well-behaved. I am sure you are capable of empathy."

"*Uru's kalka kisir*," said the Epsteinian.

"Oh," said Mudge.

Hanging the pendulum took at least an hour. At the end, though, he had it well adjusted. As the bob passed the lowest point of its arc, the cat's-whisker wire on the bottom traced a thin line in sand which had been smoothed, leveled, and wet down. Now Mudge led the sailors away; they raised the ball again and carried it to another preselected tree. Here the human mounted a ladder, knotted a piece of light rope to the bottom loop, and tied the other end to the bole. The sphere hung four meters above ground, its cable nearly taut, ready to swing when released.

"Now we fill the globe with sand to make it heavier and thus more stable," said Mudge, "and then I believe we can, er, call it a day."

He demonstrated. The sailors formed a bucket brigade up the ladder and began loading the ball. They had almost completed that task when Ulrica Ormstad appeared.

Behind her trailed Captain Zalakun and a bemedaled, beswreded, bemonocled Epsteinian whom Mudge had not seen before. Ardabadur whistled and fell on his face. The sailors tumbled from the ladder and followed suit. Mudge gaped.

"Good heavens," he said.

"This is Feridur of Beradura," explained the girl. "He owns this expedition. I mean that almost literally."

Her face was tight and anxious. Though the wind blew cool, there was sweat on her wide brow, and an uncharacteristic lock of hair had broken loose to stream over one ear.

"Mudge," she said, "we are in trouble."

"I know," he agreed.

Her temper ripped across. "Don't get sarcastic with me, you little worm!" she yelled.

"But I wasn't . . . I didn't—" Mudge swallowed. Ulrica was a beautiful sight, he thought. So, however, was a hungry tiger.

He had had no experience with the modern frontier type of woman. His mother disapproved of them. In his inmost soul he admitted hoping he would meet a young lady on this planet, where no one would jealously interfere, who could become Mrs. Mudge. But someone well-bred and well-read, with civilized ways, please!

"What have you been doing, anyhow?" snapped Ulrica.

"I told you," said Mudge, after husking once or twice. "I have been correcting my watch. I have a correction factor now, or will as soon as I make the calculations from my data, and then we will know exact Greenwich time." He paused. "I admit that is making no allowance for relativistic laws . . . simultaneity is an approximational concept at best . . . but this is a refinement which the data book does not take into account either. So—"

"Shut your big mouth before I reach in and pull you inside out!" screamed Ulrica.

Mudge cowered.

Ulrica expressed herself richly for several seconds. Mudge would have covered his ears, but was too stunned. He had never heard most of those words. The context, though, made their meaning all too hideously evident. Good heavens! Cultivated society, conversing at tea time in Boston, seemed five hundred light-years away.

He remembered with a shock that it *was* five hundred light-years away.

A part of him gibbered that the spaceship had headed into Virgo, and surely people would not make remarks like this in the region of Virgo.

Reason came back to him as Ulrica ran down. She put arms akimbo and said grimly: "All right. Why do you want to know Greenwich Market Time? To say your evening prayers?"

"No," gulped Mudge. "To locate us. I mean, we have to know where we are, don't we? the data book says Lonesome Landing is at 47° 32′ 4″ N., and the prime meridian has been drawn through it. But we know only that we are somewhere west of there, how far we cannot tell, and have no idea if we are north or south of it. I mean—"

"You mean," growled Ulrica, "that you have read chronometric time is necessary for navigation. So you set blindly out to find the time. You gruntbrain! Don't you know longitude reckoning depends on the *comparison* of times? How can we get local noon when we can't see the sun? How can we get the height of anything, for latitude?"

She gave the copper ball a green glare. "And what, with your kind permission, is that?"

"A . . . a Foucault pendulum," said Mudge. He squared thin shoulders. "It is a classic demonstration of the fact that a planet rotates. A pendulum will hold to its own vibrational plane—in effect, the planet turns beneath it—so that cat whisker will describe a line which gradually turns through a complete circle."

Ulrica stood speechless.

"This project has a secondary value," continued Mudge with a bit more self-confidence, "in that I am sure these Epsteinians imagine their world to be flat and fixed in space. The pendulum offers a simple proof of its rotation. Therefore they will be more inclined to accept on faith our assertion that the planet is a spheroid, and this in turn will lead them to follow our advice when—"

"Great," said Ulrica. "Leaping. Blue. Balls. Of. Radioactive. Muck."

Then the blast came. Mudge huddled away from it. The girl raged over his head, like the remote lightning come down to earth.

"For your blank blank information, Mister Didymus Blank Blank Mudge, I have just been talking to the captain and Feridur. They don't know which dash deleted asterisk way to steer for the obscenity station. How could they? Without a reasonably accurate vector—distance within a few hundred kilometers, direction within a compass point or less—they could search the double dash four star exclamation point ocean for an anathematized year without coming near Lonesome Blank Blank Landing. And of course they won't even attempt it. If they cruised obscenely around in any kind of crudely expressed search pattern, they'd lose their own unprintable way and risk never finding land again. If we don't give them a deep blue bearing and a sulfurous distance estimate, they're going to up anchor and head for accursed home tomorrow. AND YOU WANT TO GIVE A LECTURE ON COPERNICAN ASTRONOMY!"

Wherever You Are 141

"Oooh," moaned Ardabadur, trembling.

Exactly, thought Mudge, also trembling.

He opened his mouth, but nothing came out. At that moment, Feridur twittered. Ulrica stopped in mid-career and faced around. Feridur put the monocle in his eye and repeated the question. Captain Zalakun said something in a protesting tone of voice. Feridur made a sweet reply at which the captain shuddered and backed away. Ulrica turned quite pale.

Mudge listened intently. He heard Feridur ask, with painful distinctness: *"Uluka's kuruta yaldazir itoban urnalik?"*

"Yalgesh, Zirvan," said Ulrica, in a small subdued voice and a Swedish accent. *"Obunadun haladur erkedivir."*

The saw-toothed blade rasped from Feridur's sheath. He giggled. *"Yagatun!"*

Ulrica clenched her fists. Then, suddenly, she spat at the Harakuni's feet. The color flamed back in her cheeks. *"Yagatun zoltada, Yaldazir Feridur!"* she snapped.

"Eep!" said Feridur, horrified at such manners. Captain Zalakun sought to remedy the breach, but got nowhere. The sailors burrowed in the sand, trying to make themselves inconspicuous. Finally Zalakun himself went off in giant kangaroo leaps toward the tents.

"What is this?" whispered Mudge.

Ulrica said in a harsh tone: "Feridur wanted to know if you can locate the Earth base, since I can't. When I admitted you had only been playing games, he said he would fight me. I have explained that the vitamin pills are necessary for our life, so he knows we would soon die in any case when he turns homeward. He wants to take my skull in combat instead, for his collection."

"What?" squeaked Mudge. The island revolved around him. He stumbled, feeling blackness in his head. Ulrica caught him.

"Don't be afraid," she said in the same metallic voice. "You are not worth fighting—no glory in taking your head. They will keep you for a pet, I suppose . . . and you will have my pills . . . and it is barely possible, in that extra time a search party will chance upon you."

"But this is ghastly!" stammered Mudge. "I mean, it isn't done!"

"It seems to be." Ulrica managed a bleak grin. "Maybe I can take Feridur's head. Then I inherit his titles, properties, and skull collection, and can sail the ship where I will. Not that we have much chance anyway, without a bearing." She sighed. "This may be the better way to die."

"But listen—" wailed Mudge.

Zalakun returned with a sword, shouldered past him and said something to the girl. She nodded. Mudge tried to get a word in edgewise. "Shut up," said Ulrica. Zalakun finished by handing her the weapon.

"In case you are interested," said Ulrica, "he was explaining the rules. In effect, there aren't any. Either party can use tricks, assistants—"

Zalakun flickered a glance at Feridur, who was polishing his monocle several meters off. The captain leaned over and whispered something to the girl. She smiled a suddenly gentle smile and gave his scaly back a furtive pat.

"What is it?" gibbered Mudge. "What did he say?"

"He said no one will help Feridur," she answered curtly. "They don't like him. Of course, they are too afraid of him to take my side either. He's the leading phrenologist in Harakun."

"But . . . I can . . . I mean, that is, I have to tell you—"

"Oh, be quiet," she said. "What use would you be? Stand aside out of my way, that is all you can do."

"But you don't have to fight this barbaric thing!" yelped Mudge. "It isn't necessary! If you would only listen to me for five minutes, I can explain—"

Wherever You Are 143

"Shut up," she cut him off. He tried to continue. She whirred her blade past his nose. He jumped backward, choking. She laughed with a real, if deplorably coarse mirth, and said more kindly: "It is too late anyhow. I insulted him on purpose. Whatever I said now, he would insist on disposing of me."

Zalakun wrung her hand and scuttled off to the sidelines as Feridur turned around. The aristocrat screwed his eyeglass in more firmly, hefted his sword, and minced across the sand. Ulrica crouched, waiting. The wind fluttered her kilt and the one loose lock of hair.

Mudge put his back against the tree bole and tried to think. But that was like trying to run through glue. This was the U.S.P. Standard adventure-story situation, a beautiful girl threatened by a bulging-eyed monster, and he was a man, and it was up to him to save her, but—Feridur's blade whipped up and then down. It hit Ulrica's with a clang that hurt Mudge's eardrums. The blow would have gone halfway through him.

He huddled next to the comforting bulk of good old Ardabadur, and prayed that the beautiful girl would save him from the bug-eyed monster.

"*Yava's!*" cried Feridur.

He bounced back from Ulrica's attack. She knew fencing, but had no skill with these awkward weapons. She closed in, though, a rush and a sweep. Somehow it got past Feridur's guard, and steel teeth rattled across his scales. They did no harm. His own blade moved with a combination of thrust and stroke. Ulrica retreated, fending him off by mere fury of blows. He grinned and stalked around her, so that she must keep turning to face him. His reach was not much greater than hers, but he had every advantage of height, stride, and strength.

All at once, like a snake, his weapon darted in, slid past

Ulrica's and touched her thigh. She got away in time, with only a thin red slash, but Mudge felt sick. "Son of an improper union," she muttered, and cut loose again. "You want to saw me up alive, huh? We'll see!"

She leaped in, hewing low. Feridur hissed as she opened a gash on his left shin. Her metal was already up to block his answering cut. He brought his edge down, chopping at her ankles. She jumped high, the sword whined beneath her feet, she came down on it and it was torn from Feridur's grasp.

"Now, you miserable alligator!" she exclaimed, and assaulted his head. A small sailor emitted a very small cheer, then covered his mouth and looked around in terror of having been overheard.

Feridur whirled about, raised his tail, and struck Ulrica amidships. The wind whoofed from her. She rolled three meters and climbed dizzily to her feet. Feridur picked up his sword and advanced with deliberation. The watching sauroids looked distressed, Captain Zalakun twisted his hands together, but all seemed nailed to the spot.

"Look out!" screamed Mudge. Impulsively, he darted forward.

Ulrica waved him back. She still clutched her sword. The free hand dabbed at a bruised cheek. "No," she said. "One is enough."

"But you are a woman!" he cried. "Give me that! I'll fight for you!"

She managed a ghost of a laugh. "Dear little Didymus," she whispered. "I am an Ormstad of Clan Swenson. Get out of my way."

Feridur closed in for the kill as Mudge staggered back to Ardabadur's side. The Harakuni noble paused to readjust his monocle. He tittered.

Then Ulrica exploded into motion. Her sword became a

blur, yelled in the air, banged on Feridur's iron, knocked down his guard and slashed him across the shoulder. He hissed and jumped back. Ulrica followed, shouting.

She's splendid! thought Mudge wildly. *They don't make girls like that in Boston!* He blushed and corrected himself: *I mean, there aren't any girls like that in Boston.*

Feridur rallied and beat off the attack. Ulrica retreated. Through wind and surf, above the steady belling of steel, Mudge could hear how she clawed for breath. And once she stumbled from exhaustion. Feridur would kill her in minutes.

"I should go out and die with her." Mudge licked dry lips. "Really, I should, if I can't do anything else. I feel so useless."

"*Akrazun kulakisir,*" said Ardabadur comfortingly.

"It wouldn't be against the rules," chattered Mudge. "She told me anything goes. I could help. Only . . . only . . . to be absolutely honest, as my mother always told me to be, I'm scared."

Feridur drew blood again: a flesh wound, no more, but Ulrica's sword was now slow and heavy in her fingers.

"Of course, later I can explain, and maybe they will take me to Lonesome Landing after all," babbled Mudge. "But no, I haven't her training, I could not possibly learn the language before my vitamins ran out. I am done for, too. You had all this work for nothing, Ardabadur. Now you will never know why you made—"

The thought came to him. It was not exactly a blinding flash of intuition. Or perhaps it was. He didn't notice. By the time he was fully conscious of having an idea, it was already in execution.

"Ulrica!" he shouted. "Miss Ormstad! *Major* Ormstad! Get him . . . maneuver him onto . . . that cleared, wet space in the sand . . . under that tree . . . keep him there . . . and look out!"

Meanwhile he snatched a knife from Ardabadur's belt and went up the ladder. The carpenter whistled alarm and started after him. Frantically, Mudge kicked him on the crest, while sawing at the cord and yelling at Ulrica.

"Miss Ormstad! Work him onto that level damp patch! Quickly! Hold him . . . just a minute . . . please! I beg of you!"

Ulrica, fighting for another second of existence, heard his thin screech and croaked out of pain and despair: "Let me die by myself, Earthling."

Somehow, without planning to, scarcely aware of it, Didymus Mudge inflated his lungs and roared in a heroic tenor, so that even Zalakun jumped: *"Profanity dash blasphemy blue and green, green starred et cetera! Do what I blank unprintable tell you before I commit unspeakable violence upon your defamity person!"*

Whether the memory of drill sergeants ten years ago came back and possessed her, or whether she was suddenly given hope—or for whatever reason—Ulrica sprang away from Feridur and ran. He bounded after, jeering at her. Ulrica crossed the wet sand, twirled about, and met his charge. Saw teeth locked together as the blades met. Feridur began to shove hers aside. She threw her last strength into resisting him, though she felt it drain from muscle and bone.

Didymus Mudge cut the cord on his Foucault sphere.

Loaded with hundreds of kilos of sand, it swung across the beach, gathering velocity all the way. Mudge fell off the ladder, onto Ardabadur. They went down in a tangle of arms, legs, and tail. By the time he had picked himself up, it was all over, and the Harakuni were howling as one jubilant mob around Ulrica.

Mudge limped toward her. He wanted to see, if he could, how much of an arc his pendulum was describing. Yes . . . there was definitely an elliptical path, but a narrow one. That tendency should be quite obviated when he made the official experiment tomorrow. He would burn the rope then, rather than cut it, to liberate the bob without transverse forces . . . He ducked as it whistled past. So huge a thing had not lost much energy when it hit Feridur.

Mudge saw what had happened to Feridur. For a while he was not a well man.

Captain Zalakun released Ulrica's hand, which he had been pumping in a most Earthlike fashion, and regarded the mess. Finally he shook his head and clicked his tongue. "Dear me, *Zivar* Orumastat," he said. "You really must chastise your slave. No doubt he meant well, but he has completely ruined what would have been a very fine egg-shaped skull."

A while afterward, when they sat in the captain's cabin, eating the Epsteinian food—which humans found dreary—and drinking the Epsteinian wine—which was forty proof and not bad at all—Zalakun asked Ulrica: *"Arvadur zilka itoban urnalik?"*

The girl blinked beautiful, though slightly blurred, green eyes above her goblet, in Mudge's direction. "He wants to know if you can indeed navigate us, Didymus," she said.

Mudge blushed. "Well, not exactly," he admitted. "Until we reach base and get a radio network receiver, I mean. But then he will be able to navigate himself. Ahem!" He burped and reached for his own cup. "I can, however, tell him to a fair approximation how far away Lonesome Landing is, and in what direction. That should suffice, since he has good compasses and is independent of the wind. Rather, I will be able to tell him this tomorrow, when I have all the data and finish the calculations."

"But how?" She leaned forward. "How, Didymus?" she repeated softly.

"Well," he said after catching his breath, "the data book gives the location of base, so if I know our present coordinates, it becomes a simple problem in spherical trigonometry, for which the book supplies tables, to determine—"

"Yes, yes," she said in a slightly less worshipful tone. "But how do you locate us?"

"It is a problem of finding latitude and longitude," he said. He took another swig of wine. It buzzed in his head, but helped steady his voice. Once he got going, the lecture habits of a decade took over and he talked automatically. "Ahem! We had the data book and a watch, but the watch had been running awry since the moment of the crash, so that I no longer knew within several hours what time it was. Now if I could only observe something which took a precisely known time, such as ten seconds, I could compare the watch, see by what factor it was fast or slow, and apply the correction.

"I looked up the standard value of Epsteinian gravity, one thousand twelve centimeters per second squared. Local variations would not make any significant difference. A pendulum describing short arcs has a period which is a function only of length and gravity. The carpenter made me a good small pendulum and I clocked it."

"Yes, but," said Ulrica. She paused. "But," she repeated muzzily. Wine had hidden her own weariness from her, but it made the wine all the more effective. "But you don't know the length of the pendulum. Not with, *urp*, precision."

"No," said Mudge. "However, the distance covered by a

falling body is a function only of gravity and time. Air resistance can be disregarded for low speeds. I repeated Galileo's experiment, dropping a weight through a fixed height. Actually, I rolled it down an inclined plane—so did he—to get a greater length and thus a smaller percentage of error. Though I did not know the effective height in absolute units, I took care to see that it was an integral multiple of the pendulum length; and I measured the time for a ball to roll down in terms of pendulum oscillations. I therefore have two equations in two unknowns, easy to solve. When I have computed all my data, taking the average of many observations, I will know the length of the pendulum in centimeters and, what I really wanted, the length of its period in seconds. From this I can correct the time shown by my watch."

Ulrica smiled, stretched out on the floor and laid her head on Mudge's lap.

"Goodness gracious!" Mudge gasped. "What are you doing, Miss Ormstad?"

"You were speaking about falling bodies," she murmured.

"But . . . I mean . . . Major Ormstad!"

"Ulrica is my name," she whispered.

Zalakun's leathery face assumed an avuncular expression. He said something which Mudge was afraid meant, "Bless you, my children."

"Well," gulped Mudge. "Well, if you're tired, Miss . . . er . . . Major . . . I can find a pillow."

"I'm quite comfy," said the girl. She reached up and patted his cheek. "I'm sorry for losing my temper. I wouldn't have if I had known you better, Didymus. Know what? You're cute."

Mudge ran a finger beneath his collar and plunged terror-stricken onward: "Since this planet has only solar tides, I was spared one complication. To be sure, tidal patterns are not simple; but a wave crossing the almost empty Northeast Ocean will not be much delayed either. To further help me, the data book has tide tables not only for Lonesome Landing, but for selected spots elsewhere. This will assist interpolation. In short, when my watch has been corrected, I will be able to identify any local tide as one which passed Lonesome Landing so-and-so many hours ago. Knowing the speed at which it travels, I thereby know how far westward it has come in that interval—hence, our longitude."

Ulrica frowned, with a finger laid to her chin. "No," she said, " 'cute' is the wrong word. I mean, you are cute, but you are also very much of a manfolk. When you shouted at me to do what you wanted, it was poetic. Like a saga."

"I forgot myself," said Mudge wretchedly.

"I'll help you forget some more," beamed Ulrica.

"*Ugvan urunta,*" said Zalakun.

Mudge interpreted this as a request to continue his discourse. "Latitude is a simpler problem, solvable with greater accuracy," he said very fast. "I know the angular velocity of this planet's rotation, three hundred sixty degrees in forty-six hours. Knowing the date, I could calculate latitude from length of daylight, except for the clouds. A Foucault pendulum affords a much better method. It would not turn at all at the equator; it would turn with maximum speed at either pole; in between, the rate is a sine function of latitude. I can use geometrical constructions to mark off a precise angle such as ninety degrees, clock the time the pendulum needs to sweep through this angle, and thence compute our latitude. And, and, and that's all," he finished. "I should have the information for you by nightfall tomorrow, and we can start out next day. To be sure, accumulated uncertainties will doubtless cause us to miss the island, but not by much. We can find it in time if we scout about. Though I suppose we need only come within a few hundred kilometers to be spotted by an aircraft—"

Ulrica chuckled. "And so we will arrive as great heroes," she said, "very romantic, and perhaps we had better not disappoint people about the romantic side of it, no? *Käre lille* Didymus. This is going to be so pleasant a sea voyage."

Mudge swallowed hard and wondered how to escape.

"*Istvaz tuli,*" said Zalakun with a fatuous smirk.

Mudge threw him a look of wild appeal, as if somehow the bug-eyed monster could save the man from the girl.

"Nature is strange," the narrator of this chilling little tale tells us. "There are all sorts of things that look like dangerous animals. Animals that are the killers and superior fighters of their groups have no enemies. The army ants and the wasps, the sharks, the hawk, and the felines. So there are a host of weak things that try to hide among them—to mimic them. And man is the greatest killer, the greatest hunter of them all. . . . Should man then be treated by nature differently from the other dominants, the army ants and the wasps?"

Donald A. Wollheim, publisher and editor-in-chief of DAW Books, a major science-fiction paperback imprint, is probably one of the five most influential figures in the history of modern science fiction. As writer, editor, and publisher, Wollheim (b. 1914) has shaped the course of the field significantly: he edited the first s-f anthology, *The Pocket Book of Science Fiction,* in 1943; during his tenure as editor and then editor-in-chief at Ace Books in the 1950s, 1960s, and early 1970s he published virtually every major s-f writer and discovered almost half of them; and he has published fifteen novels, one scholarly nonfiction study of the field, *The Universe Makers (1970),* and at least eighty short stories, of which "Mimic" is one of the very best.

Mimic
Donald A. Wollheim

It is less than five hundred years since an entire half of the world was discovered. It is less than two hundred years since the discovery of the last continent. The sciences of chemistry and physics go back scarcely one century. The science of aviation goes back forty years. The science of atomics is being born.

And yet we think we know a lot.

We know little or nothing. Some of the most startling

things are unknown to us. When they are discovered, they may shock us to the bone.

We search for secrets in the far islands of the Pacific and among the ice fields of the frozen North, while under our very noses, rubbing shoulders with us every day, there may walk the undiscovered. It is a curious fact of nature that that which is in plain view is oft best hidden.

I have always known of the man in the black cloak. Since I was a child he has always lived on my street, and his eccentricities are so familiar that they go unmentioned except among the casual visitor. Here, in the heart of the largest city in the world, in swarming New York, the eccentric and the odd may flourish unhindered.

As children we had hilarious fun jeering at the man in black when he displayed his fear of women. We watched, in our evil, childish way, for those moments, we tried to get him to show anger. But he ignored us completely and soon we paid him no further heed, even as our parents did.

We saw him only twice a day. Once in the early morning, when we would see his six-foot figure come out of the grimy dark hallway of the tenement at the end of the street and stride down toward the elevated to work—again when he came back at night. He was always dressed in a long, black cloak that came to his ankles, and he wore a wide-brimmed black hat down far over his face. He was a sight from some weird story out of the old lands. But he harmed nobody, and paid attention to nobody.

Nobody—except perhaps women.

When a woman crossed his path, he would stop in his stride and come to a dead halt. We could see that he closed his eyes until she had passed. Then he would snap those wide, watery blue eyes open and march on as if nothing had happened.

Mimic 155

He was never known to speak to a woman. He would buy some groceries, maybe once a week, at Antonio's—but only when there were no other patrons there. Antonio said once that he never talked, he just pointed at things he wanted and paid for them in bills that he pulled out of a pocket somewhere under his cloak. Antonio did not like him, but he never had any trouble from him either.

Now that I think of it, nobody ever did have any trouble with him.

We got used to him. We grew up on the street; we saw him occasionally when he came home and went back into the dark hallway of the house he lived in.

He never had visitors, he never spoke to anyone. And he had once built something in his room out of metal.

He had once, years ago, hauled up some long flat metal sheets, sheets of tin or iron, and they had heard a lot of hammering and banging in his room for several days. But that had stopped and that was all there was to that story.

Where he worked I don't know and never found out. He had money, for he was reputed to pay his rent regularly when the janitor asked for it.

Well, people like that inhabit big cities and nobody knows the story of their lives until they're all over. Or until something strange happens.

I grew up, I went to college, I studied.

Finally I got a job assisting a museum curator. I spent my days mounting beetles and classifying exhibits of stuffed animals and preserved plants, and hundreds and hundreds of insects from all over.

Nature is a strange thing, I learned. You learn that very clearly when you work in a museum. You realize how nature uses the art of camouflage. There are twig insects that look exactly like a leaf or a branch of a tree. Exactly.

Nature is strange and perfect that way. There is a moth

in Central America that looks like a wasp. It even has a fake stinger made of hair, which it twists and curls just like a wasp's stinger. It has the same colorings and, even though its body is soft and not armored like a wasp's, it is colored to appear shiny and armored. It even flies in the daytime when wasps do, and not at night like all other moths. It moves like a wasp. It knows somehow that it is helpless and that it can survive only by pretending to be as deadly to other insects as wasps are.

I learned about army ants, and their strange imitators.

Army ants travel in huge columns of thousands and hundreds of thousands. They move along in a flowing stream several yards across and they eat everything in their path. Everything in the jungle is afraid of them. Wasps, bees, snakes, other ants, birds, lizards, beetles—even men run away, or get eaten.

But in the midst of the army ants there also travel many other creatures—creatures that aren't ants at all, and that the army ants would kill if they knew of them. But they don't know of them because these other creatures are disguised. Some of them are beetles that look like ants. They have false markings like ant thoraxes and they run along in imitation of ant speed. There is even one that is so long it is marked like three ants in single file! It moves so fast that the real ants never give it a second glance.

There are weak caterpillars that look like big armored beetles. There are all sorts of things that look like dangerous animals. Animals that are the killers and superior fighters of their groups have no enemies. The army ants and the wasps, the sharks, the hawk, and the felines. So there are a host of weak things that try to hide among them—to mimic them.

And man is the greatest killer, the greatest hunter of them all. The whole world of nature knows man for the irresistible master. The roar of his gun, the cunning of his trap, the strength and agility of his arm place all else beneath him.

Should man then be treated by nature differently from the other dominants, the army ants and the wasps?

It was, as often happens to be the case, sheer luck that I happened to be on the street at the dawning hour when the janitor came running out of the tenement on my street shouting for help. I had been working all night mounting new exhibits.

The policeman on the beat and I were the only people besides the janitor to see the thing that we found in the two dingy rooms occupied by the stranger of the black cloak.

The janitor explained—as the officer and I dashed up the narrow, rickety stairs—that he had been awakened by the sound of heavy thuds and shrill screams in the stranger's rooms. He had gone out in the hallway to listen.

When we got there, the place was silent. A faint light shone from under the doorway. The policeman knocked, there was no answer. He put his ear to the door and so did I. We heard a faint rustling—a continuous slow rustling as of a breeze blowing paper.

The cop knocked again, but there was still no response.

Then, together, we threw our weight at the door. Two hard blows and the rotten old lock gave way. We burst in.

The room was filthy, the floor covered with scraps of torn paper, bits of detritus and garbage. The room was unfurnished, which I thought was odd.

In the corner there stood a metal box, about four feet square. A tight-box, held together with screws and ropes. It had a lid, opening at the top, which was down and fastened with a sort of wax seal.

The stranger of the black cloak lay in the middle of the floor—dead.

He was still wearing the cloak. The big slouch hat was lying on the floor some distance away. From the inside of the box the faint rustling was coming.

We turned over the stranger, took the cloak off. For several instants we saw nothing amiss and then gradually—horribly—we became aware of some things that were wrong.

His hair was short and curly brown. It stood straight up in its inch-long length. His eyes were open and staring. I noticed first that he had no eyebrows, only a curious dark line in the flesh over each eye.

It was then I realized he had no nose. But no one had ever noticed that before. His skin was oddly mottled. Where the nose should have been there were dark shadowings that made the appearance of a nose, if you only just glanced at him. Like the work of a skillful artist in a painting.

His mouth was as it should be and slightly open—but he had no teeth. His head perched upon a thin neck.

The suit was—not a suit. It was part of him. It was his body.

What we thought was a coat was a huge black wing sheath, like a beetle has. He had a thorax like an insect, only the wing sheath covered it and you couldn't notice it when he wore the cloak. The body bulged out below, tapering off into the two long, thin hind legs. His arms came out from under the top of the "coat." He had a tiny secondary pair of arms folded tightly across his chest. There was a sharp, round hole newly pierced in his chest just above the arms, still oozing a watery liquid.

The janitor fled gibbering. The officer was pale but standing by his duty. I heard him muttering under his breath an endless stream of Hail Marys over and over again.

The lower thorax—the "abdomen"—was very long and insectlike. It was crumpled up now like the wreckage of an airplane fuselage.

I recalled the appearance of a female wasp that had just laid eggs—her thorax had had that empty appearance.

The sight was a shock such as leaves one in full control. The mind rejects it, and it is only in afterthought that one can feel the dim shudder of horror.

The rustling was still coming from the box. I motioned to the white-faced cop and we went over and stood before it. He took the nightstick and knocked away the waxen seal.

Then we heaved and pulled the lid open.

A wave of noxious vapor assailed us. We staggered back as suddenly a stream of flying things shot out of the huge iron container. The window was open, and straight out into the first glow of dawn they flew.

There must have been dozens of them. They were about two or three inches long and they flew on wide gauzy beetle wings. They looked like little men, strangely terrifying as they flew—clad in their black suits, with their expressionless faces and their dots of watery blue eyes. And they flew out on transparent wings that came from under their black beetle coats.

I ran to the window, fascinated, almost hypnotized. The horror of it had not reached my mind at once. Afterward I have had spasms of numbing terror as my mind tries to put the things together. The whole business was so utterly unexpected.

We knew of army ants and their imitators, yet it never occurred to us that we too were army ants of a sort. We knew of stick insects and it never occurred to us that there might be others that disguise themselves to fool, not other animals, but the supreme animal himself—man.

We found some bones in the bottom of that iron case afterwards. But we couldn't identify them. Perhaps we did not try very hard. They might have been human. . . .

I suppose the stranger of the black cloak did not fear women so much as it distrusted them. Women notice men, perhaps, more closely than other men do. Women might become suspicious sooner of the inhumanity, the deception. And then there might perhaps have been some touch of instinctive feminine jealousy. The stranger was disguised as a man, but its sex was surely female. The things in the box were its young.

But it is the other thing I saw when I ran to the window that has shaken me the most. The policeman did not see it. Nobody else saw it but me, and I only for an instant.

Nature practices deceptions in every angle. Evolution will create a being for any niche that can be found, no matter how unlikely.

When I went to the window, I saw the small cloud of flying things rising up into the sky and sailing away into the purple distance. The dawn was breaking and the first rays of the sun were just striking over the housetops.

Shaken, I looked away from that fourth-floor tenement room over the roofs of lower buildings. Chimneys and walls and empty clotheslines made the scenery over which the tiny mass of horror passed.

And then I saw a chimney, not thirty feet away on the next roof. It was squat and of red brick and had two black pipe ends flush with its top. I saw it suddenly vibrate, oddly. And I saw its red brick surface seem to peel away, and the black pipe openings turn suddenly white.

I saw two big eyes staring into the sky.

A great, flat-winged thing detached itself silently from the surface of the real chimney and darted after the cloud of flying things.

I watched until all had lost themselves in the sky.

"The Faceless Thing" in this story is a home-grown BEM; i.e., a terrestrial rather than extraterrestrial monster—a being formed of primordial ooze, an accident of nature at once terrifying and pathetic. And its story, along with that of the old man once known as Buddy, is poignant and quite different from the usual.

Edward D. Hoch (b. 1930) is a rara avis *among contemporary professional writers: he makes his living almost entirely from short stories. He has published over 500 in the past twenty-five years, most of them mystery and detective tales, with twoscore or so in the science-fiction/fantasy field; his stories have appeared in well over 100 anthologies and have been translated into many languages. (One, "The Oblong Room," was awarded an Edgar by the Mystery Writers of America as the best mystery short of 1968.) In addition to writing short fiction, he edits the annual* Best Detective Stories of the Year *and is a recognized authority on the brief-and-criminous. Three of his four novels (all published between 1969 and 1975) are science-fiction mysteries:* The Transvection Machine, The Fellowship of the Hand, *and* The Frankenstein Factory.

The Faceless Thing

Edward D. Hoch

Sunset: golden flaming clouds draped over distant canyons barely seen in the dusk of the dying day; farmland gone to rot; fields in the foreground given over wildly to the running of the rabbit and the woodchuck; the farmhouse gray and paint-peeled, sleeping possibly but more likely dead—needing burial.

It hadn't changed much in all those years. It hadn't changed; only died.

He parked the car and got out, taking it all in with eyes

still intent and quick for all their years. Somehow he hadn't really thought it would still be standing. Farmhouses that were near collapse fifty years ago shouldn't still be standing; not when all the people, his mother and father and aunt and the rest, were all long in their graves.

He was an old man, had been an old man almost as long as he could remember. Youth to him was only memories of this farm, so many years before, romping in the hay with his little sister at his side; swinging from the barn ropes, exploring endless dark depths out beyond the last field. After that, he was old—through misty college days and marriage to a woman he hadn't loved, through a business and political career that carried him around the world. And never once in all those years had he journeyed back to this place, this farmhouse now given over to the weeds and insects. They were all dead; there was no reason to come back . . . no reason at all.

Except the memory of the ooze.

A childhood memory, a memory buried with the years, forgotten sometimes but always there, crowded into its own little space in his mind, was ready to confront him and startled him with its vividness.

The ooze was a place beyond the last field, where water always collected in the springtime and after a storm; water running over dirt and clay and rock, merging with the soil until there was nothing underfoot but a black ooze to rise above your boots. He'd followed the stream rushing with storm water, followed it to the place where it cut into the side of the hill.

It was the memory of the tunnel, really, that had brought him back—the dark tunnel leading nowhere, gurgling with rain-fed water, barely large enough for him to fit through. A tunnel floored with unseen ooze, peopled by unknown danger; that was a place for every boy.

Had he been only ten that day? Certainly he'd been no

more than eleven, leading the way while his nine-year-old sister followed. "This way. Be careful of the mud." She'd been afraid of the dark, afraid of what they might find there. But he'd called encouragement to her; after all, what could there be in all this ooze to hurt them?

How many years? Fifty?

"What *is* it, Buddy?" She'd always called him Buddy. What is it, Buddy? Only darkness, and a place maybe darker than dark, with a half-formed shadow rising from the ooze. He'd brought along his father's old lantern, and he fumbled to light it.

"Buddy!" she'd screamed—just once—and in the flare of the match he'd seen the thing, great and hairy and covered with ooze; something that lived in the darkness here, something that hated the light. In that terrifying instant it had reached out for his little sister and pulled her into the ooze.

That was the memory, a memory that came to him sometimes only at night. It had pursued him down the years like a fabled hound, coming to him, reminding him, when all was well with the world. It was like a personal demon sent from Hades to torture him. He'd never told anyone about that thing in the ooze, not even his mother. They'd cried and carried on when his sister was found the next day, and they'd said she'd drowned. He was not one to say differently.

And the years had passed. For a time, during his high school days, he read the local papers—searching for some word of the thing, some veiled news that it had come out of that forgotten cavern. But it never did; it liked the dark and damp too much. And, of course, no one else ever ventured into the stream bed. That was a pursuit only for the very young and very foolish.

By the time he was twenty, the memory was fading,

merging with other thoughts, other goals, until at times he thought it only a child's dream. But then at night it would come again in all its vividness, and the thing in the ooze would beckon him.

A long life, long and crowded . . . One night he'd tried to tell his wife about it, but she wouldn't listen. That was the night he'd realized how little he'd ever loved her. Perhaps he'd only married her because, in a certain light, she reminded him of that sister of his youth. But the love that sometimes comes later came not at all to the two of them. She was gone now, like his youth, like his family and friends. There was only this memory remaining. The memory of a thing in the ooze.

Now the weeds were tall, beating against his legs, stirring nameless insects to flight with every step. He pressed a handkerchief against his brow, sponging the sweat that was forming there. Would the dark place still be there, or had fifty years of rain and dirt sealed it forever?

"Hello there," a voice called out. It was an old voice, barely carrying with the breeze. He turned and saw someone on the porch of the deserted farmhouse. An old woman, ancient and wrinkled.

"Do I know you?" he asked, moving closer.

"You may," she answered. "You're Buddy, aren't you? My, how old I've gotten. I used to live at the next farm, when you were just a boy. I was young then myself. I remember you."

"Oh! Mrs. . . . ?" The name escaped him, but it wasn't important.

"Why did you come back, Buddy? Why, after all these years?"

He was an old man. Was it necessary to explain his actions to this woman from the past? "I just wanted to see the place," he answered. "Memories, you know."

"Bitter memories. Your little sister died here, did she not?" The old woman should have been dead, should have been dead and in her grave long ago.

He paused in the shade of the porch roof. "She died here, yes, but that was fifty years ago."

"How old we grow, how ancient! Is that why you returned?"

"In a way. I wanted to see the spot."

"Ah! The little brook back there beyond the last field. Let me walk that way with you. These old legs need exercise."

"Do you live here?" he asked, wanting to escape her now but knowing not how.

"No, still down the road. All alone now. Are you all alone, too?"

"I suppose so." The high grass made walking difficult.

"You know what they all said at the time, don't you? They all said you were fooling around, like you always did, and pushed her into the water."

There was a pain in his chest from breathing so hard. He was an old man. "Do you believe that?"

"What does it matter?" she answered. "After all these fifty years, what does it matter?"

"Would you believe me," he began, then hesitated into silence. Of course she wouldn't believe him, but he had to tell now. "Would you believe me if I told you what happened?"

She was a very old woman and she panted to keep up even his slow pace. She was ancient even to his old eyes, even in his world where now everyone was old. "I would believe you," she said.

"There was something in the ooze. Call it a monster, a

demon, if you want. I saw it in the light of a match, and I can remember it as if it were yesterday. It took her."

"Perhaps," she said.

"You don't believe me."

"I said I would. This sun is hot today, even at twilight."

"It will be gone soon. I hate to hurry you, old woman, but I must reach the stream before dark."

"The last field is in sight."

Yes, it was in sight. But how would he ever fit through that small opening, how would he face the thing, even if by some miracle it still waited there in the ooze? Fifty years was a long long time.

"Wait here," he said as they reached the little stream at last. It hadn't changed much, not really.

"You won't find it." He lowered his aged body into the bed of the stream, feeling once again the familiar forgotten ooze closing over his shoes.

"No one has to know," she called after him. "Even if there was something, that was fifty years ago."

But he went on, to the place where the water vanished into the rock. He held his breath and groped for the little flashlight in his pocket. Then he ducked his head and followed the water into the black.

It was steamy here, steamy and hot with the sweat of the earth. He flipped on the flashlight with trembling hands and followed its narrow beam with his eyes. The place was almost like a room in the side of the hill, a room perhaps seven feet high, with a floor of mud and ooze that seemed almost to bubble as he watched.

"Come on," he said softly, almost to himself. "I know you're there. You've got to be there."

And then he saw it, rising slowly from the ooze. A shapeless thing without a face, a thing that moved so slowly it might have been dead. An old, very old thing. For a long time he watched it, unable to move, unable to cry out. And even as he watched, the thing settled back softly into the ooze, as if even this small exertion had tired it.

"Rest," he said, very quietly. "We are all so old now."

And then he made his way back out of the cave, along the stream, and finally pulled himself from the clinging ooze. The ancient woman was still waiting on the bank, with fireflies playing about her in the dusk.

"Did you find anything?" she asked him.

"Nothing," he answered.

"Fifty years is a long time. You shouldn't have come back."

He sighed and fell into step beside her. "It was something I had to do."

"Come up to my house, if you want. I can make you a bit of tea."

His breath was coming better now, and the distance back to the farmhouse seemed shorter than he'd remembered. "I think I'd like that," he said....

"The Rull" is pure 1940s space opera, but that is in no way meant to be a negative comment. Space opera at its best was exciting, suspenseful, and rich in imagery and invention—all of which qualities are abundant in this strong story of a one-on-one confrontation between an Earthman and a wormlike BEM, two opposing players in a thousand-year war for control of the galaxy.

A. E. Van Vogt (b. 1912) was one of the six major writers of John Campbell's 1940s Astounding *(the others being Robert Heinlein, Isaac Asimov, Lester del Rey, Theodore Sturgeon, and the interchangeable Henry Kuttner/C. L. Moore) who centered the so-called Golden Age of Science Fiction and helped pivot the field toward mass-audience respectability. His novels of the period, such as* Slan, The World of Null A, The Players of Null A, *and* The Weapon Shops of Isher, *remain in the contemporary repertory, as do several of his short stories. Between 1950 and 1965 he ceased for all intents and purposes to write fiction, but has subsequently returned with novels and occasional short-story appearances. The indescribable and awful alien was one of Van Vogt's obsessive themes of the forties and he does it characteristically well in "The Rull."*

The Rull

A. E. Van Vogt

Professor Jamieson saw the other space boat out of the corner of one eye. He was sitting in a hollow about a dozen yards from the edge of the precipice, and some score of feet from the doorway of his own lifeboat. He had been intent on his survey book, annotating a comment beside the voice graph to the effect that Laertes III was so close to the invisible dividing line between Earth-controlled and Rull-controlled space that its prior discovery by man was in itself a major victory in the Rull–human war.

It was at that point that he saw the other boat, above and somewhat to his left, approaching the tableland. He glanced up at it—and froze where he was, torn between two opposing purposes.

His first impulse, to run for the lifeboat, yielded to the realization that the movement would be seen instantly by the electronic reflexes of the other ship. For a moment, then, he had the dim hope that if he remained quiet enough, neither he nor his ship would be observed.

Even as he sat there, perspiring with indecision, his tensed eyes noted the Rull markings and the rakish design of the other vessel. His vast knowledge of things Rull enabled him to catalogue it instantly as a survey craft.

A *survey* craft. The Rulls had discovered the Laertes sun.

The terrible potentiality was that behind this small craft might be fleets of battleships, whereas he was alone. His own lifeboat had been dropped by the *Orion* nearly a parsec away while the big ship was proceeding at antigravity speeds. That was to insure that Rull energy traces did not record its passage through this area of space.

The *Orion* was to head for the nearest base, load up with planetary defense equipment, and return. She was due in ten days.

Ten days. Jamieson groaned inwardly, and drew his legs under him and clenched his survey book in the fingers of one hand. But still the possibility that his ship, partially hidden under a clump of trees, might escape notice if he remained quiet, held him there in the open. His head tilted up, his eyes glared at the alien, and his brain willed it to turn aside.

Once more, flashingly, while he waited, the implications of the disaster that could be here struck deep. In all the universe there had never been so dangerous an intelligence as the Rull. At once remorseless and immune to all attempts at establishing communication, Rulls killed human beings on sight. A human-manned warship that ventured into Rull-patrolled space was attacked until it withdrew or was destroyed. Rull ships that entered Earth-controlled space *never* withdrew once they were attacked. In the beginning, man had been reluctant to engage in a death struggle for the galaxy. But the inexorable enemy had forced him finally to match in every respect the tenacious and murderous policies of the Rull.

The thought ended. The Rull ship was a hundred yards away, and showed no signs of changing its course. In seconds, it would cross the clump of trees that half-hid the lifeboat.

In a spasm of a movement, Jamieson launched himself from his chair. Like a shot from a gun, with utter abandon, he dived for the open doorway of his machine. As the door clanged behind him, the boat shook as if it had been struck by a giant. Part of the ceiling sagged; the floor staggered toward him, and the air grew hot and suffocating.

Gasping, Jamieson slid into the control chair and struck at the main emergency switch. The rapid-fire blasters huzzaed into automatic firing positions and let go with a hum and deep-throated *ping*. The refrigerators whined with power; a cold blast of air blew at his body. The relief was so quick that a second passed before Jamieson realized that the atomic engines had failed to respond, and that the lifeboat, which should already have been sliding into the air, was still lying inert in an exposed position.

Tense, he stared into the visiplates. It took a moment to locate the Rull ship. It was at the lower edge of one plate, tumbling slowly out of sight beyond a clump of trees a quarter of a mile away. As he watched, it disappeared; and then the crash of the landing came clear and unmistakable from the sound board in front of him.

The relief that came was weighted with an awful reaction. Jamieson sank back into the cushions of the control chair, weak from the narrowness of his escape. The weakness ended abruptly as a thought struck him. There had been a sedateness about the way the enemy ship fell. *The crash hadn't killed the Rulls aboard.*

He was alone in a damaged lifeboat on an impassable mountain with one or more of the most remorseless creatures ever spawned. For ten days, he must fight in the hope that man would still be able to seize the most valuable planet discovered in a century.

He saw in his visiplate that it was growing darker outside.

Jamieson took another antisleep pill and made a more definite examination of the atomic motors. It didn't take long to verify his earlier diagnosis. The basic graviton pile had been thoroughly frustrated. Until it could be reactivated on the *Orion*, the motors were useless.

The conclusive examination braced Jamieson. He was committed irrevocably to the battle of the tableland, with all its intricate possibilities. The idea that had been turning over in his mind during the prolonged night took on new meaning. This was the first time in his knowledge that a Rull and a human being had faced each other on a limited field of action, where neither was a prisoner. The great battles in space were ship against ship and fleet against fleet. Survivors either escaped or were picked up by overwhelming forces. Actually, both humans and Rulls, captured or facing capture, were conditioned to kill themselves. Rulls did it by a mental *willing* that had never been circumvented. Men had to use mechanical methods, and in some cases that had proved impossible. The result was that Rulls had had occasional opportunities to experiment on living, conscious men.

Unless he was bested before he could get organized, here was a priceless opportunity to try some tests on Rulls—and without delay. Every moment of daylight must be utilized to the uttermost limit.

By the time the Laertes sun peered palely over the horizon that was the northeast cliff's edge, the assault was under way. The automatic defensors, which he had set up the night before, moved slowly from point to point ahead of the mobile blaster.

Jamieson cautiously saw to it that one of the three defensors also brought up his rear. He augmented that basic protection by crawling from one projecting rock after another. The machines he manipulated from a tiny hand control, which was connected to the visiplate that poked out from his headgear just above his eyes. With tensed eyes he watched the wavering needles that would indicate movement or that the defensor screens were being subjected to energy opposition.

Nothing happened.

As he came within sight of the Rull craft, Jamieson stalled his attack while he seriously pondered the problem of no resistance. He didn't like it. It was possible that all the Rulls aboard *had* been killed, but he doubted it mightily. Rulls were almost boneless. Except for half a dozen strategically linked cartilages, they were all muscles.

With bleak eyes, Jamieson studied the wreck through the telescopic eyes of one of the defensors. It lay in a shallow indentation, its nose buried in a wall of gravel. Its lower plates were collapsed versions of the originals. His single-energy blast the evening before, completely automatic though it had been, had really dealt a smashing blow to the Rull ship.

The overall effect was of utter lifelessness. If it were a trick, then it was a very skillful one. Fortunately, there were tests he could make, not absolutely final but evidential and indicative.

He made them.

The echoless height of the most unique mountain ever discovered hummed with the fire-sound of the mobile blaster. The noise grew to a roar as the unit's pile warmed to its task and developed its maximum kilo-curie activity.

Under that barrage, the hull of the enemy craft trembled a little and changed color slightly, but that was all. After ten minutes, Jamieson cut the power and sat baffled and indecisive.

The defensive screens of the Rull ship were full on. Had they gone on automatically after his first shot of the evening before? Or had they been put up deliberately to nullify just such an attack as this?

He couldn't be sure. That was the trouble; he had no positive knowledge. The Rulls could be lying inside dead. They could be wounded and incapable of doing anything against him. They could have spent the night marking up the tableland with *elled* nerve-control lines—he'd have to make sure he never looked directly at the ground—or they could simply be waiting for the arrival of the greater ship that had dropped it onto the planet.

Jamieson refused to consider the last possibility. That way was death, without qualification or hope.

Frowningly, he studied the visible damage he had done the ship. All the hard metals had held together so far as he could see, but the whole bottom of the ship was dented to a depth that varied from one to four feet. Some radiation must have got in, and the question was, what would it have damaged?

He had examined dozens of captured Rull survey craft, and if this one ran to the pattern, then in the front would be the control center, with a sealed-off blaster chamber. In the rear the engine room, two storerooms, one for fuel and equipment, the other for food and—

For food. Jamieson jumped, and then with wide eyes noted how the food section had suffered greater damage than any other part of the ship.

Surely, surely, some radiation must have got into it, poisoning it, ruining it, and instantly putting the Rull, with his swift digestive system, into a deadly position.

Jamieson sighed with the intensity of his hope, and prepared to retreat. As he turned away, quite accidentally, he glanced at the rock behind which he had shielded himself from possible direct fire.

Glanced at it, and saw the *elled* lines in it. Intricate lines, based on a profound and inhuman study of the human nervous system. Jamieson recognized them, and stiffened in horror. He thought in anguish: *Where, where am I supposed to fall? Which cliff?*

With a desperate will, with all his strength, he fought to retain his senses a moment longer. He strove to see the lines again. He saw, briefly, flashingly, five vertical and above them three lines that pointed east with their wavering ends.

The pressure built up, up, up inside him, but still he fought to keep his thoughts moving. Fought to remember if there were any wide ledges near the top of the east cliff.

There were. He recalled them in a final agony of hope. *There,* he thought. *That one, that one. Let me fall on that one.* He strained to hold the ledge image he wanted, and to repeat, repeat the command that might save his life. His last, dreary thought was that here was the answer to his doubts. The Rull *was* alive.

Blackness came like a curtain of pure essence of night.

Somberly, the Rull glided toward the man's lifeboat. From a safe distance, he examined it. The defense screens were up, but he couldn't be sure they had been put up before the attack of the morning, or had been raised since then, or had come on automatically at his approach.

He couldn't be sure. That was the trouble. Everywhere, on the tableland around him, was a barrenness, a desolation unlike anything else he had ever known. The man could be dead, his smashed body lying at the remote bottom of the mountain. He could be inside the ship badly injured; he had, unfortunately, *had* time to get back to the safety of his craft. Or he could be waiting inside, alert, aggressive, and conscious of his enemy's uncertainty, determined to take full advantage of that uncertainty.

The Rull set up a watching device that would apprise him when the door opened. Then he returned to the tunnel that led into his ship, laboriously crawled through it, and settled himself to wait out the emergency.

The hunger in him was an expanding force, hourly taking on a greater urgency. It was time to stop moving around. He would need all his energy for the crisis.

The days passed.

Jamieson stirred in an effluvium of pain. At first it seemed all-enveloping, a mist of anguish that bathed him in sweat from head to toe. Gradually, then, it localized in the region of his lower left leg.

The pulse of the pain made a rhythm in his nerves. The minutes lengthened into an hour, and then he finally thought: *Why, I've got a sprained ankle!* He had more than that, of course. The pressure that had driven him here clung like a gravitonic plate. How long he lay there, partly conscious, was not clear, but when he finally opened his eyes, the sun was still shining on him, though it was almost directly overhead.

He watched it with the mindlessness of a dreamer as it withdrew slowly past the edge of the overhanging precipice. It was not until the shadow of the cliff suddenly plopped across his face that he started to full consciousness with a sudden memory of deadly danger.

It took a while to shake the remnants of the *elled* "take" from his brain. And, even as it was fading, he sized up, to some extent, the difficulties of his position. He saw that he had tumbled over the edge of a cliff to a steep slope. The angle of descent of the slope was a sharp fifty-five degrees, and what had saved him was that his body had been caught in the tangled growth near the edge of the greater precipice beyond.

His foot must have twisted in those roots, and sprained.

As he finally realized the nature of his injuries, Jamieson braced up. He was safe. In spite of having suffered an accidental defeat of major proportions, his intense concentration on this slope, his desperate will to make *this* the place where he must fall, had worked out.

He began to climb. It was easy enough on the slope, steep as it was; the ground was rough, rocky, and scraggly with brush. It was when he came to the ten-foot overhanging cliff that his ankle proved what an obstacle it could be.

Four times he slid back, reluctantly; and then, on the fifth try, his fingers, groping desperately over the top of the cliff, caught an unbreakable root. Triumphantly, he dragged himself to the safety of the tableland.

Now that the sound of his scraping and struggling was gone, only his heavy breathing broke the silence of the emptiness. His anxious eyes studied the uneven terrain. The tableland spread before him with not a sign of a moving figure anywhere.

To one side, he could see his lifeboat. Jamieson began to crawl toward it, taking care to stay on rock as much as possible. What had happened to the Rull he did not know.

And since, for several days, his ankle would keep him inside his ship, he might as well keep his enemy guessing during that time.

Professor Jamieson lay in his bunk, thinking. He could hear the beating of his heart. There were the occasional sounds when he dragged himself out of bed. But that was almost all. The radio, when he turned it on, was dead. No static, not even the fading in and out of a wave. At this colossal distance, even subspace radio was impossible.

He listened on all the more active Rull wave lengths. But the silence was there, too. Not that they would be broadcasting if they were in the vicinity.

He was cut off here in this tiny ship on an uninhabited planet, with useless motors.

He tried not to think of it like that. "Here," he told himself, "is the opportunity of a lifetime for an experiment."

He warmed to the idea as a moth to flame. Live Rulls were hard to get hold of. About one a year was captured in the unconscious state, and these were regarded as priceless treasures. But here was an even more ideal situation.

We're prisoners, both of us. That was the way he tried to picture it. Prisoners of an environment, and, therefore, in a curious fashion, prisoners of each other. Only each was free of the conditioned need to kill himself.

There were things a man might discover. The great mysteries—as far as men were concerned—that motivated Rull actions. Why did they want to destroy other races totally? Why did they needlessly sacrifice valuable ships in attacking Earth machines that ventured into their sectors of space when they knew that the intruders would leave in a few weeks anyway? And why did prisoners who could kill themselves at will commit suicide without waiting to find out what fate was intended for them? Sometimes they were merely wanted as messengers.

Was it possible the Rulls were trying to conceal a terrible weakness in their make-up of which man had not yet found an inkling?

The potentialities of this fight of man against Rull on a lonely mountain exhilarated Jamieson as he lay on his bunk, scheming, turning the problem over in his mind.

There were times during those dog days when he crawled over to the control chair and peered for an hour at a stretch into the visiplates. He saw the tableland and the vista of distance beyond it. He saw the sky of Laertes III, bluish pink sky, silent and lifeless.

He saw the prison. Caught here, he thought bleakly. Professor Jamieson, whose appearance on an inhabited planet would bring out unwieldy crowds, whose quiet voice in the council chambers of Earth's galactic empire spoke with final authority—that Jamieson was here, alone, lying in a bunk, waiting for a leg to heal, so that he might conduct an experiment with a Rull.

It seemed incredible. But he grew to believe it as the days passed.

On the third day, he was able to move around sufficiently to handle a few heavy objects. He began work immediately on the mental screen. On the fifth day it was finished. Then the story had to be recorded. That was easy. Each sequence had been so carefully worked out in bed that it flowed from his mind onto the visiwire.

He set it up about two hundred yards from the lifeboat, behind a screening of trees. He tossed a can of food a dozen feet to one side of the screen.

The rest of the day dragged. It was the sixth day since

the arrival of the Rull, the fifth since he had sprained his ankle.

Came the night.

A gliding shadow, undulating under the starlight of Laertes III, the Rull approached the screen the man had set up. How bright it was, shining in the darkness of the tableland, a blob of light in a black universe of uneven ground and dwarf shrubbery.

When he was a hundred feet from the light, he sensed the food—and realized that here was a trap.

For the Rull, six days without food had meant a stupendous loss of energy, visual blackouts on a dozen color levels, a dimness of life-force that fitted with the shadows, not the sun. That inner world of disjointed nervous system was like a run-down battery, with a score of organic "instruments" disconnecting one by one as the energy level fell. The *yeli* recognized dimly, but with a savage anxiety, that only a part of that nervous system would ever be restored to complete usage. And even for that speed was essential. A few more steps downward, and then the old, old conditioning of mandatory self-inflicted death would apply even to the high Aaish of the Yeell.

The worm body grew quiet. The visual center behind each eye accepted light on a narrow band from the screen. From beginning to end, he watched the story as it unfolded, and then watched it again, craving repetition with all the ardor of a primitive.

The picture began in deep space with a man's lifeboat being dropped from a launching lock of a battleship. It showed the battleship going on to a military base, and there taking on supplies and acquiring a vast fleet of reinforcements, and then starting on the return journey. The scene switched to the lifeboat dropping down on Laertes

III, showed everything that had subsequently happened, suggested the situation was dangerous to them both—and pointed out the only safe solution.

The final sequence of each showing of the story was of the Rull approaching the can to the left of the screen and opening it. The method was shown in detail, as was the visualization of the Rull busily eating the food inside.

Each time that sequence drew near, a tension came over the Rull, a will to make the story real. But it was not until the seventh showing had run its course that he glided forward, closing the last gap between himself and the can. It was a trap, he knew, perhaps even death—it didn't matter. To live, he had to take the chance. Only by this means, by risking what was in the can, could he hope to remain alive for the necessary time.

How long it would take for the commanders cruising up there in the black of space in their myriad ships—how long it would be before they would decide to supersede his command, he didn't know. But they would come. Even if they waited until the enemy ships arrived before they dared to act against his strict orders, they would come.

At that point they could come down without fear of suffering from his ire.

Until then he would need all the food he could get.

Gingerly, he extended a sucker, and activated the automatic opener of the can.

It was shortly after four in the morning when Professor Jamieson awakened to the sound of an alarm ringing softly. It was still pitch dark outside—the Laertes day was twenty-six sidereal hours long; he had set his clocks the first day to coordinate—and at this season dawn was still three hours away.

Jamieson did not get up at once. The alarm had been activated by the opening of the can of food. It continued to ring for a full fifteen minutes, which was just about perfect. The alarm was tuned to the electronic pattern emitted by the can once it was opened, and so long as any food remained in it. The lapse of time involved fitted with the capacity of one of the Rull's suckers in absorbing three pounds of pork.

For fifteen minutes, accordingly, a member of the Rull race, man's mortal enemy, had been subjected to a pattern of mental vibrations corresponding to its own thoughts. It was a pattern to which the nervous system of other Rulls had responded in laboratory experiments. Unfortunately, those others had killed themselves on awakening, and so no definite results had been proved. But it had been established by the ecphoriometer that the unconscious and not the conscious mind was affected.

Jamieson lay in bed, smiling quietly to himself. He turned over finally to go back to sleep, and then he realized how excited he was.

The greatest moment in the history of Rull–human warfare. Surely, he wasn't going to let it pass unremarked. He climbed out of bed and poured himself a drink.

The attempt of the Rull to attack him through his unconscious mind had emphasized his own possible actions in that direction. Each race had discovered some of the weaknesses of the other.

Rulls used their knowledge to exterminate. Men tried for communication, and hoped for association. Both were ruthless, murderous, pitiless, in their methods. Outsiders sometimes had difficulty distinguishing one from the other.

But the difference in purpose was as great as the difference between black and white, the absence as compared to the presence of light.

There was only one trouble with the immediate situation. Now that the Rull had food, he might develop a few plans of his own.

Jamieson returned to bed, and lay staring into the darkness. He did not underrate the resources of the Rull, but since he had decided to conduct an experiment, no chance must be considered too great.

He turned over finally, and slept the sleep of a man determined that things were working in his favor.

Morning. Jamieson put on his cold-proof clothes and went out into the chilly dawn. Again he savored the silence and the atmosphere of isolated grandeur. A strong wind was blowing from the east, and there was an iciness in it that stung his face. Snow? He wondered.

He forgot that. He had things to do on this morning of mornings. He would do them with his usual caution.

Paced by defensors and the mobile blaster, he headed for the mental screen. It stood in open high ground where it would be visible from a dozen different hiding places, and so far as he could see it was undamaged. He tested the automatic mechanism, and for good measure ran the picture through one showing.

He had already tossed another can of food in the grass near the screen and he was turning away when he thought: *That's odd. The metal framework looks as if it's been polished.*

He studied the phenomena in a de-energizing mirror, and saw that the metal had been varnished with a clear substance. He felt sick as he recognized it.

He decided in agony, *If the cue is not to fire at all, I won't do it. I'll fire even if the blaster turns on me.*

He scraped some of the "varnish" into a receptacle, began his retreat to the lifeboat. He was thinking violently: *Where does he get all this stuff? That isn't part of the equipment of a survey craft.*

The first deadly suspicion was on him that what was happening was not just an accident. He was pondering the vast implications of that, narrow-eyed, when, off to one side, he saw the Rull.

For the first time in his many days on the tableland, he saw the Rull.

What's the cue?

Memory of purpose came to the Rull shortly after he had eaten. It was dim at first, but it grew stronger.

It was not the only sensation of his returning energy.

His visual centers interpreted more light. The starlit tableland grew brighter—not as bright as it it could be for him, by a very large percentage, but the direction was up instead of down. It would never again be normal. Vision was in the mind, and that part of his mind no longer had the power of interpretation.

He felt unutterably fortunate that it was no worse.

He had been gliding along the edge of the precipice. Now, he paused to peer down. Even with his partial night vision, the view was breathtaking. There was distance below and distance afar. From a spaceship, the height was almost minimum. But gazing down that wall of gravel into those depths was a different experience. It emphasized how completely he had been caught by an accident. And it reminded him of what he had been doing before the hunger.

He turned instantly away from the cliff and hurried to where the wreckage of his ship had gathered dust for days. Bent and twisted wreckage, half buried in the hard ground of Laertes III. He glided over the dented plates inside to one in which he had the day before sensed a quiver of antigravity oscillation. Tiny, potent, tremendous minutiae of oscillation, capable of being influenced.

The Rull worked with intensity and purposefulness. The plate was still firmly attached to the frame of the ship. And the first job, the heartbreakingly difficult job, was to tear it completely free. The hours passed.

R-r-i-i-i-pp! The hard plate yielded to the slight re-arrangement of its nucleonic structure. The shift was infinitesimal, partly because the directing nervous energy of his body was not at norm, and partly because it had better be infinitesimal. There was such a thing as releasing energy enough to blow up a mountain.

Not, he discovered finally, that there was danger in this plate. He found that out the moment he crawled onto it. The sensation of power that aura-ed out of it was so dim that, briefly, he doubted if it would lift from the ground.

But it did. The test run lasted seven feet, and gave him his measurement of the limited force he had available. Enough for an attack only.

He had no doubts in his mind. The experiment was over. His only purpose must be to kill the man, and the question was, how could he insure that the man did not kill him while he was doing it? The varnish!

He applied it painstakingly, dried it with a drier, and then, picking up the plate again, he carried it on his back to the hiding place he wanted.

When he had buried it and himself under the dead leaves of a clump of brush, he grew calmer. He recognized that the veneer of his civilization was off. It shocked him, but he did not regret it.

In giving him the food, the two-legged being was obviously doing something to him. Something dangerous. The only answer to the entire problem of the experiment of the tableland was to deal death without delay.

He lay tense, ferocious, beyond the power of any vagrant thoughts, waiting for the man to come.

It looked as desperate a venture as Jamieson had seen in Service. Normally, he would have handled it effortlessly. But he was watching intently—*intently*—for the paralysis to strike him, the negation that was of the varnish.

And so, it was the unexpected normal quality that nearly ruined him. The Rull flew out of a clump of trees mounted on an antigravity plate. The surprise of that was so great that it almost succeeded. The plates had been drained of all such energies, according to his tests the first morning. Yet here was one alive again and light again with the special antigravity lightness which Rull scientists had brought to the peak of perfection.

The action of movement through space toward him was, of course, based on the motion of the planet as it turned on its axis. The speed of the attack, starting as it did from zero, did not come near the eight-hundred-mile-an-hour velocity of the spinning planet, but it was swift enough.

The apparition of metal and six-foot worm charged at him through the air. And even as he drew his weapon and fired at it, he had a choice to make, a restraint to exercise: *Do not kill!*

That was hard, oh, hard. The necessity exercised his capacity for integration and imposed so stern a limitation that during the second it took him to adjust the Rull came to within ten feet of him.

What saved him was the pressure of the air on the metal plate. The air tilted it like a wing of a plane becoming airborne. At the bottom of that metal he fired his irresistible weapon, seared it, burned it, deflected it to a crash landing in a clump of bushes twenty feet to his right.

Jamieson was deliberately slow in following up his success. When he reached the bushes, the Rull was fifty feet beyond it gliding on its multiple suckers over the top of a hillock. It disappeared into a clump of trees.

He did not pursue it or fire a second time. Instead, he gingerly pulled the Rull antigravity plate out of the brush and examined it. The question was, how had the Rull degravitized it without the elaborate machinery necessary?

And if it was capable of creating such a "parachute" for itself why hadn't it floated down to the forest land far below where food would be available and where it would be safe from its human enemy?

One question was answered the moment he lifted the plate. It was "normal" weight, its energy apparently exhausted after traveling less than a hundred feet. It had obviously never been capable of making the mile-and-a-half trip to the forest and plain below.

Jamieson took no chances. He dropped the plate over the nearest precipice and watched it fall into distance. He was back in the lifeboat when he remembered the varnish.

Why, there had been no cue, not yet.

He tested the scraping he had brought with him. Chemically, it turned out to be a simple resin, used to make varnishes. Atomically, it was stabilized. Electronically, it transformed light into energy on the vibration level of human thought.

It was alive, all right. But what was the recording?

Jamieson made a graph of every material and energy level, for comparison purposes. As soon as he had established that it had been altered on the electronic level—which had been obvious, but which, still, had to be proved—he recorded the images on a visiwire. The result was a hodgepodge of dreamlike fantasies.

Symbols. He took down his book, "Symbol Interpretations of the Unconscious," and found the cross reference: "Inhibitions, Mental."

On the referred page and line, he read: "Do not kill!"

"Well, I'll be—" Jamieson said aloud into the silence of the lifeboat interior. "That's what happened."

He was relieved, and then not so relieved. It had been his personal intention not to kill at this stage. But the Rull hadn't known that. By working such a subtle inhibition, it had dominated the attack even in defeat.

That was the trouble. So far he had got *out* of situations, but had created no successful ones in retaliation. He had a hope, but that wasn't enough.

He must take no more risks. Even his final experiment must wait until the day the *Orion* was due to arrive.

Human beings were just a little too weak in certain directions. Their very life cells had impulses which could be stirred by the cunning and the remorseless.

He did not doubt that, in the final issue, the Rull would try to stir.

On the ninth night, the day before the *Orion* was due, Jamieson refrained from putting out a can of food. The following morning he spent half an hour at the radio, trying to contact the battleship. He made a point of broadcasting a detailed account of what had happened so far, and he described what his plans were, including his intention of testing the Rull to see if it had suffered any injury from its period of hunger.

Subspace was as silent as death. Not a single pulse of vibration answered his call.

He finally abandoned the attempt to establish contact and went outside. Swiftly, he set up the instruments he would need for his experiment. The tableland had the air of a deserted wilderness. He tested his equipment, then looked at his watch. It showed eleven minutes of noon. Suddenly jittery, he decided not to wait the extra minutes.

He walked over, hesitated, and then pressed a button. From a source near the screen, a rhythm on a very high energy level was being broadcast. It was a variation of the rhythm pattern to which the Rull had been subjected for four nights.

Slowly, Jamieson retreated toward the lifeboat. He wanted to try again to contact the *Orion*. Looking back, he saw the Rull glide into the clearing and head straight for the source of the vibration.

As Jamieson paused involuntarily, fascinated, the main alarm system of the lifeboat went off with a roar. The sound echoed with an alien eeriness on the wings of the icy wind that was blowing, and it acted like a cue. His wrist radio snapped on, synchronizing automatically with the powerful radio in the lifeboat. A voice said urgently:

"Professor Jamieson, this is the battleship *Orion*. We heard your earlier calls but refrained from answering. An entire Rull fleet is cruising in the vicinity of the Laertes sun.

"In approximately five minutes, an attempt will be made to pick you up. Meanwhile—*drop everything*."

Jamieson dropped. It was a physical movement, not a mental one. Out of the corner of one eye, even as he heard his own radio, he saw a movement in the sky. Two dark blobs that resolved into vast shapes. There was a roar as the Rull super-battleships flashed by overhead. A cyclone followed their passage that nearly tore him from the ground, where he clung desperately to the roots of intertwining brush.

At top speed, obviously traveling under gravitonic power, the enemy warships turned a sharp somersault and came back toward the tableland. Expecting death, and beginning to realize some of the truth of the situation on the tableland, Jamieson quailed. But the fire flashed past him, not at him. The thunder of the shot rolled toward Jamieson, a colossal sound that yet did not blot out his sense awareness of what had happened. His lifeboat. They had fired at his lifeboat.

He groaned as he pictured it destroyed in one burst of

intolerable flame. And then, for a moment, there was no time for thought or anguish.

A third warship came into view, but, as Jamieson strained to make out its contours, it turned and fled. His wrist radio clicked on:

"Cannot help you now. Save yourself. Our four accompanying battleships and attendant squadrons will engage the Rull fleet and try to draw them toward our great battle group cruising near the star, Bianca, and then re—"

A flash of vivid fire in the distant sky ended the message. It was a full minute before the cold air of Laertes III echoed to the remote thunder of the broadside. The sound died slowly, reluctantly, as if endless little overtones of it were clinging to each molecule of air.

The silence that settled finally was, strangely, not peaceful, but like the calm before a storm, a fateful, quiescent stillness, alive with unmeasurable threat.

Shakily, Jamieson climbed to his feet. It was time to assess the immediate danger that had befallen him. The greater danger he dared not even think about.

Jamieson headed first for his lifeboat. He didn't have to go all the way. The entire section of the cliff had been sheared away. Of the ship there was no sign.

It pulled him up short. He had expected it, but the shock of the reality was terrific.

He crouched like an animal and stared up into the sky, into the menacing limits of the sky. It was empty of machines. Not a movement was there, not a sound came out of it, except the sound of the east wind. He was alone in a universe between heaven and earth, a mind poised at the edge of an abyss.

Into his mind, tensely waiting, pierced a sharp understanding. The Rull ships had flown once over the mountain to size up the situation on the tableland, and then had tried to destroy him.

Who was the Rull here with him, that super-battleships should roar down to insure that no danger remained for it on the tableland?

Well, they hadn't quite succeeded. Jamieson showed his teeth to the wind. Not quite. But he'd have to hurry. At any moment they might risk one of their destroyers in a rescue landing.

As he ran, he felt himself one with the wind. He knew that feeling, that sense of returning primitiveness during moments of excitement. It was like that in battles, and the important thing was to yield one's whole body and soul to it. There was no such thing as fighting efficiently with half your mind or half your body. All, all, was demanded.

He expected falls, and he had them. Each time he got up, almost unconscious of the pain, and ran on again. He arrived bleeding—but he arrived.

The sky was silent.

From the shelter of a line of brush, he peered at the Rull.

The captive Rull, *his* Rull to do with as he pleased. To watch, to force, to educate—the fastest education in the history of the world. There wasn't any time for a leisurely exchange of information.

From where he lay, he manipulated the controls of the screen.

The Rull had been moving back and forth in front of the screen. Now, it speeded up, then slowed, then speeded up again, according to his will.

Some thousands of years before, in the twentieth century, the classic and timeless investigation had been made of which this was one end result. A man called Pavlov fed a laboratory dog at regular intervals, to the accompaniment of the ringing of a bell. Soon, the dog's digestive system responded as readily to the ringing of the bell without the food as to the food and the bell together.

Pavlov himself never did realize the most important reality behind his conditioning process. But what began on that remote day ended with a science that could control animals and aliens—and men—almost at will. Only the Rulls baffled the master experimenters in the later centuries when it was an exact science. Defeated by the will to death of all Rull captives, the scientists foresaw the doom of Earth's galactic empire unless some beginning could be made in penetrating the minds of Rulls.

It was his desperate bad luck that he had no time for real penetrations.

There was death here for those who lingered.

But even what he had to do, the bare minimum of what he had to do, would take precious time. Back and forth, back and forth; the rhythm of obedience had to be established.

The image of the Rull on the screen was as lifelike as the original. It was three-dimensional, and its movements were like an automaton. The challenger was actually irresistible. Basic nerve centers were affected. The Rull could no more help falling into step than it could resist the call of the food impulse.

After it had followed that mindless pattern for fifteen minutes, changing pace at his direction, Jamieson started the Rull and its image climbing trees. Up, then down again, half a dozen times. At that point, Jamieson introduced an image of himself.

Tensely, with one eye on the sky and one on the scene before him, he watched the reactions of the Rull—watched them with narrowed eyes and a sharp understanding of Rull responses to the presence of human beings. Rulls were digestively stimulated by the odor of man. It showed in the way their suckers opened and closed. When, a few minutes later, he substituted himself for his image, he was satisfied that this Rull had temporarily lost its normal automatic hunger when it saw a human being.

And now that he had reached the stage of final control, he hesitated. It was time to make his tests. Could he afford the time?

He realized that he had to. This opportunity might not occur again in a hundred years.

When he finished the tests twenty-five minutes later, he was pale with excitement. He thought: *This is it. We've got it.*

He spent ten precious minutes broadcasting his discovery by means of his wrist radio—hoping that the transmitter on his lifeboat had survived its fall down the mountain, and was picking up the thready message of the smaller instrument and sending it out through subspace.

During the entire ten minutes, there was not a single answer to his call.

Aware that he had done what he could, Jamieson headed for the cliff's edge he had selected as a starting point. He looked down and shuddered, then remembered what the *Orion* had said: "An entire Rull fleet cruising . . ."

Hurry!

He lowered the Rull to the first ledge. A moment later he fastened the harness around his own body, and stepped into space. Sedately, with easy strength, the Rull gripped the other end of the rope, and lowered him down to the ledge beside it.

They continued on down and down. It was hard work, although they used a very simple system.

A long plastic rope spanned the spaces for them. A metal climbing rod, used to scale the smooth vastness of a spaceship's side, held position after position while the rope did its work.

On each ledge, Jamieson burned the rod at a downward

slant into solid rock. The rope slid through an arrangement of pulleys in the metal as the Rull and he, in turn, lowered each other to ledges farther down.

The moment they were both safely in the clear of one ledge, Jamieson would explode the rod out of the rock, and it would drop down ready for use again.

The day sank towards darkness like a restless man into sleep—slowly, wearily. Jamieson grew hot and tired, and filled with the melancholy of the fatigue that dragged at his muscles.

He could see that the Rull was growing more aware of him. It still cooperated, but it watched him with intent eyes each time it swung him down.

The conditioned state was ending. The Rull was emerging from its trance. The process should be completed before night.

There was a time, then, when Jamieson despaired of ever getting down before the shadows fell. He had chosen the western, sunny side for that fantastic descent down a black-brown cliff the like of which did not exist elsewhere in the known worlds of space. He found himself watching the Rull with quick, nervous glances. When it swung him down onto a ledge beside it, he watched its blue eyes, its staring blue eyes, come closer and closer to him, and then as his legs swung below the level of those strange eyes, they twisted to follow him.

The intent eyes of the other reminded Jamieson of his discovery. He felt a fury at himself that he had never reasoned it out before. For centuries man had known that his own effort to see clearly required a good twenty-five per cent of the energy of his whole body. Human scientists should have guessed that the vast wave compass of Rull eyes was the product of a balancing of glandular activity on a fantastically high energy level. A balancing which, if disturbed, would surely affect the mind itself either temporarily or permanently.

He had discovered that the impairment was permanent.

What would a prolonged period of starvation diet do to such a nervous system?

The possibilities altered the nature of the war. It explained why Rull ships had never attacked human food sources or supply lines; they didn't want to risk retaliation. It explained why Rull ships fought so remorselessly against Earth ships that intruded into their sectors of the galaxy. It explained their ruthless destruction of the other races. They lived in terror that their terrible weakness would be found out.

Jamieson smiled with a savage anticipation. If his message had got through, or if he escaped, Rulls would soon feel the pinch of hunger. Earth ships would concentrate on that basic form of attack in the future. The food supplies of entire planetary groups would be poisoned, convoys would be raided without regard for casualties. Everywhere at once the attack would be pressed without letup and without mercy.

It shouldn't be long before the Rulls began their retreat to their own galaxy. That was the only solution that would be acceptable. The invader must be driven back and back, forced to give up his conquests of a thousand years.

Four P.M. Jamieson had to pause again for a rest. He walked to the side of the ledge away from the Rull and sank down on the rock. The sky was a brassy blue, silent and windless now, a curtain drawn across the black space above, concealing what must already be the greatest Rull–human battle in ten years.

It was a tribute to the five Earth battleships and their

escort that no Rull ship had yet attempted to rescue the Rull on the tableland.

Possibly, of course, they didn't want to give away the presence of one of their own kind.

Jamieson gave up the futile speculation. Wearily, he compared the height of the cliff above with the depth that remained below. He estimated they had come two-thirds of the distance. He saw that the Rull was staring out over the valley. Jamieson turned and gazed with it.

The scene which they took in with their different eyes and different brains was fairly drab and very familiar, yet withal strange and wonderful. The forest began a quarter of a mile from the bottom of the cliff, and it almost literally had no end. It rolled up over the hills and down into the shallow valleys. It faltered at the edge of a broad river, then billowed out again and climbed the slopes of mountains that sprawled mistily in the distance.

His watch showed four-fifteen. Time to get going again.

At twenty-five minutes after six, they reached a ledge a hundred and fifty feet above the uneven plain. The distance strained the capacity of the rope, but the initial operation of lowering the Rull to freedom and safety was achieved without incident. Jamieson gazed down curiously at the worm. What would it do now that it was in the clear?

It looked up at him and waited.

That made him grim. Because this was a chance he was not taking. Jamieson waved imperatively at the Rull, and took out his blaster. The Rull backed away, but only into the safety of a gigantic rock. Blood-red, the sun was sinking behind the mountains. Darkness moved over the land. Jamieson ate his dinner. It was as he was finishing it that he saw a movement below.

He watched as the Rull glided along close to the edge of the precipice.

It disappeared beyond an outjut of the cliff.

Jamieson waited briefly, then swung out on the rope. The descent drained his strength, but there was solid ground at the bottom. Three quarters of the way down, he cut his finger on a section of the rope that was unexpectedly rough.

When he reached the ground, he noticed that his finger was turning an odd gray. In the dimness, it looked strange and unhealthy.

As Jamieson stared at it, the color drained from his face. He thought in a bitter anger, *The Rull must have smeared it on the rope on his way down.*

A pang went through his body. It was knife sharp, and it was followed instantly by a stiffness. With a gasp, he grabbed at his blaster, to kill himself. His hand froze in midair. He fell to the ground. The stiffness held him there, froze him there motionless.

The will to death is in all life. Every organic cell ecphorizes the inherited engrams of its inorganic origin. The pulse of life is a squamous film superimposed on an underlying matter so intricate in its delicate balancing of different energies that life itself is but a brief, vain straining against that balance.

For an instant of eternity, a pattern is attempted. It takes many forms, but these are apparent. The real shape is always a time and not a space shape. And that shape is a curve. Up and then down. Up from the darkness into the light, then down again into the blackness.

The male salmon sprays his mist of milt onto the eggs of the female. And instantly he is seized with a mortal melancholy. The male bee collapses from the embrace of the queen he has won back into that inorganic mold from which he climbed for one single moment of ecstasy. In man, the fateful pattern is repressed into quadrillions of individual cells.

But the pattern is there. Waiting.

Long before, the sharp-minded Rull scientists, probing for chemical substances that would shock man's system into its primitive forms, found the special secret of man's will to death.

The *yeli*, Meeesh, gliding back toward Jamieson, did not think of the process. He had been waiting for the opportunity. It had occurred. He was intent on his own purposes.

Briskly, he removed the man's blaster; then he searched for the key to the lifeboat. And then he carried Jamieson a quarter of a mile around the base of the cliff to where the man's ship had been catapulted by the blast from the Rull warship.

Five minutes later, the powerful radio inside was broadcasting on Rull wavelengths an imperative command to the Rull fleet.

Dimness. Inside and outside his skin. He felt himself at the bottom of a well, peering out of night into twilight. As he lay, a pressure of something swelled around him, lifted him higher and higher and near to the mouth of the well.

He struggled the last few feet, a distinct mental effort, and looked over the edge. Consciousness.

He was lying on a raised table inside a room which had several large mouselike openings at the floor level, openings that led to other chambers. Doors, he realized, odd-shaped, alien, unhuman. Jamieson cringed with the stunning shock of recognition.

He was inside a Rull warship.

There was a slithering of movement behind him. He turned his head and rolled his eyes in their sockets.

In the shadows, three Rulls were gliding across the floor toward a bank of instruments that reared up behind and to one side of him. They pirouetted up an inclined plane and poised above him. Their pale eyes, shiny in the dusk of that unnatural chamber, peered down at him.

Jamieson tried to move. His body writhed in the confines of the bonds that held him. That brought a sharp remembrance of the death-will chemical that the Rull had used. Relief came surging. He was not dead. *Not dead.* NOT DEAD. The Rull must have helped him, forced him to move, and so broken the downward curve of his descent to dust.

He was alive—for what?

The thought slowed his joy. His hope snuffed out like a flame. His brain froze into a tensed, terrible mask of anticipation.

As he watched with staring eyes, expecting pain, one of the Rulls pressed a button. Part of the table on which Jamieson was lying lifted. He was raised to a sitting position.

What now?

He couldn't see the Rulls. He tried to turn, but two head shields clamped into the side of his head and held him firmly.

He saw that there was a square of silvery sheen on the wall which he faced. A light sprang onto it, and then a picture. It was a curiously familiar picture, but at first because there was a reversal of position Jamieson couldn't place the familiarity.

Abruptly, he realized.

It was a twisted version of the picture that he had shown the Rull, first when he was feeding it, and then with more weighty arguments after he discovered the vulnerability of man's mortal enemy.

He had shown how the Rull race would be destroyed unless it agreed to peace.

In the picture he was being shown it was the Rull that urged cooperation between the two races. They seemed unaware that he had not yet definitely transmitted his knowledge to other human beings. Or perhaps that fact was blurred by the conditioning he had given to the Rull when he fed it and controlled it.

As he glared at the screen, the picture ended—and then started again. By the time it had finished a second time, there was no doubt. Jamieson collapsed back against the table. They would not show him such a picture unless he was to be used as a messenger.

He would be returned home to carry the message that man had wanted to hear for a thousand years. He would also carry the information that would give meaning to the offer.

The Rull–human war was over.

The monster in this chilling exercise in science-fictional horror is not, as you might think, the alien creature with one large eye, several appendages, and an external muscle system. No, the true monster here is the Earthman—the fugitive killer, the one whose life has been "viler than maggots, more loathsome than carrion"—the man called Smith. What happens to him, therefore, is most fitting indeed....

*Although Cyril M. Kornbluth (1924–1958) is best known for his collaborative novels with Frederick Pohl—*The Space Merchants, Gladiator-at-Law, Wolfbane—*and although he published such solo science-fiction novels of distinction as* The Syndic, *his greatest accomplishment was probably in the short story. He published close to 100 in his brief career, and many of them, such as "Friend to Man," were both so good and so dangerous as perceived through the inimical taboo-screens of the decade, that they wound up in* 10-Story Fantasy, *as this one did, and other second-line publications. Kornbluth's sudden, shocking death in 1958 (and the equally tragic death just one month earlier of another premier writer in the field, Henry Kuttner, at age forty-four) signaled the end of science fiction's greatest decade of fertility and accomplishment.*

Friend to Man

C. M. Kornbluth

Call him, if anything, Smith. He had answered to that and to other names in the past. Occupation, fugitive. His flight, it is true, had days before slowed to a walk and then to a crawl, but still he moved, a speck of gray, across the vast and featureless red plain of a planet not his own.

Nobody was following Smith, he sometimes realized, and then he would rest for a while, but not long. After a minute or an hour the posse of his mind would reform and spur behind him; reason would cry no and still he would heave himself to his feet and begin again to inch across the sand.

The posse, imaginary and terrible, faded from front to rear. Perhaps in the very last rank of pursuers was a dim shadow of a schoolmate. Smith had never been one to fight fair. More solid were the images of his first commercial venture, the hijacking job. A truck driver with his chest burned out namelessly pursued; by his side a faceless cop. The ranks of the posse grew crowded then, for Smith had been a sort of organizer after that, but never an organizer too proud to demonstrate his skill. An immemorially old-fashioned garrotting-wire trailed inches from the nape of Winkle's neck, for Winkle had nearly sung to the police.

"Squealer!" shrieked Smith abruptly, startling himself. Shaking, he closed his eyes and still Winkle plodded after him, the tails of wire bobbing with every step, stiffly.

A solid, businesslike patrolman eclipsed him, drilled through the throat; beside him was the miraculously resurrected shade of Henderson.

The twelve-man crew of a pirated lighter marched, as you would expect, in military formation, but they bled ceaselessly from their ears and eyes as people do when shot into space without helmets.

These he could bear, but, somehow, Smith did not like to look at the leader of the posse. It was odd, but he did not like to look at her.

She had no business there! If they were ghosts why was she there? He hadn't killed her, and, as far as he knew, Amy was alive and doing business in the Open Quarter at Portsmouth. It wasn't fair, Smith wearily thought. He inched across the featureless plain and Amy followed with her eyes.

Friend to Man 205

Let us! Let us! We have waited so long!
Wait longer, little ones. Wait longer.

Smith, arriving at the planet, had gravitated to the Open Quarter and found, of course, that his reputation had preceded him. Little, sharp-faced men had sidled up to pay their respects, and they happened to know of a job waiting for the right touch—

He brushed them off.

Smith found the virginal, gray-eyed Amy punching tapes for the Transport Company, tepidly engaged to a junior executive. The daughter of the Board Chairman, she fancied herself daring to work in the rough office at the port.

First was the child's play of banishing her young man. A minor operation, it was managed with the smoothness and dispatch one learns after years of such things. Young Square-Jaw had been quite willing to be seduced by a talented young woman from the Open Quarter, and had been so comically astonished when the photographs appeared on the office bulletin board!

He had left by the next freighter, sweltering in a bunk by the tube butts, and the forlorn gray eyes were wet for him.

But how much longer must we wait?
Much longer, little ones. It is weak—too weak.

The posse, Smith thought vaguely, was closing in. That meant, he supposed, that he was dying. It would not be too bad to be dead, quickly and cleanly. He had a horror of filth.

Really, he thought, this was too bad! The posse was in front of him—

It was not the posse; it was a spindly, complicated creature that, after a minute of bleary staring, he recognized as a native of the planet.

Smith thought and thought as he stared and could think of nothing to do about it. The problem was one of the few that he had never considered and debated within himself. If it had been a cop he would have acted; if it had been any human being he would have acted, but this—

He could think of nothing more logical to do than to lie down, pull the hood across his face and go to sleep.

He woke in an underground chamber big enough for half a dozen men. It was egg-shaped and cool, illuminated by sunlight red-filtered through the top half. He touched the red-lit surface and found it to be composed of glass marbles cemented together with a translucent plastic. The marbles he knew; the red desert was full of them, wind-polished against each other for millennia, rarely perfectly round, as all of these were. They had been most carefully collected. The bottom half of the egg-shaped cave was a mosaic of flatter, opaque pebbles, cemented with the same plastic.

Smith found himself thinking clear, dry, level thoughts. The posse was gone and he was sane and there had been a native and this must be the native's burrow. He had been cached there as food, of course, so he would kill the native and possibly drink its body fluids, for his canteen had been empty for a long time. He drew a knife and wondered how to kill, his eyes on the dark circle which led from the burrow to the surface.

Silently the dark circle was filled with the tangled appendages of the creature, and in the midst of the appendages was, insanely, a Standard Transport Corporation five-liter can.

The STC monogram had been worn down, but was unmistakable. The can had heft to it.

Water? The creature seemed to hold it out. He reached

into the tangle and the can was smoothly released to him. The catch flipped up and he drank flat, distilled water in great gulps.

He felt that he bulged with the stuff when he stopped, and knew the first uneasy intimations of inevitable cramp. The native was not moving, but something that could have been an eye turned on him.

"Salt?" asked Smith, his voice thin in the thin air. "I need salt with water."

The thing rubbed two appendages together and he saw a drop of amber exude and spread on them. It was, he realized a moment later, rosining the bow, for the appendages drew across each other and he heard a whining, vibrating cricket-voice say: "S-s-z-z-aw-w?"

"Salt," said Smith.

It did better the next time. The amber drop spread, and—"S-z-aw-t?" was sounded, with a little tap of the bow for the final phoneme.

It vanished, and Smith leaned back with the cramps beginning. His stomach convulsed and he lost the water he had drunk. It seeped without a trace into the floor. He doubled up and groaned—once. The groan had not eased him in body or mind; he would groan no more but let the cramps run their course.

Nothing but what is useful had always been his tacit motto. There had not been a false step in the episode of Amy. When Square-Jaw had been disposed of, Smith had waited until her father, perhaps worldly enough to know his game, certain at all events not to like the way he played it, left on one of his regular inspection trips. He had been formally introduced to her by a mutual friend who owed money to a dangerous man in the Quarter, but who had not yet been found out by the tight little clique that thought it ruled the commercial world of that planet.

With precision he had initiated her into the Open

Quarter by such easy stages that at no one point could she ever suddenly realize that she was in it or the gray eyes ever fill with shock. Smith had, unknown to her, disposed of some of her friends, chosen other new ones, stage-managed entire days for her, gently forcing opinions and attitudes, insistent, withdrawing at the slightest token of counter-pressure, always urging again when the counter-pressure relaxed.

The night she had taken Optol had been prepared for by a magazine article—notorious in the profession as a whitewash—a chance conversation in which chance did not figure at all, a televised lecture on addiction, and a trip to an Optol joint at which everybody had been gay and healthy. On the second visit, Amy had pleaded for the stuff—just out of curiosity, of course, and he had reluctantly called the unfrocked medic, who injected the gray eyes with the oil.

It had been worth his minute pains; he had got 200 feet of film while she staggered and reeled loathsomely. And she had, after the Optol evaporated, described with amazed delight how *different* everything had looked, and how exquisitely she had danced....

"S-z-aw-t!" announced the native from the mouth of the burrow. It bowled at him marbles of rock-salt from the surface, where rain never fell to dissolve them.

He licked one, then cautiously sipped water. He looked at the native, thought, and put his knife away. It came into the burrow and reclined at the opposite end from Smith.

It knows what a knife is, and water and salt, and something about language, he thought between sips. What's the racket?

But when? But when?
Wait longer, little ones. Wait longer.

"You understand me?" Smith asked abruptly.

The amber drop exuded, and the native played whiningly: *"A-ah-nn-nah-t-ann."*

"Well," said Smith, "thanks."

He never really knew where the water came from, but guessed that it had been distilled in some fashion within the body of the native. He had, certainly, seen the thing shovel indiscriminate loads of crystals into its mouth—calcium carbonate, aluminum hydroxide, anything—and later emit amorphous powders from one vent and water from another. His food, brought on half an STC can, was utterly unrecognizable—a jelly, with bits of crystal embedded in it that he had to spit out.

What it did for a living was never clear. It would lie for hours in torpor, disappear on mysterious errands, bring him food and water, sweep out the burrow with a specialized limb, converse when requested.

It was days before Smith really *saw* the creature. In the middle of a talk with it he recognized it as a fellow organism rather than as a machine, or gadget, or nightmare, or alien monster. It was, for Smith, a vast step to take.

Not easily he compared his own body with the native's, and admitted that, of course, his was inferior. The cunning jointing of the limbs, the marvelously practical detail of the eye, the economy of the external muscle system, were admirable.

Now and then at night the posse would return and crowd about him as he lay dreaming, and he knew that he screamed then, reverberatingly in the burrow. He awoke to find the most humanoid of the native's limbs resting on his brow, soothingly, and he was grateful for the new favor; he had begun to take his food and water for granted.

The conversations with the creature were whimsy as much as anything else. It was, he thought, the rarest of Samaritans, who had no interest in the private life of its wounded wayfarer.

He told it of life in the cities of the planet, and it sawed out politely that the cities were very big indeed. He told it of the pleasures of human beings, and it politely agreed that their pleasures were most pleasant.

Under its cool benevolence he stammered and faltered in his ruthlessness. On the nights when he woke screaming and was comforted by it he would demand to know why it cared to comfort him.

It would saw out: *"S-z-lee-p mm-ah-ee-nn-d s-z-rahng."* And from that he could conjecture that sound sleep makes the mind strong, or that the mind must be strong for the body to be strong, or whatever else he wished. It was *kindness*, he knew, and he felt shifty and rotted when he thought of, say, Amy.

> *It will be soon, will it not? Soon?*
> *Quite soon, little ones. Quite, quite soon.*

Amy had not fallen; she had been led, slowly, carefully, by the hand. She had gone delightfully down, night after night. He had been amused to note that there was a night not long after the night of Optol when he had urged her to abstain from further indulgence in a certain diversion which had no name that anyone used, an Avernian pleasure the penalties against which were so severe that one would not compromise himself so far as admitting that he knew it existed and was practiced. Smith had urged her to abstain, and had most sincerely this time meant it. She was heading for the inevitable collapse, and her father was due back from his inspection tour. The whole process had taken some fifty days.

Her father, another gray-eyed booby. . . . A projection room. "A hoax." "Fifty thousand in small, unmarked . . ." The flickering reel-change. "It *can't* be—" "You should know that scar." "I'll kill you first!" "That won't burn the prints." The lights. "The last one—I don't believe . . ." "Fifty thousand." "I'll kill you—"

But he hadn't. He'd killed himself, for no good reason that Smith could understand. Disgustedly, no longer a blackmailer, much out of pocket by this deal that had fizzled, he turned hawker and peddled prints of the film to the sort of person who would buy such things. He almost got his expenses back. After the week of concentration on his sudden mercantile enterprise, he had thought to inquire about Amy.

She had had her smashup, lost her job tape-punching now that her father was dead and her really scandalous behavior could no longer be ignored. She had got an unconventional job in the Open Quarter. She had left it. She appeared, hanging around the shops at Standard Transport, where the watchmen had orders to drive her away. She always came back, and one day, evidently, got what she wanted.

For on the Portsmouth-Jamestown run, which Smith was making to see a man who had a bar with a small theater in what was ostensibly a storeroom, his ship had parted at the seams.

"Dumped me where you found me—mid-desert."
"T-urr-ss-t-ee," sawed the native.
There seemed to be some reproach in the word, and Smith chided himself for imagining that a creature which

spoke by stridulation could charge its language with the same emotional overtones as those who used lungs and vocal cords.

But there the note was again: "Ei-m-m-ee—t-urr-ss-t—t-oo."

Amy thirst too. A stridulating moralist. But still ... one had to admit ... in his frosty way, Smith was reasoning, but a wash of emotion blurred the diagrams, the cold diagrams by which he had always lived.

It's getting me, he thought—it's getting me at last. He'd seen it happen before, and always admitted that it might happen to him—but it was a shock.

Hesitantly, which was strange for him, he asked if he could somehow find his way across the desert to Portsmouth. The creature ticked approvingly, brought in sand and with one delicate appendage began to trace what might be a map.

He was going to do it. He was going to be clean again, he who had always had a horror of filth and never until now had seen that his life was viler than maggots, more loathsome than carrion. A warm glow of self-approval filled him while he bent over the map. Yes, he was going to perform the incredible hike and somehow make restitution to her. Who would have thought an inhuman creature like his benefactor could have done this to him? With all the enthusiasm of any convert, he felt young again, with life before him, a life where he could choose between fair and foul. He chuckled with the newness of it.

But to work! Good intentions were not enough. There was the map to memorize, his bearings to establish, some portable food supply to be gathered—

He followed the map with his finger. The tracing appendage of the creature guided him, another quietly lay around him, its tip at the small of his back. He accepted it, though it itched somewhat. Not for an itch would he risk offending the bearer of his new life.

He was going to get Amy to a cure, give her money, bear her abuse—she could not understand all at once that he was another man—turn his undoubted talent to an honest—

Farewell! Farewell!
Farewell, little ones. Farewell.

The map blurred a bit before Smith's eyes. Then the map toppled and slid and became the red-lit ceiling of the burrow. Then Smith tried to move and could not. The itching in his back was a torment.

The screy mother did not look at the prostrate host as she turned and crawled up from the incubator to the surface. Something like fond humor wrinkled the surface of her thoughts as she remembered the little ones and their impatience. Heigh-ho! She had given them the best she could, letting many a smaller host go by until this fine, big host came her way. It had taken feeding and humoring, but it would last many and many a month while the little wrigglers grew and ate and grew within it. Heigh-ho! Life went on, she thought; one did the best one could. . . .

There are people who claim to have seen and communicated with alien beings, either here on Earth or inside alien spacecraft; there are even people who are convinced that creatures from the stars—BEMs with multicolored tentacles, perhaps—are bent on invasion and ultimate takeover of the planet. It is generally felt that these individuals are suffering from delusions of one kind or another and might be cured by extensive psychotherapy. But what if such a person went to his psychiatrist to discuss what he believed was an alien invasion, and discovered that the shrink had been replaced by a BEM? This is what happens to Cavender, the protagonist of "The Last One Left," and with rather startling results.

Despite the fact that they live 3,000 miles apart, Bill Pronzini (b. 1943) and Barry N. Malzberg (b. 1939) have been collaborating since the early 1970s. Working together, they have produced three suspense novels, three previous anthologies of science fiction, and some thirty mystery and s-f short stories. Individually, Pronzini has published fifteen novels and more than 200 short stories and articles, and is the editor of one fantasy (Werewolf!) and three mystery anthologies; and Malzberg has authored seventy novels, 250 short works of fiction and nonfiction, and six collections, and has co-edited four additional science-fiction anthologies with Edward L. Ferman and Martin Harry Greenberg.

The Last One Left

Bill Pronzini and
Barry N. Malzberg

The alien leans toward Cavender and folds two of its six tentacles on the desk blotter. Bright green eyes on slender stalks regard him gravely. "Now then," it says, "what did you say is disturbing you? It would be best to get right to the point. Of course," it adds in gentle tones, "if you'd prefer not to discuss it at the present moment that would be all right too. Ultimately you must be the judge, the controller, the captain, as it were, of your life."

Cavender smiles. He winks at the alien; it pretends not to notice. He is used to this kind of thing by now and is not even surprised that Doctor Fount has been replaced. His own wife, his secretary, half of his office staff in the last week; surely his psychiatrist was inevitable. He sees Fount twice a week, was somewhat surprised the replacement had not been accomplished on Tuesday.

When the aliens first appeared, just one week ago, they had started at the fringes: marginal people, beggars, cleaning ladies, token sellers, busboys and the like. The next day it had been the children and white-collar workers. Last night it had been Eunice and three-quarters of the opera company. And now it was his shrink. Ah well. He had never got along with Fount anyway.

It doesn't really matter, he thinks. What does matter is finding out why they have moved in and from where they've come. And why nobody but him seems to have been aware of the replacements when they started; no pandemonium on the streets, no newspaper articles, routine applause at the City Opera last night. Is he the only one who can see them?

Once he has the answers to these questions Cavender is sure he will be able to find a way to banish or destroy the aliens. *He* will have to save the world—that occurred to him during the sextet, just before all six of the singers sprouted tentacles. Not to put too fine a point on it, but the fate of Mankind is in his hands. Which is not unusual. He has been cleaning up weaker people's messes all of his life, it seems.

"All of my life," he says, and realizes that he has spoken most of this aloud. An old trait, this talking to himself, which has increased markedly in the past couple of days, what with the pressures and losing Eunice and all. Who could blame a man for becoming a little less stable under these circumstances?

The alien, who has been listening to him with polite attention, says, "This is very interesting, Albert. Why do you think this is so? Why does the fate of Mankind, that is to say, rest exclusively upon you?"

Like Fount, the alien replacement is humoring him. It must have read the files, listened to the tapes. No matter; Cavender loves to be humored. Why pay a hundred dollars for forty-five minutes if not for that? He has always enjoyed psychotherapy, although now of course he can hardly continue.

"Because," he says, "I seem to be the only one aware of the invasion. Your invasion, I mean, through which one by one you've usurped almost all the population of New York. I wonder if it's this way in the midwest, to say nothing of the Eastern bloc?"

The alien regards him sadly. "How long have you felt this way?"

"Oh come on," Cavender says, "I've been in this shrinking game for four years and I know all the tricks better than you. You don't have to deal with me as if this is reactive depression with paranoid focus."

"Come again?"

"Never mind," Cavender says. He pauses. "What I want to find out," he says, "is why you're doing this. I mean, what's your primary motivation? Simple conquest of an inferior race? Or what? And what happens to all the good folks you've replaced? Are they simply being eliminated or are they transferred to your home planet, whatever strange place that must be, and put to work in mines or labor communes?"

The alien holds a pencil between two of its tentacles and assumes an expression of professional concern. It seems to be waiting with interest for him to continue.

"Labor communes would be my guess," Cavender says. "Let's see. You needed to take over a new world because living conditions on your planet are becoming intolerable. Pollution, overpopulation, that sort of thing."

"Mmm," the alien says noncommittally.

"But you don't want to just abandon your home because there are plenty of natural resources left. None of your people want to stay there and work in the communes, so that's where we come in. Where the ones you've replaced come in, rather. How about that? Am I on the right track?"

One of the alien's eyestalks flicks aside. Nothing else changes in its expression and it doesn't speak, but Cavender thinks: Aha! On target, all right.

"Now the next question is," he says, "why am I exempt? Why haven't I been replaced and why is it I can see you for what you are and nobody else suspected a thing?"

"Perhaps you'd care to venture another guess there, Albert," the alien says.

Cavender nods, considers, and has what he takes to be another insight. "Maybe you aliens are only able to replace people who don't need shrinks," he says. "The unimaginative masses, the normal ones. Normal ones," he says again, because he likes the sound of the phrase. "Does that make any sense?"

"What do you think, Albert? It's you on whom all of this must focus, after all. Are *you* pleased with your insights?"

"Stop patronizing me," Cavender says. "I'm one of the last ones left and you know it. Maybe I'm even the *last* one by now, who knows?" He pauses, suddenly at a loss. "I'm quite disturbed by all of this," he adds after a while.

"I'm sure you are, Albert," the alien says in a sympathetic way. "Of course you realize I have no answers. The only answers must come from you, as I have explained in the past."

The alien's color has shifted, Cavender notices. It is the most delicate of orange now, its tentacles a pastoral and bucolic blue, as blue as an inverted bowl of sky against the earth-colored speckles of the upper and lower extremities. His perspective lurches; he feels a moment of confusion. *Another* moment of confusion?

"I think I'm going to leave," he says.

"That is your decision. You don't have to talk, though: we can just sit here if you like."

There is a beauty to the tentacles; they have the symmetry and the fine detail of the backs of old violins. "No," Cavender says, "I want to leave. You'll bill me, I guess. Do aliens send out bills?"

"Of course I'll bill you, Albert," the alien says kindly. "But why don't you lie down on the couch and rest for a time? You still have twenty minutes left and you want to get full value for your money, don't you?"

"You have no mercy," Cavender says. "I'm not bitter about that but it's the truth. No mercy at all."

"Why do you say that? Why do you think I have no mercy?"

"Because you don't. You could make it easier for me by admitting the truth, but you just won't do it."

"What truth, Albert?"

"Oh all right," Cavender says irritably and stands. The beauty of the tentacles is beginning to unnerve him. "An invasion is an invasion. You people are obviously superior to us in every way and your mass hypnosis and transferral program is almost a hundred percent effective. You hold all the advantages. For now," he adds in a cryptic tone. "For now."

"We'll continue this next Tuesday," the alien says. "Unless you'd care to change your mind and stay on for the rest of your session—"

Cavender shakes his head, turns, and leaves the office. He notes as he walks through the reception area that in the interim Fount's secretary has also become an alien—a small, delicate, five-tentacled creature in fetching magenta with multicolored eye-stalks. It is all slipping away very quickly; he should have known that they would make a second sweep of all clerical personnel. He sighs and goes through the outer door, waits in the corridor by the elevator.

Three aliens emerge wobbling from the periodontist's office adjacent and stand by him, complaining to each other about excessive bleeding and the perils of anesthesia. Aliens, it would seem, have the same dental problems as humans. He must keep that in mind, Cavender thinks; it might be a flaw in their armament. Perhaps it can be worked with, used against them as a means of saving the world. If there is any world left to save, that is. If he is not already the last human left.

The elevator comes and takes them all silently to the lobby, where they part. Cavender walks toward the entrance at a brisk pace, and then he—

—rolls through the flickering doors. Comes into a burning and omnipresent sunlight. Conditions here are not nearly so good as advertised, he thinks; there is too much sunlight and too much air. At the very least they could have denextified the amorlets for the Crossing, piped through a little inductivity. But then, Headquarters gives grattl about the amenities. All they care about is ranking and rendling, ninking and bocck, and little compassion for the furnerraghts as always.

Waving his tentacles meditatively, denextifying as best he can unsupported, Szzlvey Trg establishes rolicular modal control and warkles toward Cavender's hutch.

The BEM in "Hostess," like those in most stories in this anthology, is atypical: a doctor from a world called Hawkin's Planet comes to Earth to study a deadly phenomenon known as the Inhibition Death. The story begins when he is invited to stay in the home of a noted biologist and her "policeman" husband—and develops into a grim, suspenseful (and scientifically exacting) account of one of the strangest of all fictional triangles, with a superior twist at the end.

Isaac Asimov (b. 1920) last year published his 200th book—twice. That is to say, his 200th and 201st were brought out at the same time, by his two leading publishers, so that both may lay claim to the honor; they are Opus 200 *(Houghton Mifflin) and* In Memory Yet Green: The Autobiography of Isaac Asimov, Part One *(Doubleday). His 199 previous books include works of science fiction, mystery fiction, popular science, encyclopedic scholasticism—and some that defy categorization. Perhaps the most famous and most prolific writer in the United States (certainly the one with the highest visual recognition), Dr. Asimov lives in New York City with his wife, Janet, and continues to amass a staggeringly impressive body of work.*

Hostess

Isaac Asimov

Rose Smollett was happy about it; almost triumphant. She peeled off her gloves, put her hat away, and turned her brightening eyes upon her husband.

She said, "Drake, we're going to have him here."

Drake looked at her with annoyance. "You've missed supper. I thought you were going to be back by seven."

"Oh, that doesn't matter. I ate something on the way home. But, Drake, we're going to have him here!"

"*Who* here? What are you talking about?"

"The doctor from Hawkin's Planet! Didn't you realize that was what today's conference was about? We spent all day talking about it. It's the most exciting thing that could possibly have happened!"

Drake Smollett removed the pipe from the vicinity of his face. He stared first at it and then at his wife. "Let me get this straight. When you say the doctor from Hawkin's Planet, do you mean the Hawkinsite you've got at the Institute?"

"Well, of course. Who else could I possibly mean?"

"And may I ask what the devil you mean by saying we'll have him here?"

"Drake, don't you understand?"

"What is there to understand? Your Institute may be interested in the thing, but I'm not. What have we do with it personally? It's Institute business, isn't it?"

"But, darling," Rose said, patiently, "the Hawkinsite would like to stay at a private house somewhere, where he won't be bothered with official ceremony, and where he'll be able to proceed more according to his own likes and dislikes. I find it quite understandable."

"Why at *our* house?"

"Because our place is convenient for the purpose, I suppose. They asked if I would allow it, and frankly," she added with some stiffness, "I consider it a privilege."

"Look!" Drake put his fingers through his brown hair and succeeded in rumpling it. "We've got a convenient little place here—granted! It's not the most elegant place in the world, but it does well enough for us. However, I don't see where we've got room for extraterrestrial visitors."

Rose began to look worried. She removed her glasses and put them away in their case. "He can stay in the spare room. He'll take care of it himself. I've spoken to him and he's very pleasant. Honestly, all we have to do is show a certain amount of adaptability."

Drake said, "Sure, just a little adaptability! The Hawkinsites breathe cyanide. We'll just adapt ourselves to that, I suppose!"

"He carries the cyanide in a little cylinder. You won't even notice it."

"And what else about them that I won't notice?"

"*Nothing* else. They're perfectly harmless. Goodness, they're even vegetarians."

"And what does that mean? Do we feed him a bale of hay for dinner?"

Rose's lower lip trembled. "Drake, you're being deliberately hateful. There are many vegetarians on Earth; they don't eat hay."

"And what about us? Do we eat meat ourselves or will that make us look like cannibals to him? I won't live on salads to suit him; I warn you."

"You're being quite ridiculous."

Rose felt helpless. She had married late in life, comparatively. Her career had been chosen; she herself had seemed well settled in it. She was a fellow in biology at the Jenkins Institute for the Natural Sciences, with over twenty publications to her credit. In a word, the line was hewed, the path cleared; she had been set for a career and spinsterhood. And now, at thirty-five, she was still a little amazed to find herself a bride of less than a year.

Occasionally, it embarrassed her, too, since she sometimes found that she had not the slightest idea of how to handle her husband. What *did* one do when the man of the family became mulish? That was not included in any of her courses. As a woman of independent mind and career, she couldn't bring herself to cajolery.

So she looked at him steadily and said simply, "It means very much to me."

"Why?"

"Because, Drake, if he stays here for any length of time, I can study him really closely. Very little work has been done on the biology and psychology of the individual Hawkinsites or of any of the extraterrestrial intelligences. We have some on their sociology and history, of course, but that's all. Surely, you must see the opportunity. He stays here; we watch him, speak to him, observe his habits—"

"Not interested."

"Oh, Drake, I don't understand you."

"You're going to say I'm not usually like this, I suppose."

"Well, you're not."

Drake was silent for a while. He seemed withdrawn and his high cheekbones and large chin were twisted and frozen into a brooding position.

He said, finally, "Look, I've heard a bit about the Hawkinsites in the way of my own business. You say there have been investigations of their sociology, but not of their biology. Sure. It's because the Hawkinsites don't like to be studied as specimens any more than we would. I've spoken to men who were in charge of security groups watching various Hawkinsite missions on Earth. The missions stay in the rooms assigned to them and don't leave for anything but the most important official business. They have nothing to do with Earthmen. It's quite obvious that they are as revolted by us as I personally am by them.

"In fact, I just don't understand why this Hawkinsite at the Institute should be any different. It seems to me to be against all the rules to have him come here by himself, anyway—and to have him want to stay in an Earthman's home just puts the maraschino cherry on top."

Rose said, wearily, "This is different. I'm surprised you can't understand it, Drake. He's a doctor. He's coming here in the way of medical research, and I'll grant you that he probably doesn't enjoy staying with human beings and will find us perfectly horrible. But he must stay just the same! Do you suppose human doctors enjoy going into the tropics, or that they are particularly fond of letting themselves be bitten by infected mosquitoes?"

Drake said sharply, "What's this about mosquitoes? What have they to do with it?"

"Why, nothing," Rose answered, surprised. "It just came to my mind, that's all. I was thinking of Reed and his yellow fever experiments."

Drake shrugged. "Well, have it your own way."

For a moment, Rose hesitated. "You're not angry about this, are you?" To her own ears she sounded unpleasantly girlish.

"No."

And that, Rose knew, meant that he was.

Rose surveyed herself doubtfully in the full-length mirror. She had never been beautiful and was quite reconciled to the fact; so much so that it no longer mattered. Certainly, it would not matter to a being from Hawkin's Planet. What *did* bother her was this matter of being a hostess under the very queer circumstances of having to be tactful to an extraterrestrial creature and, at the same time, to her husband as well. She wondered which would prove the more difficult.

Drake was coming home late that day; he was not due for half an hour. Rose found herself inclined to believe that he had arranged that purposely in a sullen desire to leave her alone with her problem. She found herself in a state of mild resentment.

He had called her just before noon at the Institute and had asked abruptly, "When are you taking him home?"

She answered, curtly, "In about three hours."

"All right. What's his name? His Hawkinsite name?"

"Why do you want to know?" She could not keep the chill from her words.

"Let's call it a small investigation of my own. After all, the thing will be in my house."

"Oh, for heaven's sake, Drake, don't bring your job home with you!"

Drake's voice sounded tinny and nasty in her ears. "Why not, Rose? Isn't that exactly what you're doing?"

It was, of course, so she gave him the information he wanted.

This was the first time in their married life that they had had even the semblance of a quarrel, and, as she sat there before the full-length mirror, she began to wonder if perhaps she ought not make an attempt to see his side of it. In essence, she had married a policeman. Of course he was more than simply a policeman; he was a member of the World Security Board.

It had been a surprise to her friends. The fact of the marriage itself had been the biggest surprise, but if she had decided on marriage, the attitude was, why not with another biologist? Or, if she had wanted to go afield, an anthropologist, perhaps; even a chemist; but why, of all people, a policeman? Nobody had exactly said those things, naturally, but it had been in the very atmosphere at the time of her marriage.

She had resented it then, and ever since. A man could marry whom he chose, but if a doctor of philosophy, female variety, chose to marry a man who never went past the bachelor's degree, there was shock. Why should there be? What business was it of theirs? He was handsome, in a way, intelligent, in another way, and she was perfectly satisfied with her choice.

Yet how much of this same snobbishness did she bring home with her? Didn't she always have the attitude that her own work, her biological investigations, were important, while his job was merely something to be kept within the four walls of his little office in the old U.N. buildings on the East River?

She jumped up from her seat in agitation and, with a deep breath, decided to leave such thoughts behind her. She desperately did not want to quarrel with him. And she just wasn't going to interfere with him. She was committed to accepting the Hawkinsite as guest, but otherwise she would let Drake have his own way. He was making enough of a concession as it was.

Harg Tholan was standing quietly in the middle of the living room when she came down the stairs. He was not sitting, since he was not anatomically constructed to sit. He stood on two sets of limbs placed close together, while a third pair entirely different in construction were suspended from a region that would have been the upper chest in a human being. The skin of his body was hard, glistening and ridged, while his face bore a distant resemblance to something alienly bovine. Yet he was not completely repulsive, and he wore clothes of a sort over the lower portion of his body in order to avoid offending the sensibilities of his human hosts.

He said, "Mrs. Smollett, I appreciate your hospitality beyond my ability to express it in your language," and he drooped so that his forelimbs touched the ground for a moment.

Rose knew this to be a gesture signifying gratitude among the beings of Hawkin's Planet. She was grateful that he spoke English as well as he did. The construction of his mouth, combined with an absence of incisors, gave a whistling sound to the sibilants. Aside from that, he might have been born on Earth for all the accent his speech showed.

She said, "My husband will be home soon, and then we will eat."

"Your husband?" For a moment, he said nothing more, and then added, "Yes, of course."

She let it go. If there was one source of infinite confusion among the five intelligent races of the known Galaxy, it lay in the differences among them with regard to their sex life and the social institutions that grew around it. The concept of husband and wife, for instance, existed only on Earth. The other races could achieve a sort of intellectual understanding of what it meant, but never an emotional one.

She said, "I have consulted the Institute in preparing your menu. I trust you will find nothing in it that will upset you."

The Hawkinsite blinked its eyes rapidly. Rose recalled this to be a gesture of amusement.

He said, "Proteins are proteins, my dear Mrs. Smollett. For those trace factors which I need but are not supplied in your food, I have brought concentrates that will be most adequate."

And proteins *were* proteins. Rose knew this to be true. Her concern for the creature's diet had been largely one of formal politeness. In the discovery of life on the planets of the outer stars, one of the most interesting generalizations that had developed was the fact that, although life could be formed on the basis of substances other than proteins—

even on elements other than carbon—it remained true that the only known intelligences were proteinaceous in nature. This meant that each of the five forms of intelligent life could maintain themselves over prolonged periods on the food of any of the other four.

She heard Drake's key in the door and went stiff with apprehension.

She had to admit he did well. He strode in, and, without hesitation, thrust his hand out at the Hawkinsite, saying firmly, "Good evening, Dr. Tholan."

The Hawkinsite put out his large and rather clumsy forelimb and the two, so to speak, shook hands. Rose had already gone through that procedure and knew the queer feeling of a Hawkinsite hand in her own. It had felt rough and hot and dry. She imagined that, to the Hawkinsite, her own and Drake's felt cold and slimy.

At the time of the formal greeting, she had taken the opportunity to observe the alien hand. It was an excellent case of converging evolution. Its morphological development was entirely different from that of the human hand, yet it had brought itself into a fairly approximate similarity. There were four fingers but no thumb. Each finger had five independent ball-and-socket joints. In this way, the flexibility lost with the absence of the thumb was made up for by the almost tentacular properties of the fingers. What was even more interesting to her biologist's eyes was the fact that each Hawkinsite finger ended in a vestigial hoof, very small and, to the layman, unidentifiable as such, but clearly adapted at one time to running, just as man's had been to climbing.

Drake said, in friendly enough fashion, "Are you quite comfortable, sir?"

The Hawkinsite answered, "Quite. Your wife has been most thoughtful in all her arrangements."

"Would you care for a drink?"

The Hawkinsite did not answer but looked at Rose with a slight facial contortion that indicated some emotion which, unfortunately, Rose could not interpret. She said, nervously, "On Earth there is the custom of drinking liquids which have been fortified with ethyl alcohol. We find it stimulating."

"Oh, yes. I am afraid, then, that I must decline. Ethyl alcohol would interfere most unpleasantly with my metabolism."

"Why, so it does to Earthmen, too, but I understand, Dr. Tholan," Drake replied. "Would you object to *my* drinking?"

"Of course not."

Drake passed close to Rose on his way to the sideboard and she caught only one word. He said, "God!" in a tightly controlled whisper, yet he managed to put seventeen exclamation points after it.

The Hawkinsite *stood* at the table. His fingers were models of dexterity as they wove their way around the cutlery. Rose tried not to look at him as he ate. His wide lipless mouth split his face alarmingly as he ingested food, and, in chewing, his large jaws moved disconcertingly from side to side. It was another evidence of his ungulate ancestry. Rose found herself wondering if, in the quiet of his own room, he would later chew his cud, and was then panic-stricken lest Drake get the same idea and leave the table in disgust. But Drake was taking everything quite calmly.

He said, "I imagine, Dr. Tholan, that the cylinder at your side holds cyanide?"

Rose started. She had actually not noticed it. It was a curved metal object, something like a water canteen, that fitted flatly against the creature's skin, half-hidden behind its clothing. But, then, Drake had a policeman's eyes.

The Hawkinsite was not in the least disconcerted. "Quite so," he said, and his hoofed fingers held out a thin, flexible hose that ran up his body, its tint blending into that of his yellowish skin, and entered the corner of his wide mouth. Rose felt slightly embarrassed, as though at the display of intimate articles of clothing.

Drake said, "And does it contain pure cyanide?"

The Hawkinsite humorously blinked his eyes. "I hope you are not considering possible danger to Earthites. I know the gas is highly poisonous to you and I do not need a great deal. The gas contained in the cylinder is five percent hydrogen cyanide, the remainder oxygen. None of it emerges except when I actually suck at the tube, and that need not be done frequently."

"I see. And you really must have the gas to live?"

Rose was slightly appalled. One simply did not ask such questions without careful preparation. It was impossible to foresee where the sensitive points of an alien psychology might be. And Drake *must* be doing this deliberately, since he could not help realizing that he could get answers to such questions as easily from herself. Or was it that he preferred not to ask her?

The Hawkinsite remained apparently unperturbed. "Are you not a biologist, Mr. Smollett?"

"No, Dr. Tholan."

"But you are in close association with Mrs. *Dr.* Smollett."

Drake smiled a bit. "Yes, I am married to a Mrs. doctor, but just the same I am not a biologist; merely a minor government official. My wife's friends," he added, "call me a policeman."

Rose bit the inside of her cheek. In this case it was the Hawkinsite who had impinged upon the sensitive point of an alien psychology. On Hawkin's Planet, there was a tight caste system and intercaste associations were limited. But Drake wouldn't realize that.

The Hawkinsite turned to her. "May I have your permission, Mrs. Smollett, to explain a little of our biochemistry to your husband? It will be dull for you, since I am sure you must understand it quite well already."

She said, "By all means do, Dr. Tholan."

He said, "You see, Mr. Smollett, the respiratory system in your body and in the bodies of all air-breathing creatures on Earth is controlled by certain metal-containing enzymes, I am taught. The metal is usually iron, though sometimes it is copper. In either case, small traces of cyanide would combine with these metals and immobilize the respiratory system of the terrestrial living cell. They would be prevented from using oxygen and killed in a few minutes.

"The life on my own planet is not quite so constituted. The key respiratory compounds contain neither iron nor copper; no metal at all, in fact. It is for this reason that my blood is colorless. Our compounds contain certain organic groupings which are essential to life, and these groupings can only be maintained intact in the presence of a small concentration of cyanide. Undoubtedly, this type of protein has developed through millions of years of evolution on a world which has a few tenths of a percent of hydrogen cyanide occurring naturally in the atmosphere. Its presence is maintained by a biological cycle. Various of our native micro-organisms liberate the free gas."

"You make it extremely clear, Dr. Tholan, and very interesting," Drake said. "What happens if you don't breathe it? Do you just go, like that?" He snapped his fingers.

"Not quite. It isn't equivalent to the presence of cyanide for you. In my case, the absence of cyanide would be equivalent to slow strangulation. It happens sometimes, in ill-ventilated rooms on my world, that the cyanide is gradually consumed and falls below the minimum necessary concentration. The results are very painful and difficult to treat."

Rose had to give Drake credit; he really sounded interested. And the alien, thank heaven, did not mind the catechism.

The rest of the dinner passed without incident. It was almost pleasant.

Throughout the evening, Drake remained that way; interested. Even more than that—absorbed. He drowned her out, and she was glad of it. *He* was the one who was really colorful and it was only her job, her specialized training, that stole the color from him. She looked at him gloomily and thought, *Why did he marry me?*

Drake sat, one leg crossed over the other, hands clasped and tapping his chin gently, watching the Hawkinsite intently. The Hawkinsite faced him, standing in his quadruped fashion.

Drake said, "I find it difficult to keep thinking of you as a doctor."

The Hawkinsite laughingly blinked his eyes. "I understand what you mean," he said. "I find it difficult to think of you as a policeman. On my world, policemen are very specialized and distinctive people."

"Are they?" said Drake, somewhat drily, and then changed the subject. "I gather that you are not here on a pleasure trip."

"No, I am here very much on business. I intend to study

this queer planet you call Earth, as it has never been studied before by any of my people."

"Queer?" asked Drake. "In what way?"

The Hawkinsite looked at Rose. "Does he know of the Inhibition Death?"

Rose felt embarrassed. "His work is important," she said. "I am afraid that my husband has little time to listen to the details of my work." She knew that this was not really adequate and she felt herself to be the recipient, yet again, of one of the Hawkinsite's unreadable emotions.

The extraterrestrial creature turned back to Drake. "It is always amazing to me to find how little you Earthmen understand your own unusual characteristics. Look, there are five intelligent races in the Galaxy. These have all developed independently, yet have managed to converge in remarkable fashion. It is as though, in the long run, intelligence requires a certain physical makeup to flourish. I leave that question for philosophers. But I need not belabor the point, since it must be a familiar one to you.

"Now when the differences among the intelligences are closely investigated, it is found over and over again that it is you Earthmen, more than any of the others, who are unique. For instance, it is only on Earth that life depends upon metal enzymes for respiration. Your people are the only ones which find hydrogen cyanide poisonous. Yours is the only form of intelligent life which is carnivorous. Yours is the only form of life which has not developed from a grazing animal. And, most interesting of all, yours is the only form of intelligent life known which stops growing upon reaching maturity."

Drake grinned at him. Rose felt her heart suddenly race. It was the nicest thing about him, that grin, and he was using it perfectly naturally. It wasn't forced or false. He was *adjusting* to the presence of this alien creature. He was being pleasant—and he must be doing it for her. She loved that thought and repeated it to herself. He was doing it for her; he was being nice to the Hawkinsite for her sake.

Drake was saying with his grin, "You don't look very large, Dr. Tholan, I should say that you are an inch taller than I am, which would make you six feet two inches tall. Is it that you are young, or is it that the others on your world are generally small?"

"Neither," said the Hawkinsite. "We grow at a diminishing rate with the years, so that at my age it would take fifteen years to grow an additional inch, but—and this is the important point—we never *entirely* stop. And, of course, as a consequence, we never entirely die."

Drake gasped and even Rose felt herself sitting stiffly upright. This was something new. This was something which, to her knowledge, the few expeditions to Hawkin's Planet had never brought back. She was torn with excitement but held an exclamation back and let Drake speak for her.

He said, "They don't entirely die? You're not trying to say, sir, that the people on Hawkin's Planet are immortal?"

"No people are truly immortal. If there were no other way to die, there would always be accident, and if that fails, there is boredom. Few of us live more than several centuries of your time. Still, it is unpleasant to think that death may come involuntarily. It is something which, to us, is extremely horrible. It bothers me even as I think of it now, this thought that *against my will and despite all care*, death may come."

"We," said Drake, grimly, "are quite used to it."

"You Earthmen live with the thought; we do not. And this is why we are disturbed to find that the incidence of Inhibition Death has been increasing in recent years."

"You have not yet explained," said Drake, "just what the Inhibition Death is, but let me guess. Is the Inhibition Death a pathological cessation of growth?"

"Exactly."

"And how long after growth's cessation does death follow?"

"Within the year. It is a wasting disease, a tragic one, and absolutely incurable."

"What causes it?"

The Hawkinsite paused a long time before answering, and even then there was something strained and uneasy about the way he spoke. "Mr. Smollett, we know nothing about the cause of the disease."

Drake nodded thoughtfully. Rose was following the conversation as though she were a spectator at a tennis match.

Drake said, "And why do you come to Earth to study this disease?"

"Because again Earthmen are unique. They are the only intelligent beings who are immune. The Inhibition Death affects *all* the other races. Do your biologists know that, Mrs. Smollett?"

He had addressed her suddenly, so that she jumped slightly. She said, "No, they don't."

"I am not surprised. That piece of information is the result of very recent research. The Inhibition Death is easily diagnosed incorrectly and the incidence is much lower on the other planets. In fact, it is a strange thing, something to philosophize over, that the incidence of the Death is highest on my world, which is closest to Earth, and lower on each more distant planet—so that it is lowest on the world of the star Tempora, which is farthest from Earth, while Earth itself is immune. Somewhere in the biochemistry of the Earthite, there is the secret of that immunity. How interesting it would be to find it."

Drake said, "But look here, you can't say Earth is immune. From where I sit, it looks as if the incidence is a hundred percent. All Earthmen stop growing and all Earthmen die. We've *all* got the Inhibition Death."

"Not at all. Earthmen live up to seventy years after the cessation of growth. That is not the Death as *we* know it. *Your* equivalent disease is rather one of unrestrained growth. Cancer, you call it. —But come, I bore you."

Rose protested instantly. Drake did likewise with even more vehemence, but the Hawkinsite determinedly changed the subject. It was then that Rose had her first pang of suspicion, for Drake circled Harg Tholan warily with his words, worrying him, jabbing at him, attempting always to get the information back to the point where the Hawkinsite had left off. Not baldly, not unskillfully, but Rose knew him, and could tell what he was after. And what could he be after but that which was demanded by his profession? And, as though in response to her thoughts, the Hawkinsite took up the phrase which had begun careening in her mind like a broken record on a perpetual turntable.

He asked, "Did you not say you were a policeman?"
Drake said, curtly, "Yes."
"Then there is something I would like to request you to do for me. I have been wanting to all this evening, since I discovered your profession, and yet I hesitate. I do not wish to be troublesome to my host and hostess."
"We'll do what we can."
"I have a profound curiosity as to how Earthmen live; a curiosity which is not perhaps shared by the generality of

my countrymen. So I wonder, could you show me through one of the police departments on your planet?"

"I do not belong to a police department in exactly the way you imagine," said Drake, cautiously. "However, I am known to the New York police department. I can manage it without trouble. Tomorrow?"

"That would be most convenient for me. Would I be able to visit the Missing Persons Bureau?"

"The what?"

The Hawkinsite drew his four standing legs closer together, as if he were becoming more intense. "It is a hobby of mine, a little queer corner of interest I have always had. I understand you have a group of police officers whose sole duty it is to search for men who are missing."

"And women and children," added Drake. "But why should that interest you so particularly?"

"Because there again you are unique. There is no such thing as a missing person on our planet. I can't explain the mechanism to you, of course, but among the people of the other worlds, there is always an awareness of one another's presence, especially if there is a strong, affectionate tie. We are always aware of each other's exact location, no matter where on the planet we might be."

Rose grew excited again. The scientific expeditions to Hawkin's Planet had always had the greatest difficulty in penetrating the internal emotional mechanisms of the natives, and here was one who talked freely, who would explain! She forgot to worry about Drake and intruded into the conversation. "Can you feel such awareness even now? On Earth?"

The Hawkinsite said, "You mean across space? No, I'm afraid not. But you see the importance of the matter. All the uniquenesses of Earth should be linked. If the lack of this sense can be explained, perhaps the immunity to Inhibition Death can be, also. Besides, it strikes me as very curious that any form of intelligent community life can be built up among people who lack this community awareness. How can an Earthman tell, for instance, when he has formed a congenial sub-group, a family? How can you two, for instance, know that there is a true tie between you?"

Rose found herself nodding. How strongly she missed such a sense!

But Drake only smiled. "We have our ways. It is as difficult to explain what we call 'love' to you as it is for you to explain your sense to us."

"I suppose so. Yet tell me truthfully, Mr. Smollett—if Mrs. Smollett were to leave this room and enter another without your having seen her do so, would you really not be aware of her location?"

"I really would not."

The Hawkinsite said, "Amazing." He hesitated, then added, "Please do not be offended at the fact that I find it revolting as well."

After the light in the bedroom had been put out, Rose went to the door three times, opening it a crack and peering out. She could feel Drake watching her. There was a hard kind of amusement in his voice as he asked, finally, "What's the matter?"

She said, "I want to talk to you."

"Are you afraid our friend can hear?"

Rose was whispering. She got into bed and put her head on his pillow so that she could whisper better. She said, "Why were you talking about the Inhibition Death to Dr. Tholan?"

"I am taking an interest in your work, Rose. You've always wanted me to take an interest."

"I'd rather you weren't sarcastic." She was almost violent, as nearly violent as she could be in a whisper. "I know that there's something of your own interest in this—of *police* interest, probably. What is it?"

He said, "I'll talk to you tomorrow."

"No, right now."

He put his hand under her head, lifting it. For a wild moment she thought he was going to kiss her—just kiss her on impulse the way husbands sometimes did, or as she imagined they sometimes did. Drake never did, and he didn't now.

He merely held her close and whispered, "Why are you so interested?"

His hand was almost brutally hard upon the nape of her neck, so that she stiffened and tried to draw back. Her voice was more than a whisper now. "Stop it, Drake."

He said, "I want no questions from you and no interference. You do your job, and I'll do mine."

"The nature of my job is open and known."

"The nature of my job," he retorted, "isn't, by definition. But I'll tell you this. Our six-legged friend is here in this house for some definite reason. You weren't picked as biologist in charge for any random reason. Do you know that two days ago, he'd been inquiring about me at the Commission?"

"You're joking."

"Don't believe that for a minute. There are depths to this that you know nothing about. But that's my job and I won't discuss it with you any further. Do you understand?"

"No, but I won't question you if you don't want me to."

"Then go to sleep."

She lay stiffly on her back and the minutes passed, and then the quarter-hours. She was trying to fit the pieces together. Even with what Drake had told her, the curves and colors refused to blend. She wondered what Drake would say if he knew she had a recording of that night's conversation!

One picture remained clear in her mind at that moment. It hovered over her mockingly. The Hawkinsite, at the end of the long evening, had turned to her and said gravely, "Good night, Mrs. Smollett. You are a most charming hostess."

She had desperately wanted to giggle at the time. How could he call her a charming hostess? To him, she could only be a horror, a monstrosity with too few limbs and a too-narrow face.

And then, as the Hawkinsite delivered himself of this completely meaningless piece of politeness, Drake had turned white! For one instant, his eyes had burned with something that looked like terror.

She had never before known Drake to show fear of anything, and the picture of that instant of pure panic remained with her until all her thoughts finally sagged into the oblivion of sleep.

It was noon before Rose was at her desk the next day. She had deliberately waited until Drake and the Hawkinsite had left, since only then was she able to remove the small recorder that had been behind Drake's armchair the previous evening. She had had no original intention of keeping its presence secret from him. It was just that he had come home so late, and she couldn't say anything about it with the Hawkinsite present. Later on, of course, things had changed—

The placing of the recorder had been only a routine maneuver. The Hawkinsite's statements and intonations needed to be preserved for future intensive studies by various specialists at the Institute. It had been hidden in order to avoid the distortions of self-consciousness that the visibility of such a device would bring, and now it couldn't be shown to the members of the Institute at all. It would have to serve a different function altogether. A rather nasty function.

She was going to spy on Drake.

She touched the little box with her fingers and wondered, irrelevantly, how Drake was going to manage, that day. Social intercourse between inhabited worlds was, even now, not so commonplace that the sight of a Hawkinsite on the city streets would not succeed in drawing crowds. But Drake would manage, she knew. Drake always managed.

She listened once again to the sounds of last evening, repeating the interesting moments. She was dissatisfied with what Drake had told her. Why should the Hawkinsite have been interested in the two of them particularly? Yet Drake wouldn't lie. She would have liked to check at the Security Commission, but she knew she could not do that. Besides, the thought made her feel disloyal; Drake would definitely not lie.

But, then again, why should Harg Tholan not have investigated them? He might have inquired similarly about the families of all the biologists at the Institute. It would be no more than natural to attempt to choose the home he would find most pleasant by his own standards, whatever they were.

And if he had—even if he had investigated only the Smolletts—why should that create the great change in Drake from intense hostility to intense interest? Drake undoubtedly had knowledge he was keeping to himself. Only heaven knew how much.

Her thoughts churned slowly through the possibilities of interstellar intrigue. So far, to be sure, there were no signs of hostility or ill-feeling among any of the five intelligent races known to inhabit the Galaxy. As yet they were spaced at intervals too wide for enmity. Even the barest contact among them was all but impossible. Economic and political interests just had no points at which to conflict.

But that was only her idea and she was not a member of the Security Commission. If there *were* conflict, if there *were* danger, if there *were* any reason to suspect that the mission of a Hawkinsite might be other than peaceful—Drake would know.

Yet was Drake sufficiently high in the councils of the Security Commission to know, offhand, the dangers involved in the visit of a Hawkinsite physician? She had never thought of his position as more than that of a very minor functionary in the Commission; he had never presented himself as more. And yet—

Might he be more?

She shrugged at the thought. It was reminiscent of twentieth-century spy novels and of costume dramas of the days when there existed such things as atom bomb secrets.

The thought of costume dramas decided her. Unlike Drake, she wasn't a real policeman, and she didn't know how a real policeman would go about it. But she knew how such things were done in the old dramas.

She drew a piece of paper toward her and, with a quick motion, slashed a vertical pencil mark down its center. She headed one column "Harg Tholan," the other "Drake." Under "Harg Tholan" she wrote "bonafide" and thoughtfully put three question marks after it. After all, was he a doctor at all, or was he what could only be described as an interstellar agent? What proof had even the Institute of his profession except his own statements? Was that why Drake had quizzed him so relentlessly concerning the Inhibition

Death? Had he boned up in advance and tried to catch the Hawkinsite in an error?

For a moment, she was irresolute; then, springing to her feet, she folded the paper, put it in the pocket of her short jacket, and swept out of her office. She said nothing to any of those she passed as she left the Institute. She left no word at the reception desk as to where she was going, or when she would be back.

Once outside, she hurried into the third level tube and waited for an empty compartment to pass. The two minutes that elapsed seemed unbearably long. It was all she could do to say, "New York Academy of Medicine," into the mouthpiece just above the seat.

The door of the little cubicle closed, and the sound of the air flowing past the compartment hissed upward in pitch.

The New York Academy of Medicine had been enlarged both vertically and horizontally in the past two decades. The library, alone, occupied one entire wing of the third floor. Undoubtedly, if all the books, pamphlets and periodicals it contained were in their original printed form, rather than in microfilm, the entire building, huge though it was, would not have been sufficiently vast to hold them. As it was, Rose knew there was already talk of limiting printed works to the last five years, rather than to the last ten, as was now the case.

Rose, as a member of the Academy, had free entry to the library. She hurried toward the alcoves devoted to extraterrestrial medicine and was relieved to find them unoccupied.

It might have been wiser to have enlisted the aid of a librarian, but she chose not to. The thinner and smaller the trail she left, the less likely it was that Drake might pick it up.

And so, without guidance, she was satisfied to travel along the shelves, following the titles anxiously with her fingers. The books were almost all in English, though some were in German or Russian. None, ironically enough, were in extraterrestrial symbolisms. There was a room somewhere for such originals, but they were available only to official translators.

Her traveling eye and finger stopped. She had found what she was looking for.

She dragged half a dozen volumes from the shelf and spread them out upon the small dark table. She fumbled for the light switch and opened the first of the volumes. It was entitled *Studies on Inhibition*. She leafed through it and then turned to the author index. The name of Harg Tholan was there.

One by one, she looked up the references indicated, then returned to the shelves for translations of such original papers as she could find.

She spent more than two hours in the Academy. When she was finished, she knew this much—there was a Hawkinsite doctor named Harg Tholan, who was an expert on the Inhibition Death. He was connected with the Hawkinsite research organization with which the Institute had been in correspondence. Of course, the Harg Tholan she knew might simply be impersonating an actual doctor to make the role more realistic, but why should that be necessary?

She took the paper out of her pocket and, where she had written "bonafide" with three question marks, she now wrote a YES in capitals. She went back to the Institute and at 4 P.M. was once again at her desk. She called the switchboard to say that she would not answer any phone calls and then she locked her door.

Underneath the column headed "Harg Tholan" she

now wrote two questions: "Why did Harg Tholan come to Earth alone?" She left considerable space. Then, "What is his interest in the Missing Persons Bureau?"

Certainly, the Inhibition Death was all the Hawkinsite said it was. From her reading at the Academy, it was obvious that it occupied the major share of medical effort on Hawkin's Planet. It was more feared there than cancer was on Earth. If they had thought the answer to it lay on Earth, the Hawkinsites would have sent a full-scale expedition. Was it distrust and suspicion on their part that made them send only one investigator?

What was it Harg Tholan had said the night before? The incidence of the Death was highest upon his own world, which was closest to Earth, lowest upon the world farthest from Earth. Add to that the fact implied by the Hawkinsite, and verified by her own readings at the Academy, that the incidence had expanded enormously since interstellar contact had been made with Earth . . .

Slowly and reluctantly she came to one conclusion. The inhabitants of Hawkin's Planet might have decided that somehow Earth had discovered the cause of the Inhibition Death, and was deliberately fostering it among the alien peoples of the Galaxy, with the intention, perhaps, of becoming supreme among the stars.

She rejected this conclusion with what was almost panic. It could not be; it was impossible. In the first place, Earth *wouldn't* do such a horrible thing. Secondly, it *couldn't*.

As far as scientific advance was concerned, the beings of Hawkin's Planet were certainly the equals of Earthmen. The Death had occurred there for thousands of years and their medical record was one of total failure. Surely, Earth, in its long-distance investigations into alien biochemistry, could not have succeeded so quickly. In fact, as far as she knew, there were no investigations to speak of into Hawkinsite pathology on the part of Earth biologists and physicians.

Yet all the evidence indicated that Harg Tholan had come in suspicion and had been received in suspicion. Carefully, she wrote down under the question, "Why did Harg Tholan come to Earth alone?" the answer, "Hawkin's Planet *believes* Earth is causing the Inhibition Death."

But, then, what was this business about the Bureau of Missing Persons? As a scientist, she was rigorous about the theories she developed. *All* the facts had to fit in, not merely some of them.

Missing Persons Bureau! If it was a false trail, deliberately intended to deceive Drake, it had been done clumsily, since it came only after an hour of discussion of the Inhibition Death.

Was it intended as an opportunity to study Drake? If so, why? Was this perhaps the *major* point? The Hawkinsite had investigated Drake before coming to them. Had he come because Drake was a policeman with entry to Bureaus of Missing Persons?

But why? Why?

She gave it up and turned to the column headed "Drake."

And there a question wrote itself, not in pen and ink upon the paper, but in the much more visible letters of thought on mind. *Why did he marry me?* thought Rose, and she covered her eyes with her hands so that the unfriendly light was excluded.

They had met quite by accident somewhat more than a year before, when he had moved into the apartment house in which she then lived. Polite greetings had somehow become friendly conversation and this, in turn, had led to occasional dinners in a neighborhood restaurant. It had been very friendly and normal and an excitingly new experience, and she had fallen in love.

When he asked her to marry him, she was pleased—and overwhelmed. At the time, she had many explanations for it. He appreciated her intelligence and friendliness. She was a nice girl. She would make a good wife, a splendid companion.

She had tried all those explanations and had half-believed every one of them. But half-belief was not enough.

It was not that she had any definite fault to find in Drake as a husband. He was always thoughtful, kind and a gentleman. Their married life was not one of passion, and yet it suited the paler emotional surges of the late thirties. She wasn't nineteen. What did she expect?

That was it; she wasn't nineteen. She wasn't beautiful, or charming, or glamorous. What did she expect? Could she have expected Drake—handsome and rugged, whose interest in intellectual pursuits was quite minor, who neither asked about her work in all the months of their marriage, nor offered to discuss his own with her? Why, then, did he marry her?

But there was no answer to that question, and it had nothing to do with what Rose was trying to do now. It was extraneous, she told herself fiercely; it was a childish distraction from the task she had set herself. She was acting like a girl of nineteen, after all, with no chronological excuse for it.

She found that the point of her pencil had somehow broken, and took a new one. In the column headed "Drake" she wrote, "Why is he suspicious of Harg Tholan?" and under it she put an arrow pointing to the other column.

What she had already written there was sufficient explanation. If Earth were spreading the Inhibition Death, or if Earth knew it was suspected of such a deed, then, obviously, it would be preparing for eventual retaliation on the part of the aliens. In fact, the setting would actually be one of preliminary maneuvering for the first interstellar war of history. It was an adequate but horrible explanation.

Now there was left the second question, the one she could not answer. She wrote it slowly, "Why Drake's reaction to Tholan's words, 'You are a most charming hostess'?"

She tried to bring back the exact setting. The Hawkinsite had said it innocuously, matter-of-factly, politely, and Drake had frozen at the sound of it. Over and over, she had listened to that particular passage in the recording. An Earthman might have said it in just such an inconsequential tone on leaving a routine cocktail party. The recording did not carry the sight of Drake's face; she had only her memory for that. Drake's eyes had become alive with fear and hate, and Drake was one who feared practically nothing. What was there to fear in the phrase, "You are a most charming hostess," that could upset him so? Jealousy? Absurd. The feeling that Tholan had been sarcastic? Maybe, though unlikely. She was sure Tholan was sincere.

She gave it up and put a large question mark under that second question. There were two of them now, one under "Harg Tholan" and one under "Drake." Could there be a connection between Tholan's interest in missing persons and Drake's reaction to a polite party phrase? She could think of none.

She put her head down upon her arms. It was getting dark in the office and she was very tired. For a while, she must have hovered in that queer land between waking and sleeping, when thoughts and phrases lose the control of the conscious and disport themselves erratically and surrealistically through one's head. But, no matter where they danced and leaped, they always returned to that one phrase, "You are a most charming hostess." Sometimes she heard it in Harg Tholan's cultured, lifeless voice, and sometimes in Drake's vibrant one. When Drake said it, it was full of love, full of a love she never heard from him. She liked to hear him say it.

She startled herself to wakefulness. It was quite dark in the office now, and she put on the desk light. She blinked, then frowned a little. Another thought must have come to her in that fitful half-sleep. There had been another phrase which had upset Drake. What was it? Her forehead furrowed with mental effort. It had not been last evening. It was not anything in the recorded conversation, so it must have been before that. Nothing came and she grew restless.

Looking at her watch, she gasped. It was almost eight. They would be at home waiting for her.

But she did not want to go home. She did not want to face them. Slowly, she took up the paper upon which she had scrawled her thoughts of the afternoon, tore it into little pieces and let them flutter into the little atomic-flash ashtray upon her desk. They were gone in a little flare and nothing was left of them.

If only nothing were left of the thoughts they represented as well.

It was no use. She would have to go home.

They were not there waiting for her, after all. She came upon them getting out of a gyrocab just as she emerged from the tubes on to street level. The gyrocabbie, wide-eyed, gazed after his fares for a moment, then hovered upward and away. By unspoken mutual consent, the three waited until they had entered the apartment before speaking.

Rose said disinterestedly, "I hope you have had a pleasant day, Dr. Tholan."

"Quite. And a fascinating and profitable one as well, I think."

"Have you had a chance to eat?" Though Rose had not herself eaten, she was anything but hungry.

"Yes, indeed."

Drake interrupted, "We had lunch and supper sent up to us. Sandwiches." He sounded tired.

Rose said, "Hello, Drake." It was the first time she had addressed him.

Drake scarcely looked at her. "Hello."

The Hawkinsite said, "Your tomatoes are remarkable vegetables. We have nothing to compare with them in taste on our own planet. I believe I ate two dozen, as well as an entire bottle of tomato derivative."

"Ketchup," explained Drake, briefly.

Rose said, "And your visit at the Missing Persons Bureau, Dr. Tholan? You say you found it profitable?"

"I should say so. Yes."

Rose kept her back to him. She plumped up sofa cushions as she said, "In what way?"

"I find it most interesting that the large majority of missing persons are males. Wives frequently report missing husbands, while the reverse is practically never the case."

Rose said, "Oh, that's not mysterious, Dr. Tholan. You simply don't realize the economic setup we have on Earth. On this planet, you see, it is the male who is usually the member of the family that maintains it as an economic unit. He is the one whose labor is repaid in units of currency. The wife's function is generally that of taking care of home and children."

"Surely this is not universal!"

Drake put in, "More or less. If you are thinking of my

wife, she is an example of the minority of women who are capable of making their own way in the world."

Rose looked at him swiftly. Was he being sarcastic?

The Hawkinsite said, "Your implication, Mrs. Smollett, is that women, being economically dependent upon their male companions, find it less feasible to disappear?"

"That's a gentle way of putting it," said Rose, "but that's about it."

"And would you call the Missing Persons Bureau of New York a fair sampling of such cases in the planet at large?"

"Why, I should think so."

The Hawkinsite said, abruptly, "And is there, then, an economic explanation for the fact that since interstellar travel has been developed, the percentage of young males among the missing is more pronounced than ever?"

It was Drake who answered, with a verbal snap. "Good lord, that's even less of a mystery than the other. Nowadays, the runaway has all space to disappear into. Anyone who wants to get away from trouble need only hop the nearest space freighter. They're always looking for crewmen, no questions asked, and it would be almost impossible to locate the runaway after that, if he really wanted to stay out of circulation."

"And almost always young men in their first year of marriage."

Rose laughed suddenly. She said, "Why, that's just the time a man's troubles seem the greatest. If he survives the first year, there is usually no need to disappear at all."

Drake was obviously not amused. Rose thought again that he looked tired and unhappy. *Why* did he insist on bearing the load alone? And then she thought that perhaps he had to.

The Hawkinsite said, suddenly, "Would it offend you if I disconnected for a period of time?"

Rose said, "Not at all. I hope you haven't had too exhausting a day. Since you come from a planet whose gravity is greater than that of Earth's, I'm afraid we too easily presume that you would show greater endurance than we do."

"Oh, I'm not tired in a physical sense." He looked for a moment at her legs and blinked very rapidly, indicating amusement. "You know, I keep expecting Earthmen to fall either forward or backward in view of their meager equipment of standing limbs. You must pardon me if my comment is overfamiliar, but your mention of the lesser gravity of Earth brought it to my mind. On my planet, two legs would simply not be enough. But this is all beside the point at the moment. It is just that I have been absorbing so many new and unusual concepts that I feel the desire for a little disconnection."

Rose shrugged inwardly. Well, that was as close as one race could get to another, anyway. As nearly as the expeditions to Hawkin's Planet could make out, Hawkinsites had the faculty for disconnecting their conscious mind from all its bodily functions and allowing it to sink into an undisturbed meditative process for periods of time lasting up to terrestrial days. Hawkinsites found the process pleasant, even necessary sometimes, though no Earthman could truly say what function it served.

Conversely, it had never been entirely possible for Earthmen to explain the concept of "sleep" to a Hawkinsite, or to any extraterrestrial. What an Earthman would call sleep or a dream, a Hawkinsite would view as an alarming sign of mental disintegration. Rose thought uneasily, *Here is another way Earthmen are unique.*

The Hawkinsite was backing away, drooping so that his

forelimbs swept the floor in polite farewell. Drake nodded curtly at him as he disappeared behind the bend in the corridor. They heard his door open, close, then silence.

After minutes in which the silence was thick between them, Drake's chair creaked as he shifted restlessly. With a mild horror, Rose noticed blood upon his lips. She thought to herself, *He's in some kind of trouble. I've got to talk to him. I can't let it go on like this.*

She said, "Drake!"

Drake seemed to look at her from a far, far distance. Slowly, his eyes focused closer at hand and he said, "What is it? Are you through for the day, too?"

"No, I'm ready to begin. It's the tomorrow you spoke of. Aren't you going to speak to me?"

"Pardon me?"

"Last night, you said you would speak to me tomorrow. I am ready now."

Drake frowned. His eyes withdrew beneath a lowered brow and Rose felt some of her resolution begin to leave her. He said, "I thought it was agreed that you would not question me about my business in this matter."

"I think it's too late for that. I know too much about your business by now."

"What do you mean?" he shouted, jumping to his feet. Recollecting himself, he approached, laid his hands upon her shoulders and repeated in a lower voice, "What do you mean?"

Rose kept her eyes upon her hands, which rested limply in her lap. She bore the painfully gripping fingers patiently, and said slowly, "Dr. Tholan thinks that Earth is spreading the Inhibition Death purposely. That's it, isn't it?"

She waited. Slowly, the grip relaxed and he was standing

there, hands at his side, face baffled and unhappy. He said, "Where did you get that notion?"

"It's true, isn't it?"

He said breathlessly, unnaturally, "I want to know exactly why you say that. Don't play foolish games with me, Rose. This is for keeps."

"If I tell you, will you answer one question?"

"What question?"

"Is Earth spreading the disease deliberately, Drake?"

Drake flung his hands upward. "Oh, for Heaven's sake!"

He knelt before her. He took both her hands in his and she could feel their trembling. He was forcing his voice into soothing, loving syllables.

He was saying, "Rose dear, look, you've got something red-hot by the tail and you think you can use it to tease me in a little husband-wife repartee. Now, I'm not asking much. Just tell me exactly what causes you to say what—what you have just said." He was terribly earnest about it.

"I was at the New York Academy of Medicine this afternoon. I did some reading there."

"But why? What made you do it?"

"You seemed so interested in the Inhibition Death, for one thing. And Dr. Tholan made those statements about the incidence increasing since interstellar travel, and being the highest on the planet nearest Earth." She paused.

"And your reading?" he prompted. "What about your reading, Rose?"

She said, "It backs him up. All I could do was to skim hastily into the direction of their research in recent decades. It seems obvious to me, though, that at least some of the Hawkinsites are considering the possibility the Inhibition Death originates on Earth."

"Do they say so outright?"

"No. Or, if they have, I haven't seen it." She gazed at him in surprise. In a matter like this, certainly the government would have investigated Hawkinsite research on the matter. She said, gently, "Don't you know about Hawkinsite research in the matter, Drake? The government—"

"Never mind about that." Drake had moved away from her and now he turned again. His eyes were bright. He said, as though making a wonderful discovery, "Why, you're an expert in this!"

Was she? Did he find that out only now that he needed her? Her nostrils flared and she said flatly, "I am a biologist."

He said, "Yes, I know that, but I mean your particular specialty is growth. Didn't you once tell me you had done work on growth?"

"You might call it that. I've had twenty papers published on the relationship of nucleic acid 'fine structure' and embryonic development on my Cancer Society grant."

"Good. I should have thought of that." He was choked with a new excitement. "Tell me, Rose— Look, I'm sorry if I lost my temper with you a moment ago. You'd be as competent as anyone to understand the direction of their researches if you read about it, wouldn't you?"

"Fairly competent, yes."

"Then tell me how they think the disease is spread. The details, I mean."

"Oh, now look, that's asking a little too much. I spent a few hours in the Academy, that's all. I'd need much more time than that to be able to answer your question."

"An intelligent guess, at least. You can't imagine how important it is."

She said, doubtfully, "Of course, 'Studies on Inhibition' is a major treatise in the field. It would summarize all of the available research data."

"Yes? And how recent is it?"

"It's one of those periodic things. The last volume is about a year old."

"Does it have any account of *his* work in it?" His finger jabbed in the direction of Harg Tholan's bedroom.

"More than anyone else's. He's an outstanding worker in the field. I looked over his papers especially."

"And what are his theories about the origin of the disease? Try to remember, Rose."

She shook her head at him. "I could swear he blames Earth, but he admits they know nothing about how the disease is spread. I could swear to that, too."

He stood stiffly before her. His strong hands were clenched into fists as his side and his words were scarcely more than a mutter. "It could be a matter of complete overestimation. Who knows—"

He whirled away. "I'll find out about this right now, Rose. Thank you for your help."

She ran after him. "What are you going to do?"

"Ask him a few questions." He was rummaging through the drawers of his desk and now his right hand withdrew. It held a needle-gun.

She cried, "No, Drake!"

He shook her off roughly, and turned down the corridor toward the Hawkinsite's bedroom.

Drake threw the door open and entered. Rose was at his heels, still trying to grasp his arm, but now she stopped and looked at Harg Tholan.

The Hawkinsite was standing there motionless, eyes unfocused, his four standing limbs sprawled out in four directions as far as they would go. Rose felt ashamed of intruding, as though she were violating an intimate rite. But Drake, apparently unconcerned, walked to within four feet of the creature and stood there. They were face to face,

Drake holding the needle-gun easily at a level of about the center of the Hawkinsite's torso.

Drake said, "Now keep quiet. He'll gradually become aware of me."

"How do you know?"

The answer was flat. "I *know*. Not get out of here."

But she did not move and Drake was too absorbed to pay her further attention.

Portions of the skin on the Hawkinsite's face were beginning to quiver slightly. It was rather repulsive and Rose found herself preferring not to watch.

Drake said suddenly, "That's about all, Dr. Tholan. Don't throw in connection with any of the limbs. Your sense organs and voice box will be quite enough."

The Hawkinsite's voice was dim. "Why do you invade my disconnection chamber?" Then, more strongly, "and why are you armed?"

His head wobbled slightly atop a still frozen torso. He had, apparently, followed Drake's suggestion against limb connection. Rose wondered how Drake knew such partial reconnection to be possible. She herself had not known of it.

The Hawkinsite spoke again. "What do you want?"

And this time Drake answered. He said, "The answer to certain questions."

"With a gun in your hand? I would not humor your discourtesy so far."

"You would not merely be humoring me. You might be saving your own life."

"That would be a matter of considerable indifference to me, under the circumstances. I am sorry, Mr. Smollett, that the duties toward a guest are so badly understood on Earth."

"You are no guest of mine, Dr. Tholan," said Drake.

"You entered my house on false pretenses. You had some reason for it, some way you had planned of using me to further your own purposes. I have no compunction in reversing the process."

"You had better shoot. It will save time."

"You are convinced that you will answer no questions? That, in itself, is suspicious. It seems that you consider certain answers to be more important than your life."

"I consider the principles of courtesy to be very important. You, as an Earthman, may not understand."

"Perhaps not. But I, as an Earthman, understand one thing." Drake had jumped forward, faster than Rose could cry out, faster than the Hawkinsite could connect his limbs. When he sprang backward, the flexible hose of Harg Tholan's cyanide cylinder was in his hand. At the corner of the Hawkinsite's wide mouth, where the hose had once been affixed, a droplet of colorless liquid oozed sluggishly from a break in the rough skin, and slowly solidified into a brown jellylike globule, as it oxidized.

Drake yanked at the hose and the cylinder jerked free. He plunged home the knob that controlled the needle valve at the head of the cylinder and the small hissing ceased.

"I doubt," said Drake, "that enough will have escaped to endanger us. I hope, however, that you realize what will happen to you *now*, if you do not answer the questions I am going to ask you—and answer them in such a way that I am convinced you are being truthful."

"Give me back my cylinder," said the Hawkinsite, slowly. "If not, it will be necessary for me to attack you and then it will be necessary for you to kill me."

Drake stepped back. "Not at all. Attack me and I shoot your legs from under you. You will lose them; all four, if necessary, but you will still live, in a horrible way. You will live to die of cyanide lack. It would be a most uncomfortable death. I am only an Earthman and I can't appreciate its true horrors, but you can, can't you?"

The Hawkinsite's mouth was open and something within quivered yellow-green. Rose wanted to throw up. She wanted to scream, *Give him back the cylinder, Drake!* But nothing would come. She couldn't even turn her head.

Drake said, "You have about an hour, I think, before the effects are irreversible. Talk quickly, Dr. Tholan, and you will have your cylinder back."

"And after that—" said the Hawkinsite.

"After that, what does it matter to you? Even if I kill you then, it will be a clean death; not cyanide lack."

Something seemed to pass out of the Hawkinsite. His voice grew guttural and his words blurred as though he no longer had the energy to keep his English perfect. He said, "What are your questions?" and as he spoke, his eyes followed the cylinder in Drake's hand.

Drake swung it deliberately, tantalizingly, and the creature's eyes followed—followed—

Drake said, "What are your theories concerning the Inhibition Death? Why did you really come to Earth? What is your interest in the Missing Persons Bureau?"

Rose found herself waiting in breathless anxiety. These were the questions she would like to have asked, too. Not in this manner, perhaps, but in Drake's job, kindness and humanity had to take second place to necessity.

She repeated that to herself several times in an effort to counteract the fact that she found herself loathing Drake for what he was doing to Dr. Tholan.

The Hawkinsite said, "The proper answer would take more than the hour I have left me. You have bitterly shamed me by forcing me to talk under duress. On my own planet, you could not have done so under any circumstances. It is only here, on this revolting planet, that I can be deprived of cyanide."

"You are wasting your hour, Dr. Tholan."

"I would have told you this eventually, Mr. Smollett. I needed your help. It is why I came here."

"You are still not answering my questions."

"I will answer them now. For years, in addition to my regular scientific work, I have been privately investigating the cells of my patients suffering from Inhibition Death. I have been forced to use the utmost secrecy and to work without assistance, since the methods I used to investigate the bodies of my patients were frowned upon by my people. Your society would have similar feelings against human vivisection, for instance. For this reason, I could not present the results I obtained to my fellow physicians until I had verified my theories here on Earth."

"What were your theories?" demanded Drake. The feverishness had returned to his eyes.

"It became more and more obvious to me as I proceeded with my studies that the entire direction of research into the Inhibition Death was wrong. The answer was neither bacterial nor viral."

Rose interrupted, "Surely, Dr. Tholan, it isn't psychosomatic."

A thin, gray, translucent film had passed over the Hawkinsite's eyes. He no longer looked at them. He said, "No, Mrs. Smollett, it is not psychosomatic. It is a true infection, but more subtle than could be expected of either bacteria or viruses. I worked with Inhibition Death patients of other races than my own, and the conclusion was eventually forced upon me. There is a whole variety of infection never yet suspected by the medical science of any of the planets."

Rose said, faintly, "This is wild, impossible. You must be mistaken, Dr. Tholan."

"I am not mistaken. Until I came to Earth, I thought I might be. But my stay at the Institute, my researches at the Missing Persons Bureau have convinced me that this is not so. What is so impossible about the concept of a supremely subtle, yet unsuspected class of infections? The very subtlety would militate against their discovery. In your history and in ours, there were thousands of years in which the causes of bacterial infections were unknown. And when tools were developed capable of studying bacteria, viruses remained unknown for generations.

"Is it impossible to proceed a step further? Bacteria, by and large, are extracellular creatures. They compete with the cells of the body for foodstuffs, sometimes too successfully, and they release their waste products, or toxins, into the bloodstream. The virus goes a step further. It lives within the cell, utilizing cellular machinery for its own purposes. You know all this, Mrs. Smollett, so I need not elaborate. Perhaps your husband knows it as well."

"Go on," said Drake.

"Proceed one more stage, then. Imagine a parasite that lives not only inside the cell, but inside the *chromosomes* of the cell. In other words, a parasite that takes its place along with the genes, so that it is something we might call a pseudo-gene. It would have a hand in the manufacture of enzymes, which is the primary function of genes, and in that way a very firm finger in the biochemistry of the terrestrial organism."

Rose said, "Why particularly the terrestrial?"

"Have you not surmised that the pseudo-gene I speak of is a native of Earth? Terrestrial beings from the beginning have lived with it, have adapted to it, are unconscious of it. These pseudo-genes feed on the *organization* of the body.

Bacteria feed on the foodstuffs, viruses on the cells, pseudo-genes on the economy of the cellular macrostructure as a whole through their control of the body's biochemistry. It is why the higher species of terrestrial animals, including man, do not grow after maturity, and, eventually, die what is called natural death. It is the inevitable end result of this universal parasitic infestation."

"A disease of the soul—" Rose said, wistfully.

The Hawkinsite said, "What is the soul?"

"For heaven's sake," said Drake, abruptly, "do not get mystical, Rose!"

She flushed. "I'm sorry. Go on, Dr. Tholan."

"As a pseudo-gene, it is perfectly obvious how the universal disease is transmitted. It is placed along with the true genes in every ovum or spermatazoon formed by the infected organism. Every organism is already infected at the moment of conception. But there is another form of transmission—there *must* be to account for all the facts. Chemically, genes and viruses are similar, since both are nuclear proteins. A pseudo-gene can, therefore, exist independently of the chromosomes.

"Perhaps it infects a virus, or perhaps it forms a virus-like body itself at some stage of its development. As such, it can be transmitted in the ordinary fashion of other viral infections—by contact, by air, through waste materials and so on. Naturally, Earthmen have nothing to fear from such contact; they are already infected. On Earth, such a process is purely vestigial, dating back to the days when infections could yet be made. It is different on the extraterrestrial worlds, however."

"I see," said Rose.

"I don't," objected Drake, bluntly.

The Hawkinsite sighed. "We of the other worlds have not lived with these parasites for millions of years, as man and his ancestors had. We have not adapted ourselves to it. Our weak strains have not been killed off gradually through hundreds of generations until only the resistants were left. So, where Earthmen could survive the infection for decades with little harm, we others, once infected by the viral stage of the disease, die a quick death within a year."

Rose said, "And is that why the incidence has increased since interstellar travel between Earth and the other planets began?"

"Yes. There were infections previously. It has long been suspected that bacterial spores and virus molecules can drift off into space and through it. Absolute zero will not kill them, but rather keep them alive indefinitely. Statistically, a certain percentage of them will reach other planets. Before space travel there were cases which could be accounted for, perhaps, by such a mechanism. Since then, it has increased ten thousand times and more."

For a moment there was silence, and then the Hawkinsite said with a sudden access of energy, "Give me back my cylinder. You have your answer."

Drake said, coolly, "What about the Missing Persons Bureau?" He was swinging the cylinder again; but now the Hawkinsite did not follow its movements. The gray translucent film on his eyes had deepened and Rose wondered whether that was simply an expression of weariness or an example of the changes induced by cyanide lack.

The Hawkinsite said, "As we are not well adapted to the pseudo-genes that infest man, neither are they well adapted to us. It can live on us, but it cannot reproduce with ourselves alone as the source of its life. Infections of Inhibition Death before the advent of space travel set off tiny epidemics that would last through ten or twenty transfers, growing gradually milder, until it died out altogether. Now, the disease transfers indefinitely, getting milder where thorough quarantines are imposed and then, suddenly and erratically, growing completely virulent again."

Rose looked at him with a growing horror. "What are you implying, Dr. Tholan?"

He said, "The Earthman remains the prime host for the parasite. An Earthman may infect one of us if he remains among us. But the pseudo-gene, once located within our cells, cannot maintain its vigor indefinitely. Sooner or later, within twenty infections, perhaps, it must somehow return to an Earthman, if it expects to continue reproduction. Before interstellar travel this was possible only by returning through space, which was so unlikely as to be considered zero. Now—"

Rose said faintly, "The missing persons."

"Yes. They are the intermediate hosts. Almost all the young men who disappeared in the last decade were space-travelers. They had been on other inhabited planets at least once in their lives. Once the period of incubation within the human being has transpired, they return to an outer planet. He disappears, as far as Earth is concerned."

"But this is impossible," insisted Rose. "What you say implies that the pseudo-gene can control the actions of its host! This cannot be!"

"Why not? They control the biochemistry, at least in part, by their very role as pseudo-genes. There is no intelligence, or even instinct, behind their control. It is purely chemical. If adrenalin is injected into your bloodstream, there is no imposition of a superior intelligence that makes your heart double its rate, your breathing quicken, your clotting time decrease, your blood vessels dilate—purely chemical.

"—But I am quite ill now and cannot speak much longer. I have only this to say. In this pseudo-gene, your people and mine have a common enemy. Earthmen, too, need not die involuntarily. I thought that perhaps if I found myself unable to return to my own world with my information, due to my own infection, perhaps, I might bring it to the authorities on Earth, and ask their help in stamping out this menace. Imagine my pleasure when I found that the husband of one of the biologists at the Institute was a member of one of Earth's most important investigating bodies. Naturally, I did what I could to be a guest at his home in order that I might deal with him privately; convince him of the terrible truth; utilize his position to help in the attack on the parasites.

"This is, of course, now impossible. I cannot blame you too far. As Earthmen, you cannot be expected to understand thoroughly the psychology of my people. Nevertheless, you must understand this. I can have no further dealing with either of you. I could not even bear to remain any longer on Earth."

Drake said, "Then you, alone, of all your people have any knowledge of this theory of yours."

"I alone."

Drake held out the cylinder. "Your cyanide, Dr. Tholan."

The Hawkinsite groped for it eagerly. His supple fingers manipulated the hose and the needle valve with the utmost delicacy. In the space of ten seconds, he had it in place and was inhaling the gas in huge breaths. His eyes were growing clear and transparent.

Drake waited until the Hawkinsite's breathing had subsided to normal, and then, without expression, he raised his needle-gun and fired.

Rose screamed. The Hawkinsite remained standing. His

four lower limbs were incapable of buckling, but his head lolled and, from his suddenly flaccid mouth, the cyanide hose fell, disregarded.

Once again, Drake closed the needle valve and now he tossed the cylinder aside and stood there somberly, looking at the dead creature.

There was no external mark to show that Tholan had been killed. The needle-gun's pellet, thinner than the needle which gave the gun its name, entered the body noiselessly and easily, and exploded with devastating effect only within the abdominal cavity.

Rose ran from the room, still screaming.

Drake pursued her, seized her arm. She heard the hard, brisk sounds of his palms upon her face without feeling them and subsided into little bubbling sobs.

Drake said, "I told you to have nothing to do with this. Now, what do you think you're going to do?"

She said, "Let me go. I want to leave. I want to go away."

"Because of something it was my job to do? You heard what the creature was saying. Do you suppose I could allow him to return to his world and spread those lies? They would believe him. And what do you think would happen then? Can you guess what an interstellar war might be like? They would imagine they would have to kill us all to stop the disease."

With an effort that seemed to turn her inside out, Rose steadied. She looked firmly into Drake's eyes and said, "What Dr. Tholan said were no lies and no mistakes, Drake."

"Oh, come now, you're hysterical. You need sleep."

"No, Drake. I know what he said is so because the Security Commission knows all about that same theory, and knows it to be true."

"Why do you say such a preposterous thing?"

"Because you let that slip yourself twice."
Drake said, "Sit down."
She did so, and he stood there, looking curiously at her. He said, "So I have given myself away twice, have I? You've had a busy day of detection, my dear. You have facets you keep well hidden." He sat down and crossed his legs.

Rose thought, *Yes, I've had a busy day*. She could see the electric clock on the kitchen wall from where she sat and it was more than two hours past midnight. Harg Tholan had entered their house thirty-five hours before; and now he lay murdered in the spare bedroom.

Drake said, "Well, aren't you going to tell me where I pulled my two boners?"

"You turned white when Harg Tholan referred to me as a charming hostess. Hostess has a double meaning, you know, Drake. A host is one who harbors a parasite."

"Number one," said Drake. "What's number two?"

"That's something you did before Harg Tholan entered the house. I've been trying to remember it for hours. Do *you* remember, Drake? You spoke about how unpleasant it was for Hawkinsites to associate with Earthmen, and I said Harg Tholan was a doctor and had to. I asked you if you thought that human doctors particularly enjoyed going to the tropics, or letting infected mosquitoes bite them. Do you remember how upset you became?"

Drake laughed shortly. "I had no idea I was so transparent. Mosquitoes are hosts for the malaria and yellow fever parasites." He sighed. "I've done my best to keep you out of this, Rose. I tried to keep the Hawkinsite away. I tried threatening you. Now, there's nothing left but to tell you the truth. I must, because only the truth—or death—will keep you quiet. And I don't want to kill you."

Rose shrank back in her chair, eyes wide.

Drake said, "The Commission knows the truth, yes. It does us no good. We can only do all in our power to prevent the other worlds from finding out."

"But that is impossible! The truth can't be held down forever. Harg Tholan found out. You've killed him, but another extraterrestrial will repeat the same discovery—over and over again. You can't kill them all."

"We know that, too," agreed Drake. "But we have no choice."

"Why?" cried Rose. "Harg Tholan gave you the solution. He made no suggestions or threats regarding enmity and war between worlds. He said something, instead, for which I admired him. He suggested that we combine with the other intelligences and help to wipe out the parasite. And we can—we *can*! If we, in common with all the others, put every scrap of effort into it—"

"You mean we can trust him? Does he speak for his government? Or for the other races?"

"Can we dare to refuse the risk?"

Drake said, "No, Rose, you don't understand." He reached toward her and took one of her cold, unresisting hands between both of his. He went on, "I may seem silly trying to teach you anything about your specialty, but I want you to hear me out. Harg Tholan was right. Man and his prehistoric ancestors have been living with this pseudogene for uncounted ages; certainly for a much longer period than we have been truly *Homo sapiens*. In that interval, we have not only become adapted to it, we have become dependent upon it. It is no longer a case of parasitism. It is a case of mutual cooperation."

She tore her hand away, "What are you talking about?"

"We have a disease of our own, remember. It is a reverse

disease; one of unrestrained growth. We've mentioned it already as a contrast to the Inhibition Death. Well, what is the cause of cancer? How long have biologists, physiologists, biochemists and all the others been working on it? How much success have they had with it? Why? Can't you answer that for yourself now?"

Rose frowned at him. She said, slowly, "No, I can't. What are you talking about?"

"It's all very well to say that if we could remove the parasite, we would once again have the privilege of eternal growth and life if we wanted it; or at least until we got tired of being too big or of living too long, and did away with ourselves neatly. But how many millions of years has it been since the human body has had occasion to grow in such an unrestrained fashion? Can it do so any longer? Is the chemistry of the body adjusted to that? Has it got the proper whatchamacallits?"

"Enzymes," prompted Rose in a whisper.

"Yes, enzymes. It's impossible for us. If, for any reason, the pseudo-gene, as Harg Tholan calls it, does leave the human body, or if its relationship to the human mind is in any way impaired, growth does take place, but not in any orderly fashion. We call the growth cancer.

"And there you have it, Rose. There's no way of getting rid of the parasite. We're together for all eternity. So that to get rid of their Inhibition Death, extraterrestrials must first wipe out all vertebrate life on Earth. There is no other solution for them, and so we must keep knowledge of it from them. Do you understand?"

She rose from her chair. Her mouth was dry and it was difficult to talk. "I understand, Drake."

She noticed that his forehead was damp and that there was a line of perspiration down each cheek.

She said, tightly, "And now you'll have to get it out of the apartment."

"I know. I've made arrangements. It's late at night and I'll be able to get the body out of the building. From there on—" he turned to her— "I don't know when I'll be back."

Rose said again, "I understand, Drake."

Harg Tholan was heavy. Drake had to drag him through the apartment. Rose turned away, retching. She hid her eyes until she heard the front door close. She whispered again to herself, "I understand, Drake."

It was 3 A.M. Nearly an hour had passed since she had heard the front door click gently into place behind Drake and his burden. She didn't know where he was going, what he intended doing—

She sat there numbly. There was no desire to sleep; no desire to move. She kept her mind traveling in tight circles, away from the thing she knew and which she wanted not to know.

Pseudo-genes!

Was it only a coincidence or was it some queer racial memory, some tenuous long-sustained wisp of tradition or insight, stretching back through incredible millennia, that kept current the odd myths of human beginnings? The stories of the golden ages, the Gardens of Eden in which Man had eternal life, until he lost it.

She had called the pseudo-genes a disease of the soul. Was that the memory again? The memory of the world in which sin entered, in which the soul grew diseased, and into which, as a consequence, death entered?

Yet despite her efforts, the circle of her thoughts expanded, and returned to Drake. She shoved and it returned; she counted to herself, she recited the names of the objects in her field of vision, she cried, *No, no, no,* and it returned. It kept returning.

Drake had lied to her. It had been a plausible story. It would have held good under most circumstances; but Drake was not a biologist.

Cancer could not be, as Drake had said, a disease that was an expression of a lost ability for any normal growth.

Cancer attacked children while they were still growing; it could even attack embryonic tissue. It attacked fish, which, like extraterrestrials, never stopped growing while they lived, and died only by disease or accident. It attacked plants, for many of which the same could be said.

Cancer had nothing to do with the presence or absence of normal growth. It was the general disease of life, to which *no* tissues of *any* multicellular organism were completely immune.

He should not have bothered lying. He should not have allowed some obscure sentimental weakness to persuade him to avoid the necessity of killing her in that manner. She would tell them at the Institute. The parasite *could* be beaten! Its absence would *not* cause cancer. But who would believe her?

She put her hands over her eyes and rocked gently to and fro. The young men who disappeared were usually in the first year of their marriage. Whatever the process of rejuvenation among the strains of the pseudo-genes, it must involve close association with another strain—as in the case of conjugation among the protozoa. That was how the pseudo-genes had to spread infection; through the formation of the gametes and their subsequent fertilization, a mixing of strains.

Drake had been on Hawkin's Planet. He knew too much about Hawkinsites not to have been there at least once.

She could feel her thoughts slowly disconnect. They

would be coming to her. They would be saying, *Where is Harg Tholan?* And she would answer, *With my husband.* Only they would say, *Where is your husband?* because he would be gone, too.

She knew that, anyway. He needed her no longer. He would never return. They would never find him, because he would be out in space. She would report them both, Drake Smollett and Harg Tholan, to the Missing Persons Bureau.

She wanted to weep, but couldn't. She was dry-eyed and it was very painful.

And then she began to giggle. She couldn't stop; it just went on.

After all, it was very funny. She had looked for the answers to so many questions and had found them all. She had even found the answer to the question she thought had no bearing on the subject.

She had finally learned why Drake had married her.

Not a conjugal relationship—

Conjugation.